CLAIRE CASEY'S HAD ENOUGH

Also by Liz Alterman

Novels

HE'LL BE WAITING
THE PERFECT NEIGHBORHOOD
THE HOUSE ON COLD CREEK LANE *

Non-fiction

SAD SACKED

* *available from Severn House*

CLAIRE CASEY'S HAD ENOUGH

Liz Alterman

SEVERN HOUSE

First world edition published in Great Britain and the USA in 2025
by Severn House, an imprint of Canongate Books Ltd,
14 High Street, Edinburgh EH1 1TE.

Paperback edition first published in Great Britain and the USA in 2025
by Severn House, an imprint of Canongate Books Ltd.

severnhouse.com

Copyright © Liz Alterman, 2025

Cover and jacket design by Panagiotis Lampridis

All rights reserved including the right of reproduction in whole or in part in any
form. The right of Liz Alterman to be identified as the author of this work has been
asserted in accordance with the Copyright, Designs & Patents Act 1988.

British Library Cataloguing-in-Publication Data
A CIP catalogue record for this title is available from the British Library.

ISBN-13: 978-1-4483-1577-2 (cased)
ISBN-13: 978-1-4483-1819-3 (paper)
ISBN-13: 978-1-4483-1578-9 (e-book)

This is a work of fiction. Names, characters, places and incidents are either the
product of the author's imagination or are used fictitiously. Except where actual
historical events and characters are being described for the storyline of this novel,
all situations in this publication are fictitious and any resemblance to actual persons,
living or dead, business establishments, events or locales is purely coincidental.

No part of this book may be used or reproduced in any manner for the purpose of
training artificial intelligence technologies or systems. This work is reserved from
text and data mining (Article 4(3) Directive (EU) 2019/790).

All Severn House titles are printed on acid-free paper.

Typeset by Palimpsest Book Production Ltd.,
Falkirk, Stirlingshire, Scotland.
Printed and bound in Great Britain by
CPI Group (UK) Ltd, Croydon CR0 4YY

The manufacturer's authorised representative in the EU for product safety is
Authorised Rep Compliance Ltd, 71 Lower Baggot Street, Dublin D02 P593
Ireland (arccompliance.com)

Praise for Liz Alterman

"Charming and unexpected . . . Liz Alterman has a true talent for writing all-too-relatable characters and the challenges midlife can throw our way"
Camille Pagán, bestselling author of *Good for You*

"Hilarious and heartwarming . . . With sharp wit and relatable characters, Alterman masterfully explores love, nostalgia, and the complexities of midlife"
Ann Garvin, *USA Today* bestselling author

"A propulsive story that will have you turning the pages deep into the night"
Catherine McKenzie, *USA Today* bestselling author

"A suspenseful, shocking book about grief, loss, obsession, and revenge that will grip readers from beginning to end"
Booklist on *The House on Cold Creek Lane*

"Fresh twists . . . Alterman is off to a promising start"
Publishers Weekly on *The Perfect Neighborhood*

"Well written from start to finish . . . perfect for fans of domestic suspense!"
Manhattan Book Review on *The Perfect Neighborhood*

"Super-relatable characters and nearly unbearable suspense made it impossible to stop reading"
Sarah Warburton, author of *You Can Never Tell* on *The Perfect Neighborhood*

"Liz Alterman is a masterful storyteller"
May Cobb, award-winning author of *The Hunting Wives* on *The Perfect Neighborhood*

About the author

Liz Alterman is the author of *The House on Cold Creek Lane, The Perfect Neighborhood, He'll Be Waiting*, and *Sad Sacked*. Her work has appeared in *The New York Times, The Washington Post, McSweeney's*, and other outlets. She lives in New Jersey with her husband and three sons, where she spends most days microwaving the same cup of coffee and looking up synonyms. When Liz isn't writing, she's reading.

LizAlterman.com

For Victoria Britton. Thank you for giving Claire a home.

'Falling in love was easy. Anyone could fall. It was holding on that was tricky.'

—Liane Moriarty, *The Husband's Secret*

May 11, 2024

2:20 a.m.

At least the weather was mild, Claire consoled herself as she peed behind her shed like a fugitive. Before tugging down her black dress pants and squatting, the forty-six-year-old mom of three used her phone's flashlight to check for poison ivy. The insidious weed was practically New Jersey's state flower and it would be just Claire's luck to end up with her privates polka-dotted in angry hives by morning. Luckily, it was mid-May, too early for the ivy to begin its invasive creep.

Moaning with relief, Claire emitted a stream that could've rivaled a racehorse's. She'd been holding it the entire ride from the airport. Patting her pockets, she fished out a crumpled napkin, hoped it wasn't the one she'd used to blot pizza grease eight hours earlier, and gave herself a hasty wipe.

Like a tired sunflower, she slowly lifted her drooping head. If this – using her suburban backyard as a toilet – was captured by a neighbor's security camera, the video would end up on a community forum, shared by countless parents from her children's schools, and she'd be forced to flee the country. That sounded pleasant, actually, after the day, maybe even the last decade, she'd had.

As Claire switched off the phone's flashlight, her gaze landed on the time (2:23 a.m.) before bouncing to the back entry of her home. Beyond her French doors, Paul, her husband, the man who'd promised to pick her up from the airport, slept soundly, light from the TV casting ghostly shadows on the wall behind him. He looked ridiculous wearing their son Max's Beats headphones, iPad perched precariously on his lap, one of his employer's ongoing training modules still playing.

When she'd arrived home at close to 2 a.m., she'd knocked aggressively on those French doors. Paul still hadn't replaced the doorbell's battery at their home's front entrance, though she'd asked him to do it no less than twenty-seven times.

Even if he'd taken care of it, that was no guarantee the soft *ding-dong* would've awakened him. Paul could've slept through a Metallica concert. Their sons were surely zonked out too. Claire's mom had given them noise machines last Christmas. Max favored the sound of ocean waves while Joe slumbered to falling rain. Henry preferred the gentle crackle of the sizzling bacon setting. They'd never hear her either.

She hadn't brought keys because she hadn't expected to need them.

'Idiot!' she hissed in the direction of her husband, who lay ten yards away on the couch in the comfort of their living room, snoring no doubt.

Cold dew began to seep through Claire's cheap black flats.

'Absolute moron!' she muttered to herself as she emerged from behind the shed. Her instincts had warned her that flying to Ohio to cover a toy safety conference for MamaRama.com wasn't a great idea. But she'd only started writing for the parenting website in January, and she feared that if she refused this assignment she'd be overlooked when better offerings – like that spa review in Sedona her colleague Esme snapped up – came along.

Still, she'd questioned Paul's ability to care for their sons solo. She'd imagined returning to find her boys with face tattoos and vaping habits, tending a small petting zoo in the basement.

When she'd wondered aloud if she should go, Paul had said. 'Definitely! This sounds too important to miss.' With an outstretched arm, he'd mimed holding a cell phone in selfie position. '"Claire Casey here, reporting live from . . ."' He shifted, peeking at her from behind the imaginary device. 'Where is it again? Dayton? Canton? ". . . from somewhere in the Buckeye State, bringing you an update on which brand of building blocks are secretly coated in lead paint. Stay with me as I rank dolls with the most flammable hair and reveal how to stay calm when your toddler swallows his first marble."'

Claire sighed. It was bad enough when *she* mocked her job, but hearing her husband do it made her recent career move feel like even more of a massive misstep.

'Maybe I should stay home,' she'd said, her hopes of spending two nights in a hotel room alone vanishing faster than an earring sliding down a bathroom sink drain. She'd fantasized about lying like a starfish across a bed free of crumbs or Lego pieces, then awakening to order room service. What bold, new ideas might surface with her freed-up brain space if she didn't have to worry about her kids' schedules and fixing dinner?

As disappointment clouded her face, Paul had insisted, 'Go, Claire, really. We'll be fine. The boys are older now.'

It was true. Max was fourteen, Henry, twelve, and Joe, eight. Still.

'Seriously. I got this,' Paul assured her.

Claire peered past his shoulder to the countertops laden with crusty dinner dishes from the prior evening.

'How tough can it be?' he asked as he tossed an orange peel in the direction of the garbage can and missed.

She'd bitten her tongue to stop from telling him: 'Pretty damn tough. Managing three children while working from home is more difficult than snagging a last-minute orthodontist appointment or leaving Costco without spending double what you'd intended.' But she saved her breath. He'd find out.

She knocked on the French doors again. Paul didn't stir. Perhaps the days without her had exhausted him. Maybe, by morning, she'd discover he was a changed man, one who would not only apologize for failing to pick her up but also admit he'd had no clue how taxing her life had become.

As lovely as that sounded, she knew it would never happen. Plus, she'd done the hardest bits before leaving town. In the days before her departure, Claire had made lists of all the boys' activities, shopped so they wouldn't run out of staples, signed permission slips for end-of-the-year field trips, and attached the accompanying payments for each.

By the time she'd boarded the plane, Claire had experienced a full-body fatigue so draining it felt as if she'd fought off a pack of wild hogs. She fell asleep, drooling, head dipping toward a stranger's shoulder, before the drink cart made its way up the aisle.

Meanwhile, when Paul had gone on his golf outing in late April, his only pre-trip prep involved filling a travel mug with coffee and loading his clubs into the car. On his way out the door, he'd stopped. Foolishly, Claire thought for a moment he might say he'd miss her or mention something about spending time together when he returned. Instead, he pointed toward the cellar door.

'The sump pump stopped working,' he'd said. 'If it rains, you may want to call someone.'

With that memory fresh in her mind, Claire had been determined to wring every bit of enjoyment from her work-related getaway – or as much enjoyment as one could possibly render from a toy safety conference. Truthfully, Claire would've been happy to sit in a park and attempt to teach squirrels to French-braid their tails if it meant a few moments of solitude.

While it had been nice to travel alone, the conference had been a rather bland affair. The child safety agencies who'd organized the event tried to keep attendees engaged by hosting challenges designed to 'entertain and enlighten'.

The first involved a timed test in which Claire and her counterparts were blindfolded and asked to sort laundry pods, yogurt pouches, and cannabis gummies into separate baskets. (Claire lost.)

In the next game, a scavenger hunt required each participant to spot hidden dangers in a space curated to mimic the average living room. Since Max was born, Claire had developed a sixth sense for uncovered outlets, lit candles, and loose change. Motherhood had given her the ability to sniff out an uncapped bottle of bleach in another zip code. Competing against influencers who were at least a decade younger, Claire bested them handily.

'She must be an amazing parent,' one of her opponents murmured.

Like a glass of cheap champagne, the compliment went straight to Claire's head . . . until she heard another attendee whisper, 'or a total helicopter mom.' This gal made the *chuff chuff chuff* sound of whirling chopper blades. Claire had chalked it up to envy. After all, the prize was a playroom makeover. The last time she'd won anything had been the third-grade spelling bee when she'd taken first place for nailing the word 'disappointment'.

Flush from her latest victory, Claire made the mistake of calling her mom during the lunch break to share the news about the playroom makeover.

'Oh, honey, how will they know where to start? Your whole house is like one big playroom! There's stuff everywhere!' Her mother, Eleanor, emitted that soft, older woman chuckle that invariably led to a coughing fit.

'Get some water. We'll talk later,' Claire had said and promptly ended the call.

That afternoon, during a lecture on the perils of introducing electronics to toddlers too soon, Claire's phone had begun blowing up. A flurry of texts sent the device skittering across the table, striking fear in her heart. What was so urgent that Paul couldn't handle it? Perhaps her mother had fallen during one of her daily trips to the market? Or what if it was the school nurse?

Then her thoughts shifted in a more positive direction. Maybe it was her literary agent, Marcy, texting to say she loved Claire's latest pitches.

Eight years earlier, Claire's picture book, *A Panda for Amanda*, had been a modest hit. In the beloved story, a ring-tailed lemur named Ringo grapples with jealousy when Amanda, the child who loves and cares for him, receives a large, plush panda for her birthday.

Claire had written it to help Max adjust to his little brother Henry's arrival. She'd queried agents after Paul overheard her reading it and said, 'I think you may have something there!'

The book sold quickly. She'd been trying and failing to replicate its success ever since. Though she'd envisioned follow-ups – *A Lion for Ryan*, *A Lamb for Sam* – Marcy crushed those dreams. Only celebrities could get away with writing rhyming books now, her agent explained.

'Animals are over, btw. No one cares,' Marcy informed her. 'Readers crave stories with larger messages. Think social issues. What about climate change? Food insecurity? The global housing shortage?'

For picture books? Really? Claire had frowned while reading Marcy's email.

When she floated the idea of a memoir, her agent snarfed.

'Claire, you're nobody. Wait, that didn't come out right. What I mean is: You have no platform. You're a wonderful storyteller, but what have you *survived*? Sorry, but bake sales and book fairs don't count.'

That was her agent's way – a lukewarm compliment bookended by insults.

Sometimes Claire thought about pitching an anthology: *How Did It Come to This?* She'd compile essays penned by other middle-aged women who'd also arrived at the 'Is this all there is?' stage. While Claire loved the idea, Marcy insisted non-fiction, too, was a tough sell. *Even trauma and terminal illness aren't enough anymore. Sigh*, she'd written. *Bigger ideas, Claire! Think bold, new formats!*

When Claire's phone's pinging persisted and the panel's moderator shot her a look so filthy no stain stick could've removed it, Claire snuck out to the lobby and scrolled through her messages. Max and Henry had started a group text:

Are we out of pretzels?

What's for dinner?

I can't find my water bottle! Practice started 10 mins ago.

MOM! Help!

Where do we keep the toilet paper?

Joe's been wearing the same clothes since you left. He says he's not taking them off until you come home.

When are you coming home?

MOM! Answer!

Claire's relief that there wasn't a true emergency was swiftly replaced by white-hot rage. Paul had promised he'd take care of everything.

WHERE'S YOUR FATHER? she texted.

Napping, Henry wrote.

?? Claire shot back.

He took the hammock out of the shed and then fell asleep in it, Max added.

The hammock. Bringing herself back to her present situation, Claire glanced around the backyard. That's where she'd sleep. Threadbare and freckled with mold, it was preferable to the cold, damp grass.

As Claire collapsed, the hammock's springs groaning, she considered a potential memoir title: *She Who Sleeps with Squirrels*. It would be the modern, feminist retelling of *Dances with Wolves*. Reese Witherspoon would select it for her book club. Marcy would admit she'd underestimated Claire's talent and Claire would happily resign from MamaRama to draft an equally riveting sequel.

Before closing her eyes, Claire stared at the stars and said a prayer that raccoons wouldn't gnaw their way through her suitcase and destroy her laptop. When she'd agreed to attend the conference, Sabrina, Claire's editor, had insisted she come up with at least two 'ultra-clicky' slideshows to justify her time away. On the flight home, she'd started 'The 99 Deadliest Toys Lurking in Your Playroom', and was nine away from completing it. She'd have to work on the other: '32 Household Items Most Likely to Kill Your Baby While You Sit There & Watch' next.

Claire worried they'd anger MamaRama's toy and cleaning product advertisers, but Sabrina pooh-poohed her concerns.

'Knock these out of the park, Claire, and we'll consider sending you to the annual "What's New in Appliances" convention this fall. You'll get to review the latest in washers and dryers through a "mom lens".'

'Where's that one held?' Claire hoped the answer was 'Hawaii'.

'Just outside Detroit,' Sabrina said. 'It would be a huge opportunity for you.'

'Totally!' had been all Claire could muster.

Claire awoke to the scolding *tsk tsk tsk* of her neighbors' sprinkler. Mascara crusted in the corners of her eyes as she squinted against the early morning haze and struggled to get her bearings. The hammock pitched her toward the ground when she attempted to stand. She had to put her hands down to stop from falling on her face.

'Damnit!' she spat, wiping her muddy palms on her pants. Back and neck aching like she'd spent the week piggybacking triplets across Disneyland, Claire tucked her hair behind her ears and fetched her flats from beneath the hammock. She stuffed her feet in her shoes, their insoles feeling as squishy and moist as if a dog had relieved himself inside them.

A rising tide of anger swelled in her chest as she charged toward the house, tugging her suitcase on wheels behind her.

Paul had made Claire his last priority for too long. Leaving her stranded at the airport was not only the most recent in a string of disappointments, it was also the tipping point.

'Don't worry, I'll definitely get you,' he'd said when she'd called to tell him her flight was delayed. 'Listen, my phone's about to die. Text me when you land.'

At the airport, surrounded by families – even the ones fighting over iPads and neck pillows – Claire had found herself unexpectedly homesick.

'Did you miss me?' she asked, the airport bar's warm chardonnay making her soppy.

'Of course.' Paul sounded distracted. 'Now if we had extra toilet paper, where would that be?'

'It's—' was all she managed before she heard the familiar beeps that signaled her husband's phone had died.

After a turbulent flight seated beside a passenger who used

the safety card to clean his fingernails, Claire had staggered toward the curbside pickup shortly after 1 a.m. She'd tried Paul's phone. The call went straight to voicemail. Her text messages bounced back undelivered. He'd probably gotten distracted and hadn't charged it, Claire reasoned, as she dialed the house phone. Her own voice on the outgoing message told her no one could take her call at the moment. She could envision that phone, also dead, buried beneath a couch cushion, Paul dozing beside it with his mouth hanging open – exactly as it was now.

From the patio, Claire stared at him and contemplated hurling a rock through the French doors. The knowledge that she'd be the one who would have to call to have the glass replaced was the only thing that stopped her.

Shoulders squared, hands balled into fists, Claire rapped hard and watched as her husband slowly came to life, scratching at himself like an ape in a zoo exhibit.

He switched off the TV, gave a half-hearted wave, and lumbered toward her in plaid boxers and a Yankees T-shirt.

'Hey!' He opened the door. 'Where did you come from? I thought you were going to text me for a ride.'

'I did!' Claire hissed as she stepped inside. Her suitcase nipped at her heels and twisted between her feet, nearly tripping her.

'Shoot!' He raked a hand through his bed-head, or in this case, sofa-head. 'I forgot to charge my phone. How'd you get home?'

'I took an Uber. At 2 a.m., Paul. Do you have any idea how dangerous that can be for a woman alone?'

Paul raised an eyebrow. After sixteen years of marriage, Claire could read his thoughts.

'You think because I'm forty-six I can't still be attacked by a pervert? I'm no longer attractive to perverts?' As the words left her mouth, she was keenly aware of how nuts she sounded, and also that she'd begun to smell like a high school wrestler who'd forgotten deodorant.

'That's not . . . c'mon, Claire. I slept on the couch waiting for—'

'I slept in a hammock, Paul! A hammock coated in bird shit, in my clothes, surrounded by chipmunks!'

'Why didn't you just ring the doorbell?' Paul rubbed his eyes and returned to the couch.

'I did! It doesn't work because you never changed the battery!'

'It's on my list.' That sentence had become Paul's mantra.

'I can't keep doing this.' Claire released her grip on her suitcase handle, causing it to topple and clatter against the hardwood floor.

'Then just tell MamaRama you don't want to travel anymore.' Paul stretched out and punched an indent in a throw pillow. *Was he going back to sleep?* 'If it makes you this miserable, you should definitely skip that appliance festival.'

'Not that! *Us! This!*' She waved her hand between them. 'I can't do *this* anymore, Paul. I can't count on you to follow through. On anything! You don't care about me . . .' Her voice began to waver, but it steadied when she spotted a collection of water bottles decorating the dark wood coffee table, leaving Olympic-symbol-like rings behind no doubt, 'and I am tired of pretending that you do and then being disappointed.'

'That's not fair, Claire.' Paul propped himself up on his elbow. 'I'd planned to get you. My phone died.'

'How was I supposed to get in touch with you? Telepathically?' Claire whisper-screamed so as not to wake their children, though if they hadn't stirred at her frantic knocking the night before, why would they now? 'You are a grown man who works in IT. Charge your damn phone!'

Paul sat up and stared at her. 'Look, Claire. I'm sorry. I don't know what else you want me to say or do here.'

'I want you to leave.' A warm pins-and-needles tingle flooded her face as the words shot out of her mouth. 'I do everything – the parenting, the cleaning, the cooking, the endless driving, all of it – and seeing you sitting there is a reminder that you could be helpful and you choose not to be.'

Claire felt a dizzying rush. Saying it all aloud so quickly, so unexpectedly, was like jumping off a cliff into a cool, dark body of water – a little brave, a little crazy, but thrilling nonetheless. Words hanging there, she experienced a delicious weightlessness, as if she'd removed a knapsack full of dumbbells. She staggered backward and sank into an armchair draped in mate-less socks.

Paul rubbed his chin, the gesture he made when he stood in front of the fridge swearing they were out of ketchup when, in fact, it was inches from him.

'That's not true, Claire.' He shook his head. 'I care. You're just tired. Why don't you make some coffee? You'll feel—'

'Why don't *you* make some coffee!' Claire seethed.

'Claire, geez, you sleep outside one night and now you're feral.' He threw up his hands. 'You'll feel better after a shower. You got something . . .' He pointed at her head.

Claire plucked twigs from her tangled blonde bob and let them fall to the floor beside a tumbleweed of dust. 'You aren't a partner to me, Paul.' She took a deep breath. 'You've become my fourth son and I want you to leave. Now.'

'Leave?' he snorted. 'Claire, it's not even six a.m. Where would I go?'

Even as she was kicking him out, he expected her to provide the answers. Her brain, conditioned to solve all the family's dilemmas, served up a quick fix.

'You can stay at your parents' house. They just left for Maine.'

'Do you mean for a few hours? The whole day? Longer?' Paul stood and picked at a wedgie.

Inside Claire another surge of rage spiked. She sat straighter. Her husband was wearing boxers. No jeans or shorts in sight. Had he been planning to pick her up in his underpants? Or had he been hoping she'd take a car all along?

'I mean indefinitely.'

'What will we tell the boys?'

'I'll figure it out,' Claire pressed her fingertips to her temples, 'like I always do.'

'I know you're upset and I get it, but this feels like a bit of an overreaction.' He stepped toward her. She held up a hand stop-sign-style before he could attribute her outburst to hunger or perimenopause.

'Fine. I'll go.' As he backed out of the kitchen, he stepped on a Gatorade bottle that had fallen out of the overflowing recycling bin. Its loud crackle momentarily startled him. 'Call me when you've cooled off.'

'Oh, so you'll have your phone charged by then?'

Paul scowled. Claire, who typically swallowed her snark, licked her chapped lips. She detected a hint of garlic from the slice of airport pizza but mostly she tasted sweet satisfaction.

If Paul wasn't going to change, she would.

September 4, 2024

6:32 a.m.

Claire stretched her arm across Paul's pillow. Her husband's head had been replaced by her phone. She reached for it and hit snooze.

Self-help gurus advised against bringing devices into bed, but when Claire invariably awoke at 3 a.m. and couldn't fall back to sleep, she eased her midlife anxiety by listening to audiobooks, reading essays, or watching cat videos.

When she told Paul to leave nearly four months ago, she hadn't expected their separation to last this long. She'd been so angry with him that, initially, his departure was a relief – like sending a sulky teen to sleep-away camp.

Each day during that first week he was gone, she waited for some grand gesture: a show-stopping apology in the form of flowers, a love letter, even a call inviting her to dinner to talk things through. Perhaps together, over a bottle of wine, they could figure out how they'd gotten to this place and, more importantly, how they'd get out of it.

She didn't need him to stand beneath her window holding a boombox and declaring his love in front of the neighbors, but she expected *something*. Anything.

He did nothing. Well, actually he texted. And that made things worse.

Paul: I think I forgot my toothbrush. Can you check?

Claire: Buy another.

Paul: How do you plunge a toilet?

Claire: Google it.

Paul: Am I lactose intolerant or did we drink that funky oat milk for one of the kids?

Claire didn't respond.

She'd only told one person that she'd asked him to leave: Beatrice DiCosta, her friend Julie's mom. Beatrice – Claire's unlikely confidante – had moved in with Julie and her family in

June after she was released from rehab following a fall down her basement stairs.

Each Thursday, Claire popped in to visit Bea between 9 a.m. and noon, bridging the gap between when Julie, a lawyer, went to her Manhattan office, and the home health aide arrived.

'Don't let her know you're checking on her,' Julie had insisted. 'Pretend you're borrowing a cup of sugar or an egg.'

Though Julie lived just down the block, initially, Claire didn't know how she'd fit this detour into her workday, and yet it was the least she could do. She and Julie had been friends since their children were in diapers. They'd been there for each other through teething and potty training, laughter and tears. Over countless bottles of wine, they'd commiserated about those early years, vowing it had to get easier. In some ways it had, in many it hadn't. But they had each other and that made it bearable.

As close as they were, Claire hadn't told Julie about Paul's departure. She didn't want to talk about it until she had a better idea of where they'd go from there. Was this a permanent split or a 'break', as they'd told the boys? It wasn't easy to work 'I asked Paul to leave and he did' into casual conversation, and Julie's career, coupled with caring for her mom, left her with little free time or space for anyone else's emotional baggage.

One Thursday in early July, as Claire handed Bea a glass of iced tea, the older woman gently touched Claire's arm.

'Can I ask you something, dear?' Bea began.

Anything, as long as it's not a request for a sponge bath, Claire thought but didn't say. 'Of course.'

'Where's your husband?'

Claire's cheeks grew hot.

'I may have cataracts, dear, but I see everything.' Bea tapped her fashionable red eyeglass frames. 'Haven't you noticed how Julie puts me on the front lawn in the afternoons to "get some air"? Like I'm a golden retriever fresh out of the tub!'

Claire suppressed a smile. She had spotted Bea on a bench to the left of a Japanese maple, enormous white purse by her side.

'I haven't seen Paul coming or going – except on Wednesday evenings.'

Claire couldn't lie to her dear friend's mom, this poor woman who'd broken a hip and shattered a wrist.

Once the floodgates opened, she spilled it all: how Paul left her stranded at the airport and she'd been forced to sleep in a hammock. She was afraid that sounded petty, so she launched into Paul's other shortcomings: his ability to ignore the most pressing home repairs, his failure to remember their sons' teachers' names, his lack of career ambition, the way he didn't see her, *really* see her anymore.

She was just revving up when Bea, a captive audience in her power lift electric recliner, interjected. 'Give me the condensed version, dear. I'm seventy-eight. I want to be around for the ending.'

'That's the thing, Mrs DiCosta, I don't know the ending.' Claire had plopped on the couch and put her head in her hands.

'First, call me Bea. Second, I can't tell you the number of times I wanted to give my husband, Lou, God rest his soul, the heave-ho. Third, what do *you* want to happen, dear?'

Claire tucked her hair behind her ears. 'Well, Bea, here's where things get a bit more complicated . . .'

And then she told Bea about Alex.

Alex, whom she'd seen again at her college reunion in late June.

Alex – the real reason Claire brought her phone to bed.

She'd grown accustomed to waking up to his messages. After the reunion, the flirty exchanges with her college boyfriend had begun slowly. A line or two, a joke maybe, in the early weeks of July, then, by August, paragraphs that maxed out the text box character limits. They had to send multiple messages. Each *ping!* delivered an electric shock to Claire's heart.

When she pictured Alex's brown eyes, warm and tempting as a pot of chocolate fondue, a little jolt of excitement shot up her spine. When was the last time that happened? Not since an order for her sons' sports gear qualified for free shipping.

Since seeing Alex again, Claire felt alive, alert, filled with sudden bursts of joy. It was exhilarating but odd considering nothing beyond messaging had happened between them. While they weren't exchanging steamy love letters, their easy back-and-forth stirred up some magical chemical within Claire that propelled her through the endless tasks and trials of each day.

'Who knew words could evoke so much feeling?' she'd found herself wondering. 'Poets knew, duh,' she would answer her own rhetorical question and blush at her newfound sappiness.

Looking back, Claire couldn't believe she'd almost skipped her college's twenty-five-year reunion. All through spring, her former roommates, Stacey, Maggie, and Annabelle, texted, asking if she wanted to chip in for an Airbnb. They wondered if somehow they could stay in the house they'd rented during their senior year. They'd loved that place on North Harrington Street with its warped floors and high ceilings.

I'll pay whatever it costs to drink Sutter Home White Zinfandel with you out of Solo cups on that deck overlooking the dumpsters again, Maggie had written.

It sounded like fun but Claire wasn't convinced she needed to drive several hours to stand around old dive bars. She already kept in touch with most of the people she'd want to see via social media or holiday cards. Sure, it would be nice to catch up with some old classmates again, but after one cocktail and a quick, 'What do you do? How many kids do you have?' she imagined the time would pass interminably.

It wasn't until Paul had come home from work one evening in April while they were still living together and told her – not asked her or even opened it up for discussion – but announced, really, that he was going out of town with some high school friends for a golf weekend, that Claire made up her mind. She would attend her university's reunion in upstate New York, and she'd have an adventure of her own.

And she did.

June 14, 2024

6:44 p.m.

It wasn't the house on North Harrington Street and Maggie couldn't make it, but even so, from the moment Claire stepped inside the suite that Annabelle had reserved at the Hyatt, it felt like old times.

Stacey poured wine while Annabelle deejayed, transporting them to the mid-Nineties with the help of the Gin Blossoms and Sheryl Crow as they compared lipsticks and swapped earrings.

By the time they arrived at the bar, Claire was already tipsy, and glad she'd opted for sensible sandals rather than the heels that left Stacey and Annabelle teetering toward a circle of revelers standing beneath a green and white 'Class of 1999' banner.

Claire scanned the faces – some so familiar it was as if she'd seen them yesterday, others unrecognizable. A man stared at her. His lips froze mid-sentence before pursing in a low whistle, then breaking into a broad smile. He stood beside her old friend Patty. Perhaps this was her husband? Claire hoped not, since the guy seemed to be checking her out. She loved Patty. An Irish gal from Long Island, she could drink a frat boy under the table without slurring a single syllable. Amid the twinkling lights of Ted's Olde Town Tavern, Claire's chest warmed with a rare flush of nostalgia.

As she inched closer to Patty, the man closed the gap between them and wrapped his arms around her.

'My God, Claire, you haven't changed a bit!' His warm breath and well-groomed stubble tickled her cheek.

No, this definitely wasn't Patty's husband. A classmate, maybe?

She pulled away, unable to mask her confusion, likely caused by the room-temperature Riesling she'd guzzled at the Hyatt.

'Claire, it's me. Alex.' His palms cupped her bare shoulders.

'Oh my gosh, Alex. Of course!' Claire gushed, color flooding her face. 'Sorry, I have early onset dementia.'

Now it was Alex's turn to look confused as Claire silently berated herself. *Get it together! Stop talking!*

With his head cocked to the side, Alex's hand traveled down her arm. 'Oh, Claire, I'm so sorr—'

'No, *I'm* sorry, I was joking. I've had a long ride and too much wine. Not together. I don't drink and drive. But once I got here, you know.' Claire stared at her feet, wishing she could get an instant pedicure and a conversational do-over. 'Sorry, apparently I can no longer make small talk with adults.'

'You can, Claire!' He squeezed her hand. 'You just need more to drink. I'm buying. What'll it be?'

She glanced around. Blue Moons seemed to be the beverage of choice. She loved to see the orange wedges floating like friendly smiles in a glass. She studied the long line of taps gleaming above the mahogany bar and knew her answer should've been, 'water', but instead said, 'A pint of Stella would be perfect.'

As he headed to the bar, Annabelle let out a faint purr. 'He turned out well. I wonder if he still has that little red Miata.'

Alex Larson. How could she have forgotten? They'd dated before graduation – a lovely but short-lived whirlwind.

After her longtime boyfriend, Neal, blindsided her with a breakup, Alex had been like a human defibrillator, getting her broken heart pumping again. Had he always been this cute? How had she not at least Googled him in all the intervening years?

She knew for sure she wouldn't bump into Neal. She'd checked his band's website. They were performing at a farmers' market thousands of miles away in a Seattle suburb.

'Not exactly T-Mobile Arena,' she'd cackled with smug delight after reading that the stage was located between a face-painting tent and a gourmet pickle truck.

When Alex returned with two frosty glasses, they toasted. 'To old friends and new beginnings,' he said.

'To getting annihilated and not spending the night watching Little League games and eating rubbery leftovers at nine p.m.!' Claire was tempted to add, but didn't want to come off like a boozy-and-bitchy mom cliché.

'How have you been?' she asked, genuinely curious.

'Good. Better now.' Alex's warm brown eyes, shining inside a broader, more distinguished face, triggered something, and her brain morphed into a slideshow similar to the ones she created for MamaRama. A montage of times they'd spent together flashed through her mind. She pictured him standing beneath a leafless birch tree in the middle of campus handing her a tissue, asking her out at a pub in London, kissing passionately on his hotel bed hours later, lighting cigarettes on a moonlit street.

'Do you still smoke?' she asked a little too enthusiastically.

'Does a fat baby sweat?' He winked. 'Let's go.'

Together, they slipped away to the patio, carrying their chalices of Stella Artois, Robin Thicke's 'Blurred Lines' blaring in the background.

Alex lit a Camel Light and passed it to Claire. 'So, did you become a writer?'

He'd remembered!

'Sort of.' Claire took a long drag. My God, how she'd missed this! Smoking. That first inhale sending her head reeling like a carnival ride, but also talking about life in a larger sense instead of all the minutiae that consumed her days – school fundraisers, laundry, who stole whose goggles. 'I wrote a book – a childr—'

'That's amazing!'

Embarrassed, Claire ashed on her toes, then stomped her foot like a circus horse and tried to pass it off as a dance move. 'It's just a children's book and that was eight years ago.'

Alex blew a plume of smoke over his shoulder and shook his head. 'Don't do that.'

Claire frowned. 'What?' she asked innocently. Had he noticed the way she'd muffled a belch with a fake cough?

'Don't undercut your accomplishments. Who cares if it was eight years ago? I bet it's fantastic. What's the title?' He pulled out his phone. 'I'm going to buy it right now.'

'*A Panda for Amanda* but you really don't have—'

Alex jerked his head back. 'For real? I love that one!'

'Oh, you know it?' Claire arched an eyebrow. 'Really? A picture book about a jealous primate?'

'Don't believe me?' Alex's forehead furrowed in concentration while his voice rose an octave. '"My heart is so big I can love you both!" cried Amanda. Ringo snuggled close and whispered, "Welcome!" to the panda.'

Claire rocked up on her toes. 'No way!'

'Yes way! I read it to my older two when my youngest was born.'

'Wow!'

'I may have lost it in the divorce, but if I find it, will you sign it?'

Divorce. If Claire were a German shepherd, this was the moment when her ears would've swiveled and pricked to attention.

'I'll mail you a new copy. I only have six dozen in my attic.'

'Cool, thanks.' He stubbed out his cigarette. 'I didn't put it together – your name on the cover, I mean.'

'Yeah, I used my married name.'

'Married, got it.' He nodded and took a drink. The beer left a foam mustache above his full lips. Claire fought the sudden urge to lick it off.

'Separated now . . . sort of . . .' What was she doing? She hadn't even told Stacey or Annabelle about the problems in her marriage.

'Sorry – not sorry.' Alex smiled. Had he always had those dimples?

Claire bit the inside of her cheek to keep from grinning like a hyena.

She expected him to flip the conversation back to himself, the way so many of her sons' friends' dads did. But Alex kept the focus on her. 'So, what else have you been up to?'

Claire inhaled. 'Well, I took this full-time job at a parenting website back in January. It's been kind of a nightmare, actually.' She stopped. How could she tell him that she'd recently compiled a slideshow ranking Disney princesses in order of who gave you the most major hair envy? 'I've wanted to start a new book but I haven't . . .'

Claire typically blamed the constant swirl of kid-related activities for her lack of creativity, but with the boys spending every other weekend with Paul, she could no longer use that as an excuse. If she were honest with herself, maybe she was afraid of putting in all that effort only to face the rejection that accompanied the writing life – and at a time when she felt like she was failing at her marriage and her career . . .

But seeing Alex, hearing him recite lines from her picture book, convinced her she needed to take her writing seriously again.

'. . . I haven't quite gotten around to it yet,' she said.

'Don't be so hard on yourself, Claire.' The kindness in Alex's eyes made her insides flutter. 'It's awesome that you're pursuing your dreams. You'll get there. You've got plenty of time.'

September 4, 2024

6:41 a.m.

Time. The phone's alarm buzzed in Claire's palm, pulling her back to the present. How did nine minutes pass like three seconds? What day was it? She rubbed the gritty sleep sand from her eyes. Thursday. Which tiresome tasks awaited her? She needed to get moving, but first she'd check to see if Alex had messaged her. Just knowing that he was thinking of her lifted her spirits. She found herself floating through the arduous early morning duties, buoyed by his attention.

Over the past month she learned that he rose before dawn to work out. After he did, he wrote to her.

Sliding her index finger across the screen, Claire tapped the app and held her breath. There it was. One new message. Sent at 5:42 a.m. A single line that acted like a triple shot of espresso.

What are you doing tonight?

Claire's heart galloped the way it did when she momentarily lost Joe in the supermarket. It pulsed in her throat, elbows, the area just above her ankles.

Was this a casual ask? Like, was he going to recommend a show she should binge-watch, a game the boys might want to catch? Or, was this a lead-in to an invitation?

What *was* she doing tonight? Claire scanned her mental calendar and kid-slash-work to-do lists but couldn't think clearly. Involuntarily, her legs swung over the side of the bed. She sat upright, blinked multiple times, and re-read Alex's message.

What are you doing tonight?

Why was he asking? How should she respond?

Before she had a chance to compose a reply, screams ripped through the previously silent second floor of her home.

'MOM!!!' Max bellowed. 'Henry's stealing my socks again!'

September 4, 2024

6:47 a.m.

Claire tightened her bathrobe belt, readying for battle. In the hallway, Max and Henry engaged in a tug of war over a maroon sock.

'Mom! He won't give it back!'

Claire looked at her oldest son's feet, already ensconced in navy socks. 'Max, we've been over this. You can only wear one pair at a time. Give your brother the sock. I'll wash them tonight.'

Tonight. She wanted to dart back to her bedroom and write to Alex. But what would she tell him?

'That's not the point,' Max shouted. 'Henry has his own socks. He should just wear those.'

She couldn't believe this was what her life had devolved into – endless negotiations over nonsense.

'Think of it as flattery, honey. Henry loves you so much; he wants to be just like you. When Joe wears my dresses, I don't get upset.'

Humor had always been Claire's go-to strategy when it came to defusing conflict. But the boys were becoming an increasingly tough audience.

'Mom, stop!' Henry snorted. 'If Joe wants to wear your dresses, you can't get upset. As his family, it's our job to support him if he decides to explore his identity. But because you're so big and he's so small, your clothes would be huge on him – not that I'm fat-shaming you or height-shaming him.'

Of course, Claire wanted to raise sensitive young men, but this level of political correctness was overwhelming. Last week when she'd used the word 'cheesy' to describe the ending of a Tom Hanks movie, the boys had ganged up on her for maligning the dairy industry. It was a lot.

'I need these socks,' Max insisted. 'I've got soccer practice this afternoon, Mom, don't forget.'

In the spring, Claire had accidentally missed an 'important' parent meeting. Max and his coach treated her like an amnesia victim ever since.

'And I'm checking out the debate club, because I'm *debating* joining.' Henry doubled over laughing at his own joke as Max whacked him on the back with the sock he'd wrangled from his brother's hands.

Joe opened his bedroom door and rubbed his head. 'Can we have Belgian waffles for breakfast?'

It wasn't even 7 a.m. and Claire already wished the day were done.

What are you doing tonight? The words floated through her mind again, giving her a little shiver. Why was Alex asking?

If she could just make it through the next ninety minutes and get everyone to school, she'd find out.

September 4, 2024

7:11 a.m.

Claire filled the kettle and lit the burner – its familiar *tic, tic, tic* an even more welcome sound than its evening counterpart: the *pop* of a cork eased from the neck of a wine bottle. She reached for the coffee beans and grinder. She'd recently said goodbye to those stale pods and the hulking machine Paul had given her – a castoff from his office's kitchen renovation – for her last birthday.

Alex told her pour-over was the way to go, and he'd been right. Richer, fresher, more flavorful. Watching the dark brew drip into a sleek, glass carafe, Claire felt like a chemist with exquisite taste. Yes, she was making changes.

As she waited for the water to boil, she prepared the boys' lunches: PB&J for Max and Joe. Salami with stone-ground mustard on a sesame-seed roll for Henry, whose tastes had never bordered on childlike. Her middle son, though only in sixth grade, seemed to have been born with the palate of a food critic. She placed each sandwich inside a plastic bag, completely forgetting that the school district had asked parents and students to commit to packing only 'litter-less lunches' this year.

As she reached into the cabinet, Claire's gaze drifted toward the water stain on the ceiling. When she'd first noticed it months ago, Max had pointed out that it was the shape of Rhode Island. Last week, Henry suggested it had grown to resemble Colorado. Was she hallucinating, or did the mark, now the size of the Pacific Northwest, appear to be bulging this morning?

'If it bothers you that much, don't look up,' suggested her husband – or estranged husband. She never knew how to think of Paul now. For weeks, he'd been promising to 'take a look at it' when he came over for his Wednesday dinners with the boys.

Claire wanted to call a plumber, but Paul, trying to avoid the expense, insisted he'd get to it.

Their home could devolve into a waterpark and he'd offer his usual, 'It's on my to-do list!'

Claire looked away from the ceiling. As she'd been doing for weeks when something unpleasant crossed her mind, she shifted her thoughts to Alex.

As her sons crunched their way through bowls of cereal at the kitchen table (no time for Belgian waffles on a Thursday!), she hurried to the dining room to open her laptop. She'd re-read Alex's message in case her sleep-deprived brain had caused her to hallucinate.

Claire intended to go straight to it but got sidetracked by an email from her brother.

> From: Kyle Collins
> To: Claire Casey
> Sept. 3
> 11:02 p.m.
> Subject: Coupon & FF
> Hey, tell Coupon if he wants in on this fantasy league, he'd better get his money and picks in ASAP.

Coupon had been her family's nickname for Paul because of the way they'd met. No one called him that to his face, though Claire doubted Paul would've minded much anyway.

On a Saturday morning during the late summer of 2004, Claire found herself roaming the aisles of Bed Bath & Beyond. She'd gone in search of a bridal shower gift for Stacey on behalf of Annabelle, who was off in an exotic locale, somewhere apparently so fabulous it did not include the ubiquitous home goods emporium.

Hungover from attending an office happy hour the night before, Claire scanned the registry for anything close to Annabelle's one-hundred-and-fifty-dollar limit. With a dull headache and a sloppy ponytail, Claire lurched toward the checkout area carrying a cumbersome crystal punchbowl. Maroon 5's 'This Love' blared overhead, leaving her longing for a power failure.

When the guy in front of her turned and began speaking, it took Claire a moment to register that he was talking to her.

'Do you have a coupon?' the guy repeated.

'Um, no, I don't think so.' Claire didn't even pretend to look.

If she opened her purse to search for anything, it would've been a stick of gum. Her tongue felt fuzzy as a strip of Velcro, and she could still taste the Fireball shots she'd downed less than twelve hours earlier.

'I have an extra.' He wore a happy, open expression and his eyes sparkled, blue as the Caribbean, against his navy Yankees T-shirt. Unlike Claire, he appeared to have showered before his Bed Bath & Beyond outing.

'Here you go.' He smiled and placed a '20 percent off' coupon atop the enormous punchbowl box.

'Thanks,' Claire managed. What was the right amount of gratitude for this generous move? Since Annabelle, jetting in that afternoon hours before Stacey's shower, would reimburse her, this coupon wasn't really doing Claire much good. But she thought it would be rude to share any of that.

The guy held up a set of barbecue tools and another coupon. 'Housewarming gift.'

'Nice.' Claire nodded, causing her head to throb. Few things seemed less appealing than hot dogs at that moment, but she had to admit a grill set was far more practical than a punchbowl. 'What was Stacey thinking registering for this?' she murmured as the cashier one aisle over shouted, 'I'm open!'

Claire slogged her way there as if she were pulling a sled full of obese children up a snowy mountain, placed the punchbowl carefully on the counter, and handed over the coupon.

'Mmm-hmmm!' The employee whistled, scanner raised high in the air. 'You just saved twenty-eight dollars! Not too shabby.'

Again, Claire thought: *Annabelle saved it, not me.* But, once more, she kept this to herself.

The cashier put the box in a shopping bag and implored Claire to 'hold it from the bottom!'

Feeling the woman's eyes on her back, Claire cradled the punchbowl like a newborn as she approached the exit where the coupon guy studied a 'snow shovel and rock salt' display; odd considering it was August and the first snowfall was hopefully months away.

'Thanks, I owe you one,' Claire said as she passed him.

'Have dinner with me,' Coupon Guy blurted, holding an ice scraper in one hand and the barbecue tool set in the other – a man caught between opposing seasons.

Claire hesitated, her headache making her even slower than her usual Saturday morning self. A cold sweat spread across the back of her neck. She really should've gone home before that third round of shots.

'Honey, that man just saved you close to thirty bucks,' the cashier interjected. 'The least you can do is split a burger and fries with him.'

At the mention of food, Claire dropped her bag. The sound of glass shattering was overshadowed as she vomited into a gray garbage pail beside the exit.

Rather than run to his car, Coupon Guy grabbed a roll of paper towels from beneath a register and offered Claire a swath the size of a catcher's mitt.

'Don't feel bad.' He smiled and shrugged. 'Who uses a punchbowl anyway?'

The memory of Paul's kind face, the dimple in his chin, which Claire had noticed as she wiped her own with the bundle of paper towels, made the sour taste of guilt spring up in her throat now. She took a sip of the rich French roast to push it back down.

Claire felt like vomiting each time she remembered that her parents and brother had no idea that Paul no longer lived there. She was a terrible secret-keeper, but it was her life, her marriage, and until she'd made up her mind about what she wanted, she didn't care to discuss it. And, besides, her mom had enough on her plate.

Truly, Claire hadn't intended for the separation to last this long. The day before the reunion, she'd thought about suggesting couples counseling, but stopped herself. Why was it always her job to fix things? Then she saw Alex again, and his interest in her provided a delicious distraction from her troubles. It also acted like a B12 shot. She began looking forward to the start of each new day, feeling simultaneously giddy, alive, and delightfully daydreamy. Why would she want that to end? She hadn't, and suddenly days unspooled into weeks, then months.

Now it was football season and her brother wanted her husband (potentially ex-husband?) to join his fantasy league. She didn't have the time nor the headspace to deal with that.

Deleting Kyle's message, she moved on. Her next two emails updated her on delivery dates for recent online purchases – Joe's new backpack and Henry's stainless-steel thermos (for the gumbo he hoped to make).

The next message was from the middle-school principal. 'BTSN REMINDERS' the subject screamed.

BTSN? BTSN? Increasingly, Claire's emails and texts were littered with acronyms she didn't understand, making her feel as outdated as a Model-T in a Tesla world. Where had she seen these initials before? *Fifty Shades of Grey?* Was this a dangerous new viral sex challenge going around the high school and trickling down to younger students?

She opened the message, preparing for yet another thing she'd need to discuss with her sons. To her relief, the initials stood for Back-To-School Night. She must've blocked it out. She'd text Paul to remind him. If Claire had forgotten about this annual ritual, she knew there was a greater chance of Paul growing wings and taking flight than remembering it on his own.

As much as she enjoyed meeting her sons' teachers, these events had taken on a carnival feel. 'Step right up and pay your PTA dues! Don't forget your school spirit T-shirts and sweats! See who's gotten Botox, lost or gained weight over the summer!'

Claire really wasn't in the mood for any of it – especially because she'd let herself go a bit. Since she'd taken on her full-time job at MamaRama.com in January, she'd been sitting on her bottom for far too much of the day, and it showed.

For decades, Claire had believed she'd been blessed with a decent metabolism. But since turning forty, if she even glanced at a bagel, her thighs expanded and her butt sagged toward her calves. Meanwhile, Paul and the boys grazed like they were at a never-ending all-you-can-eat buffet without gaining an ounce.

In the kitchen, bowls and spoons clattered against the countertop. Nothing ever made its way into the sink or dishwasher without Claire shepherding it there.

'Brush your teeth!' she called. Would there ever come a time when she could stop issuing this reminder? 'We're leaving in five!'

Because they lived less than two miles from the middle school, they didn't qualify for bussing, so Claire needed to drive Henry and Max. Mercifully, Joe took the bus to the elementary school, saving her at least ten minutes each way.

As she listened for the *thunk, thunk, thunk* of her sons racing up the steps, she clicked furiously to retrieve Alex's message.

There it was.

What are you doing tonight?

'Think, Claire! Think!' she commanded.

Before writing back to him, she needed to check the kitchen wall calendar where she jotted down things like dental appointments and sports practices. It was a terrible system – having some commitments on paper, the rest in an online calendar. And, of course, the push pin that was supposed to secure the bulky calendar to the bulletin board never held, leaving it behind a basket of cooking magazines and take-out menus.

At the bottom of the pile, Claire spied the leather journal Paul had given her for their first wedding anniversary.

'Paper!' he'd said proudly, placing it in her hands. 'It's the traditional one-year anniversary gift. It was this or lottery tickets.'

They'd just bought the house and had about two hundred dollars left in their savings.

Inside the journal's front cover, he'd written, *To my all-time favorite character. Write that book. This is your year.*

At the time, that gift – what it symbolized; his faith in her – brought tears to her eyes.

How had *they* ended up there, beneath a stack that could've easily been tossed in the recycling? How had they ended up here? Separated. So different from the people they once were.

She skimmed through the journal. The metallic tang of guilt sprang into her mouth and, once more, she swallowed it. She'd filled half the pages with the start of a romcom based on her and Paul's early days together. But once Max was born, she found it impossible to write. The moment those two pink lines appeared on the pregnancy test, it seemed as if time had ceased to be her own.

Clutching the wall calendar, she flipped to September. Other than back-to-school night, she had no plans.

She darted to the dining room, stared at Alex's message, and considered her possible reply:

It's back-to-school-night so I'll probably spend the evening hiding behind a bookcase to avoid getting roped into chairing a plant sale or sewing costumes for the spring musical. LOL. And you?

No. If Alex was about to ask her to do something – meet in person! – then she should seem available, open to it.

But, wait. She was getting ahead of herself. Maybe Alex wasn't inviting her anywhere. Perhaps after a month of daily correspondence he'd simply run out of things to say. The question could be a substitute for the bland and generic *How are you?* But Alex wasn't bland or generic. He usually opened with a funny work anecdote, a quip from one of his boys, or an interesting observation from his evening run along the river. Then he'd ask about her, her boys, her work.

She read the lone sentence again as if the words had changed or a hidden meaning might reveal itself.

What are you doing tonight?

Sneakers squeaking against hardwood brought Claire's attention back to her blinking cursor. The fridge door opened and slammed repeatedly as each kid grabbed a water bottle. She had to hurry. The boys couldn't be late on their third day of school.

Get your shit together, Claire!

Fingers hovering above the keyboard, she took a deep breath and typed with the urgency of someone whose laptop battery was below 5 percent.

No plans. You? She hit send and stood, dizzier than if she'd stepped off a Tilt-a-Whirl.

'Mom!' Max appeared in the dining-room doorway, blocking Joe, who waited until they returned from drop-off to change out of his hand-me-down solar system pajamas. 'Let's go!'

'I'm coming! I'm coming!' Claire closed the laptop and just missed the black dots bouncing in a new text box as Alex composed his reply.

September 4, 2024

7:48 a.m.

The car line was always a shitshow the first few days of the school year as new parent volunteers learned the hand signals. *These poor people; what the hell were they thinking?* Claire wondered. She might've gotten snookered into chaperoning dances and baking brownies for sports banquets, but she drew the line at serving as an unpaid traffic cop.

From the backseat she heard a beep.

'C'mon, guys, put your phones away. I'm not your Uber driver.' In truth, she wished she'd remembered her own phone. She'd left it in her bedroom when she rushed to break up the sock fight.

Had Alex written back? And if so, what had he said? The anticipation made her feel sixteen again, but also as anxious as if she were about to bungee jump off a bridge.

'Don't forget to sign my form!' Henry called from the middle of the minivan.

Claire moaned. She'd been completing back-to-school paperwork for the past two nights, though none of the information had changed from previous years. As a test, she put Paul's name and number as the primary contact in case of emergency this time.

'Which form now?' she asked.

'For the Boy Scouts camping trip, remember?' Henry said.

Claire bit her lip and smiled. 'Ah, yes, the Scouts. I remember now.'

February 1, 1999

4:22 p.m.

Cutting across campus, Discman in her coat pocket, Claire mainlined the melancholy of Counting Crows's 'Long December', though it was February and the CD was so worn it skipped, the word 'believe' echoing in her ears.

She kept her head down, looking for wildflowers beneath last year's mulch, any sign that she could speed up time and forget all about Neal.

Neal, who'd broken her heart in December when he announced he had enough credits to graduate early and was moving to California.

'Without me?' she'd squeaked when he'd told her, laying it out as casually as he had when he stated he was dropping that James Joyce seminar they'd signed up for together.

Neal's cousin lived in LA and knew a band in need of a drummer. Neal sent some MP3s, and they'd invited him to sit in.

All those afternoons she'd thought he was studying or looking for post-graduation jobs, he'd been meeting with his advisor and apartment hunting, telling her only after it was a done deal.

They'd been together since first semester freshman year. Despite living in the same house with the same friends, returning to school in January felt strange and disorienting, like walking into a familiar room and finding all the furniture upside down.

Claire wandered the campus, her insides empty as a bongo drum, trying to adjust to life without him. It was terrible to root against someone you once loved but that's what she did. If Neal's music career failed, he'd return, humbled. And when he did, she'd make him grovel a bit, but then she'd kiss him like something straight out of a blockbuster film, music building behind them, and everything would go back to the way it had been.

As Claire lumbered uphill toward the house on North Harrington Street, something caught her eye. A pale green army-style jacket. Just like Neal's. And a black knit hat. Just like Neal's.

Was he here? Now? For her? She knew it!

Maggie, Stacey, and Annabelle told her she needed to move on, but here he was. She'd get her Hollywood ending after all.

Before she could stop herself, Claire took off running and leapt onto the back of the green-jacketed figure, throwing her arms around his neck.

'Looking for me?' she whispered, nibbling his cold pink earlobe.

'Whoa!' came a voice that definitely wasn't Neal's.

She released her grip and jumped off this stranger's back, suddenly as uncomfortable as if she'd slid down a cactus.

He turned around. No, this was not Neal.

'Claire,' said the guy, rubbing his neck and adjusting the backpack she'd inadvertently kicked off his shoulder. 'This is a nice surprise!'

She was too embarrassed to speak. She'd done such an intimate, crazy thing, she might as well have burglarized the wrong house.

'Sorry, have we met?' she asked, mortified and disoriented, staring at her feet, frozen inside her Doc Martens.

'Alex,' the guy said. 'Alex Larson. I'm in your Hemingway class.' He paused. When Claire said nothing, he continued. '"After a while I went out and left the hospital and walked back to the hotel in the rain."'

As Alex quoted the last line of *A Farewell to Arms*, Claire began to cry, soft whimpers that gave way to great gulping sobs. Neal wasn't coming back. This wasn't a movie. Just her same crappy real life.

'I know, right? Poor Frederic.' Alex looked both ways and lowered his voice. 'That ending got me a little choked up too, not gonna lie.'

Claire wiped her nose on the sleeve of her pea coat, prompting Alex to sling his backpack to the ground, unzip a section, and pull out a packet of Kleenex. Neal never would've done that. He didn't have tissues. Or cash. Not even gum. The most you could count on was a joint, a lighter, and a pair of drumsticks wrapped with grip tape.

'You carry tissues?' Claire asked, reaching for one.

'I was a Boy Scout, so you know . . .'

Claire frowned and shook her head.

'. . . always prepared!'

'Oh, right.' Claire nodded.

'Hey,' he took a tissue from the pack and patted her cheek, 'I'm gonna grab a bite and then head to the hockey game. My housemate's the goalie. Care to join me?'

We have a hockey team? Claire's universe had been so Neal-centered, what else had she missed? Still, that wasn't how she planned to spend the evening.

'I'm good, but thanks.'

'Are you good?' Alex cocked his head. 'You were just crying over Hemingway. Come out with me. We'll have a few drinks, split some wings. I'll make you forget all about Papa.'

Confused and out of practice with flirting, Claire stared blankly.

'Oof, I just heard how weird that sounded,' Alex backpedaled. '"Papa" was the nickname Hemingway chose for himself because he didn't like "Ernest", which I totally get. Not even twenty percent as cool as "Alex", right? Or "Claire" – that's a great name, too. So what do you say? If you're anti-wings, we can get something else.'

Claire's stomach rumbled at the mention of food. She was flattered by Alex's attention, his persistence. But she wouldn't join him. She was stubbornly – stupidly – stuck on giving her breakup with Neal a proper mourning period. 'That sounds fun but I have a paper due tomorrow.' *Not a lie.*

'Ah, OK, cool, yeah, this was last-minute anyway, so . . .' Alex hoisted the backpack onto his shoulder '. . . another time then.'

'Yeah, another time.'

As Claire trudged uphill, she felt a small flicker of hope bloom inside her chest. She dried her eyes and blew her nose. It made a terrible honking sound. She hoped Alex hadn't heard.

September 4, 2024

8:11 a.m.

A horn honked at the top of their street as Claire and Joe prepared to race toward the bus stop. Before leaving the house, Claire caught a glimpse of her reflection in the entryway mirror and cringed. She'd been meaning to schedule an appointment for a cut and the highlights to hide the feisty grays that were popping up (literally, straight up in the air like the bristles of a toilet brush) with an alarming frequency. Then there were the puffy purple bags beneath her eyes. She'd volunteered to test out some hyaluronic acid patches designed to reduce under-eye swelling and discoloration. After sampling a range of brands, she'd outline the results for MamaRama. Sabrina had been looking directly at her when she brought up the assignment. Her editor didn't have to say it, Claire knew she was the only one on the team old enough to tell which products truly brightened and firmed. *When was that piece due?* She needed to check her calendar – and her phone, too. She was dying to see if Alex had replied but getting Joe packed, dressed, and moving in the right direction swallowed every precious second. Plus, part of Claire was afraid to look.

What if he hadn't written back?

What if he had?

Joe grabbed her hand and tugged her down the block toward the crowd waiting between a utility pole and a Little Free Library.

Perhaps looking disheveled would work in her favor, Claire reasoned. She really didn't feel like talking to the other moms who, regardless of the early hour, always appeared showered and stylishly attired. She imagined them secretly doing those Kegel exercises her gynecologist recommended while they chatted about the best math tutors and the all-inclusive resorts they'd already booked for winter break.

Maybe if they thought Claire had just come from cleaning a garage, they'd avoid her. She worried that these women, with instincts keener than a pack of hunting dogs, had noticed that Paul was no longer coming and going from their home daily.

Thankfully, he'd been there for the first day of school. Arriving early enough to have breakfast with the boys, he'd brought Claire coffee and a bouquet of sunflowers with a note that read *Congrats on surviving another summer with our crew.* He'd even waited at the bus stop with her and Joe. That bought her some time, but how much? She'd been living in fear of her neighbors asking why they hadn't seen him for months.

Back in July, Abby McClaren jogged past the house as Claire wrestled the lid onto an overflowing garbage can and dragged it to the curb.

'Hey, Claire!' Abby chirped while running in place and tapping her Fitbit. 'Where's Paul? Shouldn't he be doing that?'

'We don't believe in restricting ourselves to traditional gender roles,' Claire wished she'd said after the interaction ended. But at that moment, she'd blushed and blurted, 'He's at his parents' house today. Helping them.'

'Huh,' Abby mumbled, as if this information confused her.

'Yes,' Claire continued, nodding. 'They're getting up there, you know. Almost eighty. Their house is small, but it's a lot for them to maintain. So—'

'But I thought—'

'Coming, boys!' Claire screamed toward her home where absolutely no one had called her. She'd nearly sprained an ankle sprinting up her porch steps. Until she had a better idea of where she and Paul stood, it seemed simpler to dodge all her neighbors and their inevitable questions.

So, as the school year began, Claire would've much preferred to kiss Joe on their porch and wave goodbye while keeping her distance. But her youngest was her baby in every sense of the word. Granted, it was only his third day of second grade, but he'd told her he wasn't ready to wait at the stop (only five houses away), without her.

'It's wonderful that he's so in touch with his emotions,' her mother had said when Claire complained about what felt like decades of standing at bus stops.

Eleanor always found a way to put a positive spin on things. Lately, it made Claire think perhaps she'd been adopted.

As Claire and Joe waited on the sidewalk, Abby approached carrying an enormous iced latte in a clear Something's Brewing tumbler.

'Ready for tonight?' she asked.

Claire's cheeks burned. Yes, Abby always inserted herself in other people's business but how did this woman know she was hoping to rekindle an old flame that very evening?

Abby, sensing Claire's confusion, heaved an exasperated sigh. 'The town council meeting! It starts at seven p.m. sharp! Be there! Please!'

Claire registered the exclamation points in Abby's voice. What was the meeting about again? Claire frowned as her neighbor tapped her nails expectantly against the tumbler's lid.

The drive-thru Starbucks! How could Claire forget? It wasn't just that Abby loathed the idea of a drive-thru popping up in their tiny suburb – potentially creating even more traffic than they already endured – but she and her husband owned the town's lone coffee shop, Something's Brewing.

'Claire!' Abby barked. 'I'm counting on you! You know how important this business is to our family. And don't forget all we do for the community. We sponsor baseball and soccer teams . . .' Abby ticked off items on her fingers.

Claire was only half-listening. She was more focused on Joe, who was aggressively scratching the back of his head. Was he developing a nervous tic because she'd kicked out his father, thereby destroying his sense of family?

'. . . they'll ruin everything we've built!' Abby screeched.

It sounded so dramatic, yet it was true. If the Seattle-based java giant came to town, surely the McClarens' shop would shutter within the month, ending the steady stream of gossip that flowed Abby's way. Without it, how would Abby (and Claire, too, for that matter) get a jump on school-related scandals or learn who was moving, and who'd fired their nanny?

'It would be great if you could cover this for the paper,' Abby said.

Claire hadn't written for *The Acorn* in two years, not since budget cuts eliminated freelancers. It shouldn't have surprised her that Abby hadn't remembered. Their friendship was based on proximity and shared complaints about garbage pickup and subpar snow plowing. Abby probably didn't even remember that Claire had accepted a new job at the start of the year.

'I'm not there any . . .'

Abby had already moved down the block, ordering more people to fight the iconic coffee company that threatened her livelihood.

Claire checked her watch. 8:22 a.m. She looked around. One by one, the other moms disappeared. Some headed to work, more to Pilates, yoga, and body sculpting.

'Where the fuck is this bus?' Claire wanted to shout into the treetops. She turned to the children and outed herself as a bad parent by asking, 'Tell me again – what time does the first bell ring?'

'Eight forty-five,' a third grader responded.

'All right.' Claire counted heads. 'One, two, three, four, five. Wait here. I'll be back in thirty seconds with the van and I'll drive everyone.'

'Thanks, Mom.' Joe clawed behind his ear and smiled, his cheeks still dotted with freckles courtesy of the summer sun.

'I'm not allowed to ride with strangers,' whined Parker Westbrook, a precocious kindergartener.

Claire thought his name sounded like the kind of law firm you retained when you were charged with a triple homicide. Though she'd only been observing him at the bus stop for the past few mornings, she could tell he was the type of kid who'd probably raise his hand in class on a Friday afternoon and say something like, 'You forgot to give us homework,' prompting a chorus of 'You suck, man!' from every corner.

She knew she should feel sorry for him, as he likely had a lifetime of bad relationships looming; instead she shrugged and offered an 'Oh well.'

When she pulled up moments later, the children piled in while Parker clung to a mailbox.

Reluctant to leave him behind on his own, Claire rolled down the passenger window and called, 'You sure you don't want a ride? You might be waiting a while by yourself. Why don't you just hop in?'

'Ahhh! Stranger Danger!' Parker shrieked, tightening his grip on the mailbox.

Out of the corner of her eye, Claire saw an older boy she didn't recognize holding a cell phone and pointing it at her. *Is he filming this?*

'Who's that?' she asked Joe, shouting to be heard above Parker's wailing.

'No clue.' Joe tugged his seatbelt over his tiny shoulder.

'His name's Noah. He's new,' someone yelled from the third row.

'Mom!' Joe squawked. 'Let's go!'

'Parker?' Claire tried again, waving this time. 'Come on. Get in. You're going to be late.'

'I don't know you!' Parker bellowed. 'Don't come any closer! Help!'

The older boy aimed the phone at Parker, then directed it toward the van. The hairs on the back of Claire's neck prickled.

'Great. Now we're all going to be late!' a girl seated in the middle row huffed.

'Suit yourself!' Claire called to Parker before muttering, 'Geez, what a baby!'

As she straightened, she noticed the older boy and his phone were still trained on her.

'Hey!' she erupted, leaning toward the open window again. 'Why don't you put that phone down and do something useful!' She hadn't meant it as harshly as it came out. That sentence had become a reflex following a whole summer of finding Max and Henry face-down in their devices, ignoring her requests to set the table or empty the dishwasher.

Wanting to get back home to see if Alex had responded made Claire jittery – or maybe it was switching to that 'robust' (Alex's word) coffee. She needed to move on before she said something worse. Her fingers turned bone white as they curled around the steering wheel and she peeled away from the curb. She avoided glancing in the rearview mirror for fear the teen had continued filming her.

With everyone buckled safely in the van, Claire barreled through the combat zone that was the elementary school drop-off line. Parent volunteers offered mixed signals, waving their stop signs like fly swatters as horns blared and kids jaywalked. Mothers from the Environmental Committee wore headbands with tiny tree branches and leaves attached as they doled out Granny Smith apples and thanked fellow parents for adhering to the strict litter-less lunch policy.

Claire was about to say to Joe, 'Environmental Committee? More like the Mental Committee,' when she remembered they weren't alone in the van.

It would've been particularly awkward because Iris (the third grader who'd told Claire when school began) and her mom had founded the committee two years earlier. The mother, daughter, and an older sister who was named for an herb Claire couldn't recall – was it Rosemary? Sage? – were also instrumental in cultivating the much-talked-about hummingbird garden.

Claire heard a buzz. At the same time, the first bell rang and her passengers began yanking at the doors as if they were hostages. She put the van in park and chirped, 'Have a good day!' which garnered no response – not even a 'you too' grunt.

'Thanks for carpooling, Claire! The Earth thanks you too!' Marjorie Watkins, head of the Environmental Committee, shouted.

'You rock!' cried one of Marjorie's underlings dressed as a pea pod. 'Together, we'll make this a litter-free, zero-waste zone!'

Joe leaned between the driver and passenger seats to let Claire kiss him goodbye, something Max and Henry no longer allowed in front of their peers.

'Mommy, I have a glitter-less lunch, right?' Joe's small forehead crinkled with concern as he scratched the back of his head.

Claire smiled, delighted that her youngest child was so creative he could envision sandwiches decked out in sparkles.

Instead of pointing out his error, she cupped his sweet face in her hands and said, 'Yes, my dear, your lunch is one hundred percent glitter-free.'

September 4, 2024

8:42 a.m.

Claire watched Joe race inside the building before putting the van's gas pedal to the floor. She had three minutes to prep for her call with Sabrina. Last night, her MamaRama editor had emailed asking to have a 'quick chat' before the 9 a.m. team-wide video meeting.

'Nothing to worry about! Just a teeny request!' Sabrina had written, sending Claire's thoughts skittering like a pack of unruly field mice. Was she about to be promoted? Fired?

Sabrina could be difficult to read. Whatever she had to say, Claire hoped she'd keep it brief. She wanted to check for a message from Alex and then, once she knew more, compose the perfect reply.

Was he about to confess that he couldn't go another minute without seeing her? Was he driving up from Philadelphia to take her somewhere magical and whisk her away from the tedium that had become her day-to-day existence? Lately, his messages had been a little bolder. He'd tell her about a hike and write *I can't wait to show you the view from the top.*

In early August, she'd written an essay about how receiving back-to-school supply lists in July ruined summer and caused undo stress for parents and students. A popular mom blogger shared it on social media and Claire's piece had gone viral – to the point that the *Today* show wanted to interview her.

She'd imagined a limo collecting her at dawn, delivering her to Rockefeller Plaza in time for hair and makeup. In reality, she'd been asked to join via video. As she waited in the virtual green room, she panicked that her mind would go blank and, when it did, she'd laugh like the Joker out of sheer panic. But her fears were unwarranted. Her segment got preempted when a celebrity chef's back-to-school lunch ideas demo ran long.

Still, the piece's popularity scored her bonus points with MamaRama's editorial team. That evening a bottle of wine (Sancerre, her favorite) waited on her porch. *Cheers to you!* the attached note read. The August humidity made the chilled bottle sweat, causing the signature to blur. She hadn't needed to read the name to know it was from Alex. *So thoughtful*, she'd smiled, though she hadn't remembered mentioning how much she liked that varietal. Maybe she'd written something about it in a summer drinks slideshow and he'd read it.

Paul had picked up the boys for the weekend so she headed to the patio, opened the bottle, and sent Alex a photo of her half-filled wine glass with the caption *Cheers!*

He'd responded with a shot of his balcony overlooking the Schuylkill River, his fingers wrapped around a highball glass, waning daylight glinting off golden liqueur. He'd written: **Drinks here soon? Just you, me, and the sunset**.

If she'd heard something like that said in one of her mom's beloved Hallmark movies, she'd have fake-gagged. But coming from Alex, at this point in her life, the words, the thought of new adventures with someone who found her appealing, sent a wild pinball-like energy zinging through her.

As much as Claire would've loved to hear his deep voice, tinged with a slight hint of a Philly accent (which she found oddly appealing), they hadn't exchanged phone numbers. Maybe it was dumb, but speaking with him seemed like it would make things more serious, more intense. The thought of phone calls took her back to those awful awkward goodbyes of her teen years. *You hang up first. No, you!* Plus, she didn't want to risk her sons overhearing a conversation and reporting back to Paul. It was better this way.

Claire pulled into the driveway, grabbed her purse, and ran toward the house, taking her porch steps two at a time, intent on reading Alex's message without further delay. Sabrina would call any second. She charged up the staircase, stumbling over the boys' carelessly abandoned flip-flops, and raced into her bedroom.

After tossing her pillows and fanning out the duvet, she found her phone twisted in the flat sheet. She sat panting, partially from the exertion of dashing up multiple flights of stairs, but mostly from anticipation. As her face unlocked the screen, the words 'Voicemail: Mom' flashed. She wanted to ignore it, but her parents were in their seventies and – since her mom's diagnosis

– Claire's first thought: *What if this is an emergency!?* guilted her into listening to the message before doing anything else:

'Hi, honey! It's your mom! I've got pork chops defrosting, and I'm calling to see if you have brown sugar for the baked beans. If not, no problem, I'll be passing stores on my way to your house. Let me know either way. See you tonight!'

She was making dinner for them tonight? *Why?* Claire struggled to recall.

'Back-to-school night!' She face-palmed and whispered, 'Oh, Mom, no, no five-course feast, please.' Sure, her mother meant well, but she'd cook up a storm, leave the kitchen looking like a tsunami had ripped through it, then either collapse in front of *Jeopardy!* or simply drive home. It seemed like so much unnecessary work, yet her mother insisted she was 'fine' and preferred to keep busy. Still, Claire worried about her overdoing it.

She started to text to say they could just order pizza when Sabrina's call came through.

Wrestling her thoughts away from her mother and Alex, Claire tried to focus on her editor. 'Hey, Sabrina.'

'Claire!' Sabrina sing-songed, stretching her name to two syllables. 'So nice to chat with you! Thanks for making the time. What I want to talk about is, well, that piece you wrote about single moms sharing their first daycare drop-off experiences was just beyond. I mean, like, really, really powerful. All the feels. I bawled.'

Claire, still trying to figure out the weird MamaRama lingo, simply said, 'Thanks so much.'

'Right, so, anyway, I totally love the quotes you got from that mom whose husband died days after their son was born. The one who said she felt like she was placing the last piece of her soulmate in a stranger's hands and asking them to nurture it? Beyond gut-wrenching.'

'I know, right?' Claire had no clue where this was heading. 'Thank you?'

As a working parent – and now a single parent (sort of) – she'd fallen into the trap of believing she should multitask at all times. With that, she sniffed at a bra lurking beneath the bed and tossed it toward the overflowing laundry basket blocking the closet. Then she grabbed tweezers from her nightstand and began plucking at her chin. In the van's rearview mirror, the dark hairs stuck out like porcupine quills, but step indoors and they hid like prairie dogs.

'As much as the team loves it, we were thinking this piece could be stronger if we took all of that out and replaced it with social media posts from MTV's *Teen Moms*. OG cast members, preferably. You follow them, right?'

'Of course,' Claire lied. She didn't follow any of it.

'Awesome. So you'll take care of that first thing? If you go back into your draft, you'll see where I've edited and removed your quotes. That's where you can just drop in the embed codes.'

'Got it.' Claire gave the phone the middle finger.

'Oh, and one more small request. This one comes from the entire editorial team . . .'

Claire braced for more bullshit, certain that Sabrina hid behind the collective noun 'team' when these were her solo 'requests'.

'We know you have so much to give. It's just that, well, we sense you're holding back.'

'Really?' Claire asked through clenched teeth. Wielding her tweezers, she attacked what appeared to be the beginnings of a mustache. Fuck peri-menopause and all the symptoms no one ever told you to expect – most of them starting the day after you turned forty-three.

'What we'd like to see are a few more exclamation points in your work,' Sabrina cooed. 'You know, sprinkled here and there. Like, even in the middle of a sentence, inside parentheses or em dashes, your choice! We just need to *feel* your intensity more. Do you know what I mean? I—'

Before she could stop herself, Claire hit the big red hang-up button, as Joe called it. Let Sabrina think the call dropped on its own.

Even just a few months ago, she never would've done something so bold. But seeing Alex again, reading his words each day and basking in the warm glow of his attention had given her a renewed sense of self-worth and caused her tolerance for foolishness to plummet to an all-time low.

Her life now seemed to be divided into halves: *Before Reconnecting with Alex and After Reconnecting with Alex*. The *After Alex* version held a lot more appeal and certainly more promise.

In eight minutes the weekly MamaRama video conference call would begin. She desperately wanted to shower, but there was no way she could wait another second to see if Alex had responded.

Claire opened the app and sank to the bed in case he hadn't replied.

There it was. One new message.

Claire exhaled and scanned the words as slowly and carefully as if she were reading a riddle at one of those escape rooms the boys loved.

Hey! Great to hear you're free. Last-minute meeting in NYC tomorrow. Staying at the W in Hoboken tonight. Not far from you, right? Would love to see you if you can slip away. I'll be in the bar at 7. If I recall correctly, you owe me a beer. – A

Claire collapsed into the mound of pillows, fireworks of joy and panic exploding inside her.

September 4, 2024

9:02 a.m.

Seated at her dining-room table, Claire stared at her laptop screen in stunned silence, her palms growing sweatier by the second.

'I think Claire's frozen,' Sabrina said. 'Claire! Claire! Can you hear us? She's not responding!'

Claire issued a silent prayer of gratitude for technical glitches as she listened to her editor carry on as if she were in a coma. 'Claire, blink if you can hear me!'

Is it possible to fake being frozen for the entirety of the meeting so I can focus on the invitation that has the power to upend my entire life? Claire thought before un-muting herself and saying, 'Can you hear me now?'

'Claire, you're echoing,' Sabrina shouted. 'Disconnect and rejoin.'

'Sure,' Claire agreed, thankful for a chance to pull herself together.

She had less than ten hours to decide if she would turn a harmless yet captivating email flirtation into a full-blown fling. Of course, she'd known something had to happen sooner or later. They were adults, not summer-camp pen-pals. Alex was a grown (single!) man. No matter how witty or fun she tried to make her messages, there was bound to come a time when they would no longer be enough. Still, she hadn't expected Alex to 'force the moment to its crisis', as T. S. Eliot wrote in one of her favorite poems, quite this soon – or so abruptly, for that matter.

Was Alex's business trip a ruse to lure her out from behind her laptop and into the real world?

Claire doubted it. Back in June, while they'd been outside enjoying cigarettes, laughing, and watching the sun set just beyond the elevated railroad tracks that stood adjacent to Ted's Olde Town Tavern, Alex told her his job took him all over the world. While she'd written exactly one children's book, he'd acquired multiple masters degrees and learned foreign languages. His intriguing background led Claire to look him up online after she'd returned from the reunion.

Normally, she wouldn't track down an old boyfriend via social media. In the not-so-distant past, she'd have chalked up seeing Alex again to an unexpected encounter that momentarily lifted her spirits and made her feel young again. She'd have left it at that, allowing another five to twenty-five years to pass before catching up with him at a future reunion.

But, by the time she bumped into Alex, it had been nearly a month since she'd asked Paul to move out, and at that point her husband had given little indication that he wanted to change or even work on their relationship. Much like the water stain on the kitchen ceiling, Claire felt like another thing Paul had willfully decided to ignore rather than tend to. In fact, the way he greeted her when she returned from the reunion made her wish she'd stayed at her university with Alex. She'd left the college town in plenty of time to make it to the start of Henry's playoff game, but she'd hit traffic.

When she'd arrived at the top of the second inning, Paul had rushed toward her, looking relieved to see her, and Claire experienced a surge of love and stupidity. In that moment, she was glad she'd hurried home before things had gone too far with Alex. Paul's eyes lit up, so blue and bright they matched the afternoon sky. How could she even think about hurting this man, this good, kind man, who obviously missed her so deeply he'd dashed off the bleachers in the punishing June humidity to be near her?

'Oh, Claire, glad you made it.' Paul had given her shoulder a fraternal squeeze. 'Listen, I forgot to bring Henry's water bottle and I left my wallet on the mantel. Do you have cash? Can you go buy him one?'

Claire's hopes that Paul might've been on the precipice of saying something meaningful skidded into the dirt, along with a player who stole second base while Henry fanned himself with his mitt.

Things were exactly as she'd left them.

Because the water fountains were broken, Claire was forced to fork out three dollars for a twelve-ounce bottle of what should be a free, natural resource. She then slumped between Paul and Joe on the bleachers, alternately waving at Henry, who'd been moved to the outfield, and seething over her estranged husband's greeting. She'd rushed back for *this*? Had Paul not even noticed that the mascara she'd slept in made her look like Courtney Love after a bar brawl?

'He doesn't see me anymore,' Claire had whispered to herself as a boy on the opposing side hit a walk-off home run.

Though Henry's team lost, the casual spectator wouldn't have known because each child was awarded a trophy the size of a lawn jockey.

'Great! Another thing to dust!' Claire might have said if she believed in proper housekeeping. She'd looked at her phone. Back on her college campus, the barbecue was kicking off. *Had Alex found someone else to wink at? To share cigarettes and old memories with?* Those thoughts circled through her mind, spinning like a CD inside her broken Discman.

She'd expected Paul to at least ask her about the reunion: *Was she glad she'd gone? On a scale of one to ten, how hungover was she?* (She was a solid twelve.) *Did she have any notable tales from her old friends?*

He'd offered a half-hearted 'Good time?' with a slight bob of his chin as they crossed the parking lot but nothing more.

'Very good.' She'd nodded back.

By Sunday, Claire experienced acute remorse that she hadn't stayed. Stacey and Annabelle texted photos from the barbecue, the bar, the 'See you in another five years!' brunch. With each, she pinched the screen in every direction scanning for Alex.

Clearly, other than serving as Henry's water boy, her presence at the game hadn't been necessary or appreciated. When she'd stood next to Alex at the reunion, every part of her came alive. She'd been more than her usual self. She'd been a person with interests, who could carry on a lively conversation. She'd felt seen and a little bit sparkly.

And so, that Sunday evening in June, she'd decided to look him up, to stare at his face once more, and see if she could recapture that same exhilaration through cyberspace. With shaky fingers, she'd typed his name. And, suddenly, there he was, looking handsome and smart in his professional headshot. She stared, butterflies flitting through her, and composed a brief but friendly message. She had to. Though she was no tech guru, Claire knew that because she'd forgotten to change her privacy settings, Alex would see that she'd looked at his LinkedIn profile. And with that, she'd sent him an 'invitation to connect'. In her opinion, reaching out through a professional networking platform seemed far less suggestive than 'friending' him on Facebook.

> So, wow, Alex, you weren't kidding about all those degrees. You make me feel like a total slacker. Anyway, I'm sorry I had to leave like that. I just wanted to say that it was great to see you and fun to catch up.

She'd agonized over the closing. *Love, Claire* seemed too familiar. *Take care, Claire* rhymed. Plus, she'd always thought that implied that the recipient was in some kind of bad situation – as in 'Take care, I'm sure you'll beat that lymphoma!'

Fondly, Claire was far too formal. She decided on **Best, Claire** and hit 'send' before she second-guessed herself further.

He'd accepted her invitation and responded within minutes. *Has he been thinking about me as much as I've been thinking of him?* Her legs turned to linguini as she read his words.

> Claire, your message is a sight for sore eyes – literally. I'm on the red-eye to LA for an early morning meeting. It was amazing to see you – as always. I totally understand why you left. BUT you do owe me a beer, which I intend to collect before another twenty-five years pass. Here's to meeting up again soon.
> – A

Claire had found herself smiling and re-reading the message again and again. *Here's to meeting up again soon.*

* * *

Meeting up. Crap! The meeting! Claire shook herself out of her revery and rejoined the meeting. She listened as Sabrina droned on about the importance of writing 'kickass Facebook prompts'. Attempting to pay attention was futile. Of course, Claire wanted to see Alex again. It was nearly all she'd thought about for the past two months. Still, was she ready to make a monumental move like meeting him in a hotel bar?

If she allowed herself this dalliance, did she really want it to happen in the birthplace of baseball and Frank Sinatra? In her mind, Hoboken, located just thirty minutes east of her New Jersey home, always seemed like Manhattan's less-worldly little sister. It wasn't as if she needed *An Affair to Remember*-like meeting atop the Empire State Building, but she did imagine something a bit more classy.

No matter where they ended up, amid the heady concoction of alcohol, physical chemistry, and a bit of flattery, could Claire trust herself to not grab Alex by the tie (the red one he was wearing in his LinkedIn headshot would be nice) and beg him to take her straight to bed?

Things seemed to be accelerating at too rapid a pace, going from zero to one hundred overnight. Was it wrong that Claire wanted to coast along on the shoulder for a little bit longer? Wasn't the unknown, the anticipation, part of the fun? Like holidays or vacations, reality rarely lived up to expectations. What if she saw Alex and that electric current that made her whole body hum had fizzled – or worse, flatlined? She wasn't ready to let it go. Or, what if being with him again surpassed her most elaborate fantasies, and, suddenly, she had her answer? Was she prepared to tell Paul their relationship was over?

Timing was another factor. Claire's in-laws, Florence and Fred, were due to return home from their seasonal rental in Maine in early October, forcing her and Paul to decide the fate of their marriage within the next few weeks. Perhaps that looming deadline had motivated Paul, because Claire had to admit, in small ways, her husband appeared to be trying to change: the sunflowers on the first day of school, the effort he made to clean the kitchen with the boys after their Wednesday dinners, the questions he asked about her work, listening thoughtfully to her answers.

But were these gestures too little, too late? Claire wasn't sure. Could she justify seeing Alex again if it helped her figure out her true feelings? Because, really, Paul – and the children – were waiting on her to determine the future of their family.

Back in May, several days after Claire had told Paul to leave, she'd asked him to return so together they could explain their new situation to the boys. Up until the moment they'd sat down in the family room, Claire had told her sons their father was keeping an eye on their grandparents' house while they were out of town. *Not a lie.*

She and Paul had huddled in the kitchen before starting the conversation she'd been dreading. She'd secretly hoped that after spending days in his childhood home, surrounded by his mother's Victorian teddy bear collection, he'd have opened this dialogue with something heartfelt – a declaration of love; a vow to be the partner she deserved; a promise to put her first from that moment on. Anything other than what he'd said, which was, 'What are we doing here, Claire?'

He'd leaned against the wall, arms folded across his chest, looking hurt and confused.

'I don't know,' she'd said.

He rubbed his forehead. 'I guess I'm used to you having all the answers.'

'That's the problem.' She strode into the family room, annoyed with herself for thinking he'd make a passionate plea to come home.

'Hey, fellas, your dad and I need to talk to you.'

Her sons' focus remained glued to the television screen, transfixed by a group of grown men pranking a senior citizen in a pizzeria.

'Boys?' She tried again before locating the remote control and switching off the TV.

'Listen, guys . . .' She closed her eyes, at a loss for how to begin this conversation. 'We're taking a break.'

'But we only just turned the TV on!' argued Max, though the boys had viewed at least four episodes that morning.

'Your dad and I are taking a break,' Claire said softly.

'It's a bit like a time-out for grown-ups,' Paul added, standing beside her.

Their sons' eyes flicked from parent to parent.

'Dad's going to stay at Grams and Gramps' for a bit while—'

'Why does Dad have to leave? He's the fun one!' Joe whined.

'Yeah, but Mom's the one who does everything, dumbass,' said Max, bopping Joe in the head with a throw pillow.

'Max!' Claire exclaimed. She couldn't decide if she should correct his language, bark at him for hitting his brother, or thank him for acknowledging that yes, she did do it all.

'Wait, are you guys getting divorced?' Henry sat up and looked from Max to Joe and then at his parents.

Claire braced for tears.

'It's OK if you are,' Henry continued. 'More than half the kids at school's parents are divorced.'

'They're so lucky!' Max interjected. 'They go on double the vacations. They get twice as many gifts at Christmas, and they eat tons of take-out 'cause the dads can't cook. It sounds lit!'

Claire didn't know whether to laugh or weep. She hadn't anticipated this reaction, but it was probably healthier than if they'd stormed out of the room or dissolved into teary puddles. She remembered crying inside her bedroom closet as a child each time her parents gave each other the silent treatment, certain they were on the brink of divorce, her whole world about to change.

'No one said anything about divorce.' Paul looked to her for guidance. When she nodded, he continued. 'We're just going to take a few weeks and see what happens.'

What had happened was Claire found validation from someone else, someone who reminded her that she was once confident, fun, and interesting. Still, in the sixteen years she and Paul had been married, she'd never even been tempted to kiss anyone else. Sure, every spring she fantasized about a meaningless romp with a sinewy landscaper, but it never went beyond a daydream – one that usually involved them groping one another beneath the pounding spray of sprinklers.

To the best of Claire's knowledge, Paul had remained faithful to her as well. Only recently did she find herself slightly concerned that he, too, might be tempted to stray.

Back in March, Paul's mother began talking about her new friend, Alice, who'd purchased the rundown Cape-Cod-style home next door. Alice was a whiz at everything: gardening, quilting, even winemaking. Claire tried not to let it irk her that Florence rarely paid her a compliment, yet beamed with pride whenever she spoke of this Alice person.

During one of their last visits, her mother-in-law had said, 'Claire, this quiche could've been really delicious with a homemade crust.'

Claire gripped the stem of her wine glass and nodded as Florence continued. 'You should taste my neighbor Alice's crust. From scratch, of course. Oh, and she's a genius with cobblers, crisps, and crumbles. I told her she should write a cookbook. She's thinking about it.'

Under other circumstances, Claire might've been jealous, but she'd assumed Alice was a lonely old widow with stooped shoulders – a byproduct of all that quilting – and enormous knobby knuckles from kneading so much dough.

It wasn't until Claire went to retrieve the boys from a weekend with Paul at her in-laws' home that she realized how wrong she'd been. As soon as she pulled into Florence and Fred's driveway, she noticed the woman. How could she not? She was as tall, tanned, and toned as an Olympic volleyball player. Pirouetting with the grace of a ballerina, she simultaneously pulled weeds and watered window boxes. This gorgeous creature appearing on the lawn of that shabby home seemed as unlikely as her father-in-law's beloved garden gnomes suddenly coming to life.

Once the van's doors closed, Claire began grilling her sons. 'So, is that Grams' friend Alice's daughter?' She'd pointed to the statuesque blonde tending the indigo hydrangeas, their perfect round blooms the size of babies' heads.

'Duh, Mom, that's Alice,' Max said. 'Don't you recognize her?'

Too stunned to admonish his 'duh', Claire backed up into another neighbor's garbage cans, and asked, 'Should I?'

'Mom! It's Alice Masters!' Henry said. 'From *Alice Masters Everything*. She's a YouTube star.'

'Grams is friends with a YouTube star?' Claire stopped herself from adding, 'I've always imagined that even prisoners in solitary confinement would prefer isolation to your grandmother's company.'

'She does these makeup and hair tutorials,' Max said. 'Girls in my class are obsessed with her.'

'Hair tutorials – we need more!' Sabrina was saying now as Claire turned her attention to the Google Meet. 'Think: braids and flat ironing techniques. How about "Champagne Extensions on a Budweiser Budget"? Anyone up for mommy-and-me 'dos? Claire, you've got boys, right? Any interest in mother-son crewcuts?'

'Um, let me talk to my boys about that,' Claire mumbled, her thoughts returning to Alice Masters.

'If she's a big star, what is she doing in *that* house?' she'd asked, certain her kids were pranking her.

'She's flipping it and documenting it all,' Henry explained. 'A construction crew starts work on the outside Monday. She'll probably get a show on HGTV.'

'She'll *totally* get one,' Max said. 'Have you seen her? She's a smokeshow.'

'Such a smokeshow,' Joe added from the third row.

'She ends every video asking, "How'd that turn out?" and her crew shouts, "Pretty darn perfect!"' Henry said.

'She's helping Dad with a secret project,' Joe chirped.

'What secret project?' Claire almost asked but bit her lip. She pictured something Alex had shared recently: *If you can't handle the answer, don't ask the question.*

Paul had dozens of projects he could've tackled at their home. Why would he start a new one with Alice? Because she was beautiful and competent. Wait until she found out Paul couldn't tell a nut from a bolt. And he certainly wasn't going to dazzle her with charm. If anyone was out of practice when it came to romance, it was her husband.

She thought back to their early dates, to one of her fondest memories. He'd taken her to see Shakespeare in the Park – this was before they admitted that neither of them enjoyed (or even understood) *Hamlet*. Paul had packed a picnic – this was during his panini phase – complete with homemade chocolate-chip cookies for dessert.

Claire had taken a gooey bite. 'Wow, yum!' Other than her mom, no one had ever prepared a meal or a homemade dessert for her.

'I bake when I'm nervous,' Paul confessed.

'Why are you nervous?' she asked.

He smiled shyly. 'I'm really into you.' He dabbed at her chin, wiping away melted chocolate, as her heart somersaulted. 'And I hope you . . .'

Since Neal and Alex, Claire had guarded her heart. But when she looked at this guy who'd braved mosquitos, the late-summer heat, and questionable community theater for her, she thought it was time to take a chance again.

'. . . hope you might feel the same—'

'I do.' She leaned closer and they kissed, lost in each other, even as Gertrude drank poison and died on stage.

She'd forgotten that Paul had made dinner most nights when they were first married. Claire would sit at the tiny table in their apartment's kitchen, attempting to outline her romcom, until her husband, in his best French waiter voice, would announce, 'Your dinner is served, madame.'

Why had Paul stopped cooking and baking? Claire was struck by a blinding flash: it was because of her. One wintry evening, he'd been on his phone, attempting to solve a work crisis. Distracted, he'd burned the meal and accidentally set an oven mitt on fire, causing the smoke alarm to blare, which woke newborn Max. Sleep-deprived and ravenous, Claire had stumbled bleary-eyed into the kitchen and tossed the flaming mitt into the sink. 'I'll make dinner from now on.'

She'd thought she was punishing him but, really, she'd screwed herself. Speaking of screwing, was she physically prepared to be with another man?

Definitely not, she thought, idly touching the soft, Shar-pei-like folds of her stomach.

As Sabrina babbled on about metrics and SEO best practices, Claire glanced down. Her body had housed three people; her vagina had forcibly spat them out. Her parts weren't the same as they'd been a quarter of a century ago. Since turning forty, she seemed to have excess skin, and much of it spilled over the elastic waistband of her black leggings.

Why had she stopped power-walking each morning with her neighbors Susie and Karen? At the end of each trek, after discussing home improvements, diets, and detoxes, Karen would tap her watch and announce how far they'd gone and how many calories they'd burned. This information often stopped Claire from having second and third helpings of the homemade macaroni and cheese Henry prepared with love and smoked gouda on chilly Sunday afternoons.

When she'd accepted her new job, Claire told Susie and Karen she couldn't walk with them anymore. They'd pressed their palms to their Lycra-covered sternums in disappointment, though she knew she hadn't added much to their outings.

She imagined joining her neighbors on their usual 10 a.m. jaunt.

But if she did, surely she'd blurt, 'Who cares if the Johnsons are installing Andersen windows? I'm having an emotional affair with a guy I dated twenty-five years ago, and I haven't felt this alive since I won that fifty-fifty raffle at the preschool Tricky Tray in the spring of 2016!'

She laughed, picturing their reactions if she shared her current situation: 'I asked Paul to move out months ago, and I'm considering sleeping with an old boyfriend. Tonight! At the W in Hoboken.'

Her neighbors could power-walk to Texas on that juicy nugget, tongues wagging all the way.

But she had no time for exercising or gossiping now. The clock was ticking. She had less than nine hours to pull herself together. While scrolling through Facebook recently, she'd seen a selfie of a woman in a tank top that read 'Fat + Tan = Muscle.' How much tanning could she pack in before she had to arrive for her usual 3 p.m. school pick-up?

Did the FDA regulate that? she wondered. *Could a fleshy, and now, thanks to peri-menopause, sometimes-pimply woman, go into a tanning salon looking as soft and pale as the Pillsbury Doughboy and come out hours later appearing to have both the curves and glow of J.Lo?*

Then, there was the matter of her undergarments. For the past decade, Claire had been buying cotton Fruit of the Loom for Her bottoms at the supermarket, same aisle as the pet supplies. In her more boring stay-at-home-mom moments, she'd wanted to spice things up and shock the kitty-litter shoppers by sweeping her arms from side to side and saying, 'For your pussy; for my pussy,' just to see their reactions.

And what about the dark forest that lay beneath those thick-as-ACE-bandages panties? After Labor Day, Claire gave her lady bits a well-deserved break from waxing and allowed things to get downright jungle-y in that region. Of course, Paul had never cared. Had he even noticed? Prior to their separation, Claire was convinced she could sit down to dinner in a tutu and a gas mask and her husband would say nothing other than, 'Is this all the chicken?'

Claire's unsightly hair issue wasn't limited to that area. Just thinking about it sparked a sudden flashback to her annual gynecologist appointment last September. At the front desk, a brochure caught her eye. On its cover, a woman crossed her arms over a hideous nude bra below the words 'Pain-Free Nipple Hair Removal'. While the receptionist was distracted, Claire had stuffed the pamphlet into her oversized purse and vowed to do something about those pesky wisps that made her feel like a boy starting puberty.

That leaflet ended up at the bottom of her handbag, buried under old grocery lists, tissues, and emergency granola bars.

She'd forgotten all about it – until last year's back-to-school night – when a fellow parent asked to borrow a pen. As Claire reached into her handbag to oblige, she'd inadvertently pulled out the nipple hair removal brochure as well. It landed face-up for all to see, as shocking as if Claire had thrown down a dildo.

Now, whenever she ran into anyone who'd sat remotely near her that evening she wanted to shout, 'Yes, I have hairy nipples! Deal with it!'

It felt almost comically unfair that women were supposed to care about so much bullshit. Had Alex, at any point while packing an overnight bag, stopped to wonder, *Do these jeans make my ass look as flat as the back of a cast-iron skillet?* She doubted it.

An overnight bag. Would Claire dare to sleep over? What was she – nine years old? This was no sleepover. In fact, she was certain there'd be very little sleep happening at all. But where would she tell Paul she was going if she didn't meet him at back-to-school night and failed to return home until the wee hours?

'My book club is pulling an all-nighter to finish *Infinite Jest* once and for all!' Even for someone as passive and unsuspecting as Paul, that would be a tough sell. But what were her other options? Sleep with Alex and then climb into her minivan, smooth her hair, and drive back to the 'burbs?

Her mother was coming with dinner for the boys. Claire still hadn't told her about the separation. If one of her kids slipped up and mentioned something, Claire would laugh, dismiss it, and say that Paul had briefly stayed at his parents' house to help with a plumbing issue or yard work.

Claire wasn't prepared to answer her mother's litany of questions. She'd need Paul to go to their home after back-to-school night and pretend that everything was normal. How odd and uncomfortable would it feel to return after being with Alex to find Paul dozing in front of the ballgame? But even if Claire came in reeking of booze and man meat, would her estranged husband simply say,

'Did you know you're out of ice cream?' his head half in the freezer.

'Is she frozen again? Claire! Claire!' Sabrina's voice pulled Claire back to her dining room.

'Yes! No! I'm here!' Claire unmuted and panicked. What had she missed while she'd been engaged in her soul-destroying body scan?

'Claire, how's the "I Tried It" under-eye-patch piece coming along?'

Claire had done little more than move the samples from her mailbox to her bathroom. Then she remembered something Alex had said, 'Confidence is key!'

'It's going great!' she enthused. 'Can't you see how well-rested I look?'

After an awkward pause, Sabrina continued, 'We need before-and-after pics! Don't forget! Close-ups, pref—'

'Claire!' Victoria, deputy editor and Sabrina's boss, interrupted, 'we also need to talk about your "Love 'Em or Leave 'Em" column.'

Claire caught herself frowning onscreen and forced her face into a more neutral expression. She'd pitched the column based on the 'Can This Marriage Be Saved' feature in her mother's *Ladies' Home Journal*, which she'd devoured as a teen.

Her editors loved the idea. Claire's responsibilities included monitoring an inbox where readers sent lengthy emails divulging their relationship problems. She selected the most compelling dilemmas, then crafted a slightly embellished rewrite. Unlike the *Journal*, MamaRama.com didn't employ a therapist to analyze couples' problems and suggest suitable compromises. Rather, the site encouraged readers to weigh in on social media, which typically resulted in divisive name-calling and cursing.

Over the past few months, Claire had gone rogue, ignoring the inbox and, instead, sharing thinly veiled issues from her own marriage. So far, reader reaction was mixed, with some viewing Paul as a 'good guy who sounds sweet and misunderstood', to 'an absolute ass-clown who needs to pack his shit and go'.

The clarity Claire hoped for remained elusive.

'Yes?' Her jaw clenched in anticipation of an insult. 'What about the column?'

'It feels really *meh* lately,' Victoria continued. 'No one cares if a dude hasn't planned a date night in a decade. Dig deeper, Claire. We need spicy, racy. More sex.'

'Oh,' Sabrina interjected, 'I was once set up with this guy who could only perform if his cats were watching. That's weird, right?'

'Yes!' Victoria shouted. 'Find shit like that, Claire! We want to hear from women whose relationships are going down in flames.'

'I'm sure your super-fan will love it,' Sabrina snorted.

Within a few weeks of starting her job, Claire's posts began receiving positive comments from a reader who went by the handle 'HotDogLuvR', a name Claire's colleagues insisted was a reference to the reader's voracious sexual appetite. Despite the unusual moniker, HotDogLuvR's comments were kind and heartening:

> You have a way with words, Ms Casey. Keep it up!
> Have you ever thought of writing a novel?
> Such insight! Sharing this with my friends and co-workers.

Claire had been flattered, especially because she knew that the internet could be a cruel wasteland where the anonymous wrote outrageous and devastating things. But not HotDogLuvR, whose praise baffled Sabrina and the rest of the staff.

Victoria gave a little cough. 'Before we go, I have a bit of news.'

Claire perked up. Maybe Victoria was getting married and would take a month-long honeymoon, allowing Claire to coast a bit in her absence.

'While we've been in this meeting, half of our marketing team has been eliminated,' Victoria said. 'Advertising's been down since those deadly toy and cleaning product slideshows pissed off sponsors.'

It was impossible to know where anyone was looking on these video calls, but Claire was certain she could feel her boss's accusatory glare burning her face through cyberspace. Those were Claire's slideshows. Sabrina's idea, but Claire's byline. Hives bloomed on her neck. She covered the splotchy patches with her hand. Was she about to follow half the marketing team to the unemployment line?

'I've arranged a really fun send-off tonight from 6 to 8 p.m. at the Slaughtered Lamb,' Victoria continued.

'Claire, we know you're remote, but it would mean a lot if you joined us!' Sabrina added.

'Tonight?' Claire gulped.

'Yes, *tonight*!' Sabrina said with an exaggerated eye roll as if Claire had nothing better to do.

February 12, 1999

5:44 p.m.

'Seriously, Claire, you've got nothing better to do,' Stacey whined. She was seated on Claire's bedroom floor, idly picking at loose carpet threads. 'Just go out with him.'

Claire loved Stacey but she suspected her housemate had ulterior motives. She and her boyfriend, Ethan, wanted to share an apartment with Claire and Neal after graduation. They'd been waiting to see which dental school Ethan got accepted by, before officially deciding where they'd live. Claire figured she could write for a local paper, build up a portfolio. Neal said he'd be cool with Boston or New York, even Austin or Nashville; anywhere with a music scene.

That was before he decided to go to LA and abandon her and their shared future. Claire knew Stacey hoped that if she found a replacement for Neal, their original plan could still work.

'I'm not picking out a new boyfriend the way I'd shop for a desk chair' she'd wanted to insist. 'Like, "Sure, yeah, any of these will do!" I can't live with a stranger so your rent is cheap and Ethan can pay off his loans faster!'

Stacey wouldn't understand. Since the day they'd met at the freshman orientation picnic, she'd been clear about her agenda: marriage by twenty-five, house by twenty-eight, baby by thirty. Maybe a short but satisfying marketing career somewhere in between. She'd shared all of that while Claire had struggled to decide between macaroni and potato salad, ultimately spooning mounds of both onto her flimsy paper plate.

'I'm happy on my own.' Claire lay on her twin bed beneath her *Exile in Guyville* poster, re-reading *The Secret History* and fantasizing about finding and befriending Donna Tartt.

Maggie leaned against the footboard. 'You need to move on,

C.C.' Mags was the only one who'd ever called Claire by her initials. She dropped her voice to a whisper, as if that would soften the blow. 'Neal hasn't even sent you a postcard.'

'I know.' Claire rolled toward the wall. Neal had promised to send some from the road, and she'd been checking the mailbox compulsively, the way her grandmother did when a new issue of *TV Guide* was due.

'Give this Alex guy a chance,' Stacey urged, jumping up to loom over Claire.

After she'd leapt on Alex's back like an absolute lunatic, he'd started waiting for her after class and walking her home, asking her about authors she admired and post-grad plans.

That afternoon, he again invited her to dinner. She'd declined, citing her housemate's birthday. *Not a lie.* It was Stacey's twenty-second. Claire, Annabelle, and Maggie had chipped in and gotten her a frozen yogurt cake, but, of course, the birthday girl planned to spend most of the evening with Ethan.

Now Claire regretted telling them anything about Alex.

'Doesn't he have a cool car?' asked Mags, who kept an index card with the quote 'It's as easy to love a rich man as it is to love a poor man' on her bulletin board, beside a black-and-white photo of the Eiffel Tower. 'A Miata, right?'

'So?' Claire put down her book and crossed her arms.

'A gal could do worse, that's all she's saying,' cooed Annabelle from the doorway.

'You guys, I don't need to date anyone.' Claire sat up, trying to short-circuit her friends' mini-intervention. 'You have no idea how bad that last one was.'

She'd agreed to get pizza with a guy who worked in the university's computer lab after he'd retrieved a lost document hours before it was due.

Over a pepperoni pie – her least favorite – he'd spent ninety minutes blathering about something called Y2K, which Claire had thought was a *Star Wars* character.

'Neal leaving is actually a good thing.' She attempted to convince her housemates and herself. A small part of Claire enjoyed moping. She felt a bit like Bridget Jones pining for Daniel Cleaver and, later, Mr Darcy. And there was no denying it, she'd written more poems in the past few months than she had in her entire life. They were mostly filled with heartbreak and 'winter as death' metaphors, but still, she was prolific. 'I finally have time to start my novel,' she added.

'Oh not this again.' Stacey threw her head back in disgust, refusing to believe that a life in the arts was possible without a trust fund or endless connections.

'Didn't you say this Alex guy could quote Hemingway?' Mags asked. 'He sounds perfect for you.'

They had a point. Neal could barely paraphrase Jimi Hendrix.

'I don't want to start anything new. Not now,' Claire said. 'Spring break's coming up. It's nice to be free, right?'

Everyone but Stacey was headed to London on a university-sponsored theater trip.

'Oh right, I forgot you're planning to hook up with Prince William.' Annabelle laughed and the others joined in.

Claire pretended to smother herself with a pillow and groaned. She pictured Alex, his broad shoulders, nice smile. She'd tried to block it out, but he'd smelled fantastic when she buried her face in his neck after she pounced on him like a street cat the afternoon she mistook him for Neal. Neal, who certainly wasn't devoting any time to thinking about her.

Stuffing the pillow beneath her head, Claire sighed. 'OK, fine. Whatever. When we get back, I'll go out with him.'

September 4, 2024

10:17 a.m.

With the meeting finally finished, Claire considered where to begin her workday. First, she had to fix the single-mom daycare drop-off feature Sabrina had butchered. Then she needed to test a dozen different under-eye patches in the next few hours without permanently destroying her skin.

After a team meeting, Claire typically allowed herself a one-minute self-pity break. She'd rest her head beside her laptop and grumble, 'How did it come to this?'

Unfortunately, she knew exactly how. Over the past year, Paul's job had grown less secure. Layoffs began last fall, convincing Claire she needed to stop freelancing and find a full-time position. Somehow Paul, the veritable dinosaur of the IT department, had managed to stay above the fray. But his luck at this mid-size insurance company couldn't hold out forever.

Each Wednesday night when he came to have dinner with the boys, he'd tell Claire that recent college grads, aka 'brogrammers', and sometimes college interns, were replacing people he'd worked with for more than a decade. If the company could let Paul go and pay a child coding prodigy half, why wouldn't they? They'd already reduced the healthcare benefits. Claire said a quick prayer of gratitude that they'd gotten Max, with his Bugs Bunny overbite, into braces right before they lost the dental plan.

But today she didn't have any spare time to wallow about the state of her career. She had big, life-changing decisions to make. She needed to get back to Alex. But what would she say? Her heart reverberated with a resounding 'Yes!' while her head offered up a decidedly stodgy 'Well, now, let's give this a bit more thought . . .'

Before she opened his message, her phone pinged. Abby.

Claire! Leaving Something's Brewing. The rumor mill's in overdrive! & U are the subject.

Claire stopped reading. Blood rushed to her face. Had her computer been hacked? Did people already know she was debating sleeping with a man who was not her husband?

No! That's crazy!

In just over an hour, she'd become completely paranoid. If she felt *this* guilty *this* fast, was she really affair material? But, technically, would this count as an affair since she and Paul were separated?

If the tables were turned, how would she feel? She pictured Paul standing beside the willowy and capable Alice Masters, handing her a nail gun, their fingertips touching, their . . .

She shook her head to clear the vision and refocused on Abby's message.

People are saying U ditched little Parker Westbrook this a.m. Left him alone at the bus stop after calling him a 'baby.' I said that was nuts! U'd never do that!

Claire breathed a sigh of relief. Abby would sort it out and defend her. She owed her. Claire had recommended the PTA get the coffee and pastries for their meetings from Abby's shop. Claire's phone pinged again.

The bus didn't pull up until 9:50 a.m. and he'd waited there ALONE that whole time. He couldn't go home because his mom gets cryotherapy in Manhattan for her migraines on Thursdays. Poor thing. As U can imagine, Parker's traumatized. Just wanted U to know the word around town is U R the 'Bus Stop Bully.' I have your back! BTW, I need a favor. Will swing by around noonish!
XOX
Abs

Claire set her phone face down and lurched toward the kitchen to refill her coffee. Her eyes landed on the water-stained ceiling. 'FML!' she whined, resorting to the acronym for Fuck My Life that she'd learned from her colleagues. A visit from Abby was the last thing she needed. If there were ever a time to run away from her entire life, today seemed like a good choice. Even if she came up with some glorious scheme whereby she could stay out until dawn like she did during her college days, she'd really only be running away for a single night.

When she returned, everything – her home with its dust and dirty fingerprints, her job with its bizarre demands, her children with their requests for Nutella crepes at all hours – would be just where she'd left them. Only *she* would be different. Could she go back to her regular life once she allowed herself to experience the passion and excitement it was missing? But by exploring things – possibly physical things – with Alex, would she officially close the door on her marriage?

Claire knew she was getting ahead of herself. Alex had simply asked her for a drink, not to elope. So, then what was this really? If they didn't give it a real go, then what would they do? Plan quarterly meetings in hotels as if they were updating shareholders?

Alex had mentioned that his ex, a chemical engineer, had accepted a 'lucrative new opportunity' in New Jersey. Maybe he'd move closer to be near his sons? While she typically devoured every word Alex wrote, admittedly, she skimmed the bits about his former wife. He'd said she was house-hunting in areas in and around Claire's town. How strange would that be to routinely bump into Alex's ex? Thinking about her ruined the illusion that they could somehow return to their carefree college days, when their biggest worries centered around writing papers and scraping together bar money.

What did Alex see in her now anyway? Did she represent a sweeter, simpler time? A sense of nostalgia? Like the way people still listened to grunge or sought out vintage clothing and kitschy lunchboxes?

While she microwaved her leftover coffee, she took a selfie. 'Christ, I'd scare my own mother!' she grumbled. Why did people always say natural light was your friend when in fact it was crueler than an amateur caricaturist at a county fair?

Claire stomped upstairs past the pile of flip-flops. In the bathroom, she sat on the lid of the closed toilet and affixed the first set of eye-patches, her thoughts messier than the cluster of shampoos, bubble baths, and rubber ducks cluttering the corners of her tub.

She had a sudden flashback to that game show her parents loved, the one where they let you phone a friend to narrow down the answer.

Whom could she call? Julie was busy at her Manhattan office. They'd been making plans to catch up all summer but life kept getting in the way.

Dinner soon? My treat! Julie would text. **You're a saint, Claire! You have no idea how much your visits mean to my mom. Seriously!** followed by a string of heart emojis. **Pick a night!**

Stop! I adore her! Claire would respond. But whenever she threw out a date, Julie had a conflict or vice versa. They'd been rescheduling since late June.

Claire hadn't talked to Mags in far too long either. At the reunion, Stacey and Annabelle were dealing with their own relationship issues. *Did that make them more or less qualified to help her figure out her next move?* None of these women even knew about her situation, and updating them would take time – time she didn't have.

Claire still needed to return her mom's call. It was 10:32 a.m. – her mother's boxing class began at 10:30. Claire would've smiled picturing her petite mom with her little cotton ball of hair wearing those enormous padded gloves if it were a fun hobby and not something suggested by her neurologist.

Back in February, Claire had noticed her mother's hands trembling. When she mentioned it, her mom clasped them around a coffee mug.

'Your father is using me as his Nespresso guinea pig,' she'd chuckled, insisting it was caffeine jitters.

Then, on a late June morning, Claire received a rare call from her brother.

'You read the email?' Kyle asked in lieu of a proper greeting.

'What email?' Claire dropped her purse and keys onto the couch. She'd just finished ferrying the boys to their summer camps: multi-sports for Max, Food Truck Fun for Henry, and Aspiring Astronauts for Joe.

'From Dad,' Kyle said. 'Read it.'

Their father had gotten in the habit of forwarding silly jokes in between warnings about lettuce recalls and corrupt politicians.

'Just tell me what it says, Kyle. I've got a busy morning.' Claire had a hard time keeping a straight face. Her first work assignment required her to compile a belly-button ring round-up, complete with a DIY guide to at-home piercings. Kyle acted as if his job at a water treatment facility was on par with a Navy Seal's. Why couldn't she pretend her role was vitally important too?

'They want us to come for dinner tonight,' Kyle said. 'Just us. Dad wrote, "Claire, leave Coupon and the kids at home. There's something your mother and I want to tell you."'

'That's weird.' Claire put the phone on speaker to scroll through her emails. She read their dad's short message while her brother rambled.

'My guess? They're finally downsizing. I wouldn't mind visiting them in Florida. Maybe Miami – like in the winter if they're close to the beach – but not in one of those over-fifty-five communities. Way too depressing.' Her brother gasped. 'What if they want us to get all of our shit out of their attic?'

'They'd never sell the house.' Claire pictured the old Victorian their parents had spent decades restoring. Before Kyle could accuse her of being sentimental about their childhood home, she added, 'Mom lives for her garden and Dad just put in those new comfort-height toilets.' She dropped into a dining-room chair and opened her laptop. 'You don't think they're splitting up, do you?'

'They're not a boy band, Claire. No, they're not splitting up.'

She'd been worrying about that on and off since she was fourteen. She could still picture their mother storming off to stay with Claire's Aunt Lorraine for several days after their father refused to accompany her to the out-of-state wedding of a former neighbor's son.

Claire hadn't wanted her family to break up, to potentially see her parents with new partners, to be shuttled between two places, neither feeling like home.

But recently she'd read an article about 'graying divorce' or 'silver singles' – mature women who'd had it with needy husbands who added nothing to their lives but more laundry and criticism. They'd grown weary from the toll of all that emotional labor, keeping every ball in the air at the expense of their health and happiness. And hadn't she just asked her own spouse to leave? Was she doing to her sons what she'd feared most as a teen?

'Guess we'll find out tonight,' Kyle said. 'I'll let you go. I know how *busy* you are. Mom sent me that video . . .' he snort-laughed '. . . of you wearing a baby bonnet and ranking diaper creams.'

Claire never would've agreed to the Instagram reel if she'd known about the bonnet. It had been a last-minute addition. Sabrina's idea. Claire drew the line at donning a pink romper and bib.

'Hard-hitting journalism, sis! Go get 'em.'

In a few quick sentences, her brother could reduce them to squabbling teens again. Claire wouldn't sink to his level, beyond giving her cell phone the middle finger. And, besides, their father's email claimed her full attention.

Because that email had arrived on a Wednesday, Paul walked through the door at 6 p.m. for dinner with the boys.

He frowned after Claire knocked Max's water bottle into the sink, dropped her phone twice, and misplaced her keys. 'You seem kind of tense. Everything OK?'

Since reading her father's message, Claire couldn't shake the creeping sense of dread. She strongly believed in mother's intuition. Was there such a thing as daughter's intuition?

'Good. Fine. Off to see my mom and dad.' She didn't want to say more, preferring to cling to the hope that whatever her parents were about to reveal was probably nothing.

Over dinner, Claire and Kyle had exchanged looks, waiting for the big announcement. Claire studied her father, who was acting like himself, adding salt and butter to the onion-soup-flavored meatloaf and scalloped potatoes before tasting them.

Her mother refilled glasses of iced tea and replenished the bread basket.

After dessert, when they'd exhausted every topic from the kids and work to politics and the weather, Kyle stood. 'Well, I'd better get back to Ginger—'

'Sit down, son,' their father said, and nodded at their mother. 'Eleanor, it's time.'

Claire's heart-rate accelerated. Her skin turned clammy. At the familiar table, in the same chair where she'd sat since before her feet touched the carpet, she felt like a child again.

Her mother cleared her throat. 'I went for my annual physical and the doctor gave me a referral to see a neurologist.'

A neurologist? A hum filled Claire's ears as she watched her mother fiddle with the corners of her placemat.

'Oh, what the heck, I'll just come out with it. I have Parkinson's disease but it's early days.'

The words knocked the wind out of Claire.

Kyle pushed his chair back from the table as if their mother were contagious. 'Did you get a second opinion?'

'Oh, honey, I don't need one. My doctor's wonderful. Such a lovely man and, oh, what a head of hair! I spent much of the appointment trying to figure out if it's a toupee. Honestly, it's like a Himalayan cat curled up on his head. And he has three grandsons! I told him, "So do I!" – so far.' She wiggled her eyebrows at Kyle. Despite the fact that his great loves were his dog, Ginger Spice, and the NFL, Eleanor never gave up hope that Kyle would settle down and father the granddaughter she longed to spoil.

'What does "early days" mean?' Kyle frowned. 'What happens next?'

Claire stared at their mother dumbly, 'Oh, Mom' the only words she could form.

'I'm fine, honey.' Her mother's blue eyes flashed, watery but resolved. 'I didn't want to worry anyone. Your father thought you should know.' She folded her Irish linen napkin in half and half again. It had belonged to Claire's grandmother. Over the last few years, Eleanor had been using all the good stuff – the Waterford wine goblets, the fancy wedding china that had spent most of Claire's life locked up, prisoners of the china cabinet. Had her mother sensed something inside her changing, coming to rob her of time?

'This is life, my dears.' Her mom smiled, her usual pale pink lipstick faded. 'We take the bad with the good. I've had a lovely run. This is but a mere bump in the road.' She stood to collect their plates. A fork clattered to the floor.

Claire wanted to help but her legs were weak. This wasn't a bump in the road – more like a terrible detour down a dark, scary path.

'Who knows? Maybe I'll meet Michael J. Fox. Claire, honey. Remember what a crush you had on him?'

'And remember how I've always said, "Never look too closely at new cars or newborns or you'll notice they're not so perfect?"' Claire's dad chimed in. 'Now you can add old people to that list!'

Claire's stomach cratered. Her father would be useless as a caregiver.

'When's your next doctor's appointment, Mom?' she asked. 'I'll go with you.'

'Your dad doesn't mind taking me,' her mom said. 'He waits in the car on a side street with his newspaper.'

'You what? Why?' Claire and Kyle blurted simultaneously.

'The practice doesn't validate for parking,' their father explained. 'Four dollars an hour they're charging for that garage. Thieves.'

'Now, there's no need to tell the boys, Claire,' her mother said. 'I don't want to worry them. I'm taking it day by day. New trials pop up all the time.'

Kyle continued asking questions while Claire struggled to digest the news along with the heavy meatloaf. Her parents drove her crazy with their endless questions – Why hadn't *A Panda for Amanda* been turned into an animated series? Was she working on a new book? Shouldn't she be more concerned about Joe's delayed reading? Why didn't Henry's baseball coach give him more playing time? Did Max have a phone addiction? Yet she couldn't imagine them any other way. And she certainly couldn't bear the thought of watching her mother, who'd selflessly taken care of everyone else, suffer.

Claire hadn't meant to, but when she walked into the house and saw Paul clearing the table, she burst into tears.

'Claire! What's wrong?' Paul set down the glasses. 'You didn't hit another deer, did you?'

The back roads that separated Claire's home from her parents' were winding and wooded, and she'd had a few run-ins over the years.

'They hit me!' Claire always wanted to correct him. It was true. The beautiful creatures had come bounding out of hedges and landed on the hood of her minivan. But her mind could only focus on one thing: 'My mom has Parkinson's disease.'

'Oh, no.' Paul opened his arms and Claire collapsed against his chest. 'I'm so sorry.'

When she'd backed out of the driveway two hours earlier, Paul and the boys were shooting hoops. His skin smelled like summer, sweat, and Henry's homemade salsa.

'She says it's early and she doesn't want the boys to know.' Claire sniffled. 'Kyle asked if they'd consider moving, but, of course, they won't. My mom walked me out to the car and she had a tough time getting back up the porch steps. My dad will be absolutely no help and you know she won't even ask him for any. Why are they so stubborn?'

'They're set in their ways,' Paul said softly. 'It's hard for people to change.'

His shoulders, like his scent, were comforting, making the tension in Claire's neck dissolve by at least 30 percent. She might not have experienced that electric jolt that surged through her when she thought of Alex, but the warm steadiness of Paul reminded her of a well-loved sweatshirt, one you picked on a snowy Sunday, when you had the flu; the kind you tunneled inside during a scary movie; the one you kept even after the hem and cuffs began to fray.

Claire closed her eyes as the front door groaned open and their sons' voices, a chorus of complaints about mosquitoes and demands for water and ice cream, filled the house.

Still, she rested her head on Paul's shoulder, until Henry backed up into the dining room making the *beep, beep, beep* of a truck reversing. 'Um, what are you doing?'

Awkwardly, Claire and Paul jerked away from one another, arms dropping to their sides.

'Nothing, pal,' Paul said.

Was it nothing? Claire thought she'd felt Paul's lips touch the top of her head ever so gently and, in that moment, she let herself believe everything would be all right.

In the upstairs bathroom, sitting on the closed toilet lid, Claire's face stung, tears welled. Was it the memory of that moment or the eye-patches?

'We must suffer for beauty,' her grandmother had insisted. As a child, Claire had loved rolling across her grandparents' king-sized bed while watching her beloved Grabby (a mashup of Grandma Betty) sit at her vanity table and tweeze off most of her eyebrows only to feather them back in with a brown pencil.

As an adult, Claire wanted less suffering and more joy. Thoughts of her grandmother led her back to Alex. During their college days, she'd shared a poem with him that she'd written about Grabby. Alex had encouraged her to submit it to a literary journal. When it was accepted, he'd brought a bottle of champagne to the house on North Harrington Street to toast her first literary success. A few weeks after graduation, he'd mailed her a framed copy of that poem. Seeing it printed on creamy paper in a simple black frame made her feel like a real writer.

She'd almost missed his note, buried beneath bubble wrap.

> Claire, this poem is as beautiful as you are.
> I leave for Spain in ten days. If I'm fired for my rudimentary Spanish and find myself back in the states, you're the first person I'll call. Thank you for the perfect ending to senior year. – A.

He hadn't been fired and he hadn't called. They'd gone their separate ways. Getting his note made her wish they'd had a chance to watch their relationship grow. The timing was terrible. Where was that poem? Her parents' attic? Their basement? She needed to see it (and that note!) again. Could she call her dad? Ask him to look for it and give it to her mother to bring that evening – poetry along with pork chops?

No, that was crazy. Her father practically needed a treasure map to find a new tube of toothpaste; he'd never unearth a framed poem from twenty-five years ago. And if he did, her mother would have a million questions about why she wanted it now and who was this Alex?

He was thoughtful and romantic, Claire mused. But was he still capable of grand gestures like that one? *Yes!* Look at the wine he'd sent to celebrate her near-appearance on the *Today* show! Was that reason enough to meet him in a hotel?

She needed to talk this through. There was one person who knew the full story – *Bea!*

September 4, 2024

10:52 a.m.

Claire grabbed her phone and hurried down the sidewalk. She'd imagined Bea would return to her own home once she'd fully recuperated, but one morning in August she found the older woman still in her cotton pajamas, mopping her eyes.

'What's wrong?' Claire had rushed to her side.

'She's selling the house.' Bea appeared pale and plain without her red glasses and her signature ruby lipstick.

'This house?' Claire gasped. Julie was a partner at her firm. It made sense that eventually she'd leave their neighborhood for greener, more sprawling pastures. Claire had no clue it would be this soon. They were beyond overdue for a catch-up.

'Not this house! *My* house!'

'Oh, Bea,' Claire sank to the couch and placed her hand on Bea's forearm, her skin soft as flour. 'I'm sorry.'

'You take a little tumble and suddenly everyone thinks you're a danger to yourself.' Bea shook her head. 'I love my daughter, but I also love my independence. After Lou passed, it took me years to adjust to living alone. I'd just started to like it.'

Claire's eyes filled in sympathy.

'Can I tell you a secret?'

'Of course.' Claire had nodded. 'You know all mine.'

'Sometimes I'd take a hot bath then I'd watch *Grey's Anatomy* in nothing but a bathrobe and eat gelato for dinner straight from the container,' she lowered her voice, 'in bed!'

'Rock star.' Claire grinned and squeezed Bea's hand.

'It wasn't supposed to turn out like this.' The older woman sighed. 'I feel so helpless.'

Claire had felt the same way over the past year. But she'd taken back a bit of control and she wanted to empower Bea, too.

'What if you could still be independent but closer? Maybe even have a little help if you wanted it?'

'I've seen where people like me end up, Claire; drooling into their mashed peas, parked at Bingo not even covering their numbers, just staring into space. No thank you.'

'Not a nursing home, Bea, an over fifty-five community. There are lovely ones, I promise.' Claire had been looking into places for her parents – not that they'd agree to even take a tour, but she wanted to be ready in case they changed their minds or it became a necessity.

She'd shown Bea websites and helped her gather information.

'I adore being here with my grandsons,' Bea had said. 'They've introduced me to two new friends – Siri and Alexa – but I want my own space.'

'I totally get that.'

Bea made Claire promise she'd help her convince Julie if her daughter showed any resistance. Claire had agreed.

Now she'd ask Bea to help her.

Claire rang the doorbell twice – their code – then sailed through the entryway, past the kitchen, and into the family room, where she found Bea in a white linen dress watching a video on her phone.

'Good morning, dear.' Bea pressed pause with a purposeful flourish. 'This woman is building birdhouses with champagne corks. It's remarkable.'

Without taking another step, Claire knew what was coming next.

'It's this wonderful program: *Alice Masters Everything*. The kids showed it to me and now I can't get enough of her. She taught me how to do this.' Bea patted her silver hair, swept up in a chignon. 'You should subscribe to her channel. Oh, and her newsletter.'

'People keep telling me that.' Claire refocused the conversation on Bea, whose turquoise bracelets jingled as she placed her phone in her lap. 'You're all dressed up today.'

'My final visit with the orthopedist.'

'Do you need a ride?' Claire offered. Maybe she could confide in Bea on the drive.

'Thank you, but I'm taking an Uber. The kids put the app on my phone and taught me to use it.'

'Impressive!'

'Trying to be more like my old self. A little more adventurous.'

'On that note . . .' Too jittery to sit, Claire paced the wide-plank floors as she spilled her news about Alex's invitation. 'What do I do?'

'Oh my.' Bea covered her open mouth. Her polished red nails matched her lipstick.

Worn out from pacing, Claire collapsed to the floor and lay on her back. 'What do I tell him? Do I go? What happens if I do?'

'How will you feel if you don't?' Bea asked. 'Nobody knows this . . .' Bea's brown eyes, magnified by her glasses, grew wider '. . . but I have a "what if" suitor in my past.'

'You do?' Claire sat up and folded her legs criss-cross applesauce.

'Marty Devlin.' Bea nodded. 'I grew up near the beach. His family rented the house across the street. The summer I was sixteen, he was seventeen. He worked in the candy store. I can still see him in his apron and paper hat. At night after the shop closed, we'd meet on the boardwalk.' She leaned forward and cupped a hand close to her mouth, indicating she was about to reveal a secret. 'I told my parents I was babysitting.' She straightened up. 'He'd bring me a little bag of Red Vines. We'd slow dance, his hand on the small of my back. And, oh Claire, he smelled so good – like cotton candy.'

'What happened?'

'We wrote to each other all fall and winter. Each time I got a letter, I'd swoon. I re-read them until the paper was thin as tissue. Then in the spring he told me his father had lost his job. They couldn't afford to rent a place that summer. I was devastated.'

Claire pressed her hands to her heart.

'My poor sister. We shared a room. She listened to me cry myself to sleep for a month.'

'Did you ever see him again?'

'I did.'

'Where?' Claire longed for Bea to say she and her first love met up years later and enjoyed a passionate rendezvous at a beachside bed and breakfast – anything that would make her desire for Alex seem completely normal, commonplace.

'Disney World.'

'Huh?'

'The girls and I were waiting for Lou and the boys to come out of the men's room and there was Marty. He had a boy on his shoulders, looked just like a mini version of the handsome guy I fell in love with all those years earlier.'

'What happened next?'

'Well, my stomach dropped same as it did when I took the kids on Space Mountain. Lou, God rest his soul, was prone to vertigo. At first I thought I'd imagined it, but then I saw a woman – his wife, I guessed – and she said, "You made sure Bobby washed his hands, Marty?" I nearly fainted. I gripped the stroller handle so I didn't fall over.'

'Then what did you do?'

'What do you think I did?' Bea laughed. 'I was a wife and mother of four. I spent the day listening to Lou complain about food prices inside the park while my children whined about long ride lines. But, privately, I did what women have done since the dawn of time: I wondered about what might have been, about all the other ways my life could've turned out. But then I laughed – if I'd ended up with Marty I'd have landed in the exact same place: Disney World, pushing the very same rental stroller.'

'Did you ever see him again?'

'No.' Bea rubbed her chin and smiled. 'I've thought about him on and off since you brought up this Alex fellow. So thank you. It's a nice memory. Now I hate to cut this short, dear but,' she unlocked her phone, 'Oscar will be here in a Toyota Camry in four minutes. I mustn't keep him waiting.'

'But, Bea, no, you can't leave yet. I don't know what I'm doing.'

'If you go, you'll know. If you don't, you'll always wonder.' Bea pressed a button to activate her power lift recliner. The chair slowly pitched her forward until she stood at her full five feet three inches. 'But that's a choice only you can make, dear.' She smoothed her dress and patted her hair. 'Now off we go!'

September 4, 2024

11:02 a.m.

Back on the sidewalk, Claire squinted against the sunlight as she opened the app on her phone and read Alex's message for the billionth time. Then she typed:

Sounds amazing. I'll try to sneak away.

With her eyes shut, and before she could change her mind, she pressed send.

Did she sound too eager? Did the word 'try' come off as breezy and non-committal? Did the phrase 'sneak away' up the clandestine factor?

She closed the app and told herself not to look at it again for a few hours. She had work to do.

September 4, 2024

11:05 a.m.

As often happened, Claire fell down a rabbit hole as she browsed the MTV *Teen Mom*s social media accounts. Initially, she'd had no idea who any of them were, but now she found herself oddly fascinated by these women and their trajectories. They'd gone from relatively tough situations to not just making a living but thriving by hawking waist-trainers and teeth-whitening kits. *Moms gotta do what moms gotta do.*

Or did they? Claire had worked hard on her original daycare drop-off piece. She'd interviewed women who'd done difficult things and generously shared their stories with her. She couldn't allow Sabrina to toss it just because they weren't reality stars.

She felt dizzy with irritation – or maybe it was hunger. She hadn't had breakfast. By Thursdays, the fridge typically stood empty, save for condiments and a few eggs. A momentary rush of relief swept through her when she remembered that her mother had dinner covered.

Claire needed to call and tell her mom that she didn't have brown sugar for the baked beans. If she didn't do it soon, her mother would call again. And this is how that would go: her mom would start off by apologizing for interrupting Claire's workday. Then, she'd launch into a twenty-minute supermarket saga explaining that the frozen dinners Claire's dad ate for lunch were on sale but rang up at their regular price. These tales always involved rejected coupons, a new cashier whom her mother would deem 'mildly incompetent', and a bumbling store manager.

Before getting to the conclusion, her mom would weave in several side conversations she'd had with the parents of Claire's former classmates whom she'd bumped into while combing the deli or produce sections.

'Skippy Tompkins is a big-time divorce attorney now,' her mom had told her last week, giving Claire pause. Was this her mom's way of fishing? Did she suspect Claire and Paul had marital problems?

When she failed to respond, her mother continued. 'Honey, you remember Skippy, don't you? Short? Face full of acne? His mom said you two had gym together all four years of high school.'

'Oh, right, it's coming back to me now.' Claire pretended to recall the classmate in question rather than doing what she wanted, which was scream, 'Why are we talking about this?'

On nights when her mother was scheduled to babysit, they'd engage in an endless back-and-forth in which Eleanor would suggest arrival times that varied by five-minute intervals.

'Honey, if it's a help, I can come as early as five twenty. But if you're not leaving until six, I should probably get your father's dinner ready, so maybe five thirty-five? Or, five thirty if you want to get going sooner?'

Guilt made Claire's heart hurt. She treasured her chats with Bea. Why was it sometimes easier to love people who weren't family?

She knew she should be more appreciative of her mom's help, especially because no one would take better care of her boys than their beloved nana, but these exchanges drained her. As Claire's patience ebbed, sadness flooded in. Who knew how much longer her mom might be willing or able to make dinner for her grandsons? She blocked the thought and stood.

Stomach rumbling, Claire considered running to her favorite sandwich shop to grab her regular: tuna on a toasted pumpernickel bagel with lettuce and tomato. But that little circle of deliciousness probably came in at no fewer than eight hundred calories. And, of course, she'd want chips and a Coke. All those carbs would have her mid-section puffing up like a blowfish in minutes.

Ninety percent of Claire's shorts and pants fit like tourniquets. She took a mental inventory of her wardrobe. The only attractive ensemble she had – black pants and a silver halter top that made her blue eyes appear almost turquoise – was the same one she'd worn to the reunion. She couldn't very well see Alex twice in twenty-five years in the exact same outfit. If she decided to meet him, should she wear a dress? Or, did that seem like she was trying too hard?

Prior to the reunion, Claire had asked Annabelle, the reigning queen of girls' night out, or GNO, as she hashtagged it in her social media posts, what she should pack for the getaway. In their group text, Annabelle wrote that all she really needed was a flattering pair of jeans, a funky shirt, and a statement necklace.

When Claire had pressed her to define 'funky', Annabelle, childless by choice, had added a series of eye-roll emojis followed by: In your case, anything without food stains will do.

Claire evaluated her options. She had dark denim that called to mind the phrase 'prison-issued', high-waisted 'mom jeans', and a pair of overalls that made her look like a farmhand. And while she might not be a fashion expert, she knew enough not to turn up at the bar of the W hotel dressed like an inmate or Old MacDonald.

Since having the boys, Claire believed her most attractive body parts were limited to the nape of her neck and the area between her shoulder and elbow. The rest seemed to be cascading toward her toes. When she allowed herself to steal a glance at her naked just-out-of-the-shower body in the full-length mirror that hung on the back of the bathroom door, Claire could hear the voice of a flight attendant: 'Caution! Cargo may have shifted.'

Cargo had *definitely* shifted.

She decided to make a couple of hard-boiled eggs, recalling an article she'd read about a supermodel who credited the protein-packed orbs with helping her shed her baby weight. 'Yeah, right, all twelve pounds of it,' Claire had scoffed. The bikini-clad new mom with washboard abs smiled mockingly from the pages of the magazine Claire had flipped through while waiting in line at the supermarket, her cart brimming with carbohydrates and glow-in-the-dark yogurt. The young woman's teeth – so smooth and even – had probably never known the pleasure of tearing into a sticky-sweet coffee roll.

Claire headed for the fridge as her phone pinged. She turned back and saw a new text from Paul.

Before she opened it, she willed her husband to have written something – anything – that might bring her back to her senses and make her cancel her date (*was it a date?*) with Alex. Maybe that meant she wasn't ready to throw away sixteen years of marriage. Still, it was a lot to hope for, considering most of Paul's messages read like ones you'd send to a personal assistant.

Before their separation, her husband's main enquiries focused on the starting time of the boys' sporting events and then, in subsequent messages, he'd ask the name of the fields where those games would take place. Requests for directions to those same fields typically followed, leaving Claire muttering, 'Put the damn address in your map app!' at her phone. Frequently, he'd want to know what was for dinner that evening. Other times, he'd ask her to run a random errand that easily could wait until the weekend.

Since he'd been living at his parents', he still texted to get the boys' sporting event details, but he'd add links to book and movie reviews he thought she'd enjoy, or tour dates for a band she'd liked that had reunited.

It was a start, yet believing Paul would suddenly write her a sonnet was about as far-fetched as expecting him to remember the name of Henry's piano teacher – another perpetual thorn in her side.

Before they separated, Claire lamented how Mrs Meyers had gotten in the habit of starting Henry's piano lessons three minutes late and wrapping up five minutes early.

'If you're paying thirty-six dollars for a thirty-minute lesson, then, technically, Mrs Meyers owes you nine dollars and sixty cents for eight missed minutes,' Henry, her math whiz, had calculated.

'I'm sorry, you keep talking about this Mrs Meyers lady as if I should know who she is,' Paul had said, bewildered.

If the boys hadn't been there, Claire would've said something snide like, 'She's the widow I keep tied to the furnace.'

'Geez, Dad, duh,' said Henry, doing the dirty work for her.

'She's my piano teacher. She's been coming to our house every Wednesday for the past two years.'

Normally, Claire would have reprimanded her son for saying 'duh' to his father, but in this case Paul had it coming.

In light of this history, it was pointless to hope Paul's text would include scintillating content. Still, she wanted a sign that he was making some sort of effort to win her back.

As she swiped to open the message, Claire's eyes landed on the word 'Tonight'. Her heart stopped. Was Paul referring to Alex's invitation? Had he used spyware to read her messages? He was a programmer, after all, so it was within his skillset, but he'd never shown that much initiative or interest. Even when they'd dated, Paul didn't have a jealous bone in his body. At the time, she'd thought of him as evolved, secure in their relationship. But, over the past few years, she'd become convinced Paul's confidence stemmed from his belief that no one would ever be attracted to her – especially now that, in certain lights, she looked like Gary Busey.

Claire took a deep breath and forced herself to read the message.

Tonight is back-to-school night, right? What time does it start? While you're out today, if you could pick up floss that would be great. Joe keeps using it to turn my mom's teddy bears into mummies. Thx

'While you're out.' That part of the message annoyed her most – as if she just drove around town in a circle all day. Wasn't he technically 'out' too? Surely, somewhere between his parents' house and his Manhattan office, he'd find a CVS or a Walgreens?

She fought back the urge to write, 'Oh no! Have you been banned from convenience stores??'

And maybe she was reading too much into it, but it also felt as if Paul had implied that she hadn't taught their youngest the basics of oral hygiene.

She typed **BTSN starts at 7**, hit send, and added floss to the growing grocery list she kept beside her computer. Hard bits of rice from the previous evening's dinner crunched beneath her notepad as she scribbled.

Though she'd tried to resist the temptation all summer, Claire couldn't help but compare Paul to Alex. She thought about a message Alex had sent her in early July – the one that made her realize she was falling for him. Hard.

Claire, there's something I've always wanted to tell you.

She braced for an admission so crazy and awful that it would abruptly end the fantasy that had sustained her through her silly work assignments, Joe's early swim team practices, and summer camp pick-ups.

She'd continued reading, oblivious to the fact that she was grinding her teeth in anticipation of Alex revealing that he was a registered sex offender or had an equally horrifying character flaw.

> I wanted to thank you. Sophomore year you waved to me across campus, it changed everything. I was walking back to my dorm. I'd just failed an econ test – not the first time that had happened in that class or others that semester.
>
> My dad had been diagnosed with cancer a couple of months earlier. I was falling apart. I wanted to go home, but my parents kept saying that the best thing for my dad was for me to stay in school, try my hardest. You know, the same thing you'd tell your own kids. I'd been put on academic probation and I'd decided the easiest thing to do would be to fail everything and go home, return to my part-time job at Blockbuster. (Remember those? Clearly, this was not a well-thought-out plan.)
>
> Then you waved to me, Claire, and it made me want to stay, to try. You were wearing jeans and a white top with blue flowers, and you had this glow, and I thought to myself, 'I'm going to fix this. I'm going to come back here in the fall, and I'm going to date that girl.' Of course, it didn't happen like that.
>
> My dad passed away this spring, and it made me understand how crucial it is to do and say the things that matter and not wait until it's too late to acknowledge the intersection of the ordinary and the remarkable.
>
> After you waved and we got closer you looked confused, sweet but confused, and I realized that you'd mistaken me for someone else. But I didn't care. I wanted to be that guy you thought you were waving to, and that was enough.
>
> So, Claire, this is my long overdue thank you. If it weren't for you, I'd be standing inside a vacant storefront holding the last VHS copy of *Animal House*.
>
> You saved me.
>
> Sleep well.

His words had had the opposite effect; Claire hadn't slept well. At all. In fact, though she'd read his email early the morning after he'd written it, she'd barely been able to fall asleep that night or the one that followed.

As a woman who wore a uniform of black stretch pants and oversized T-shirts, whose mantra had been reduced to 'What's that smell?', it seemed impossible to believe that she could've ever made an impression like that on anyone. The very notion that her existence had entwined with someone else's – and possibly improved it – made her feel as euphoric as George Bailey at the end of *It's a Wonderful Life*.

Claire found the idea magical, and it made her think that their paths had been destined to cross once again just as they had all those years ago.

Only this time, he was saving her.

March 12, 1999

11:11 p.m.

Claire and Maggie stood in the dungeon-like basement of a bar, listening to a punk band, the bass so powerful, Claire's chest throbbed. Amid the dim lighting, she thought she recognized the guy staring at her from across the crowded space. Was it Alex? She squinted and waved at him as she always did. The jacket got her every time.

Though they'd been in London for three days, she hadn't realized he'd been on the school trip until that moment. Seconds later, he crossed the stone floor, flickering candles casting shadows across his handsome face.

Above the lead singer's screams, Claire heard him loud and clear as he leaned in close to her ear.

'You look fantastic.' His warm breath tickled her neck, sending goosebumps up and down her bare arms.

'Thank you!' Claire smiled and clinked her glass against his. 'Going for a "new country, new me" thing.' She'd borrowed a sleeveless black faux-leather minidress from Annabelle, and paired it with hoop earrings and ankle boots. The ensemble gave her curves and confidence. 'Speaking of new, you need a new jacket.' If Claire's second Cosmo loosened her up, the third made her liquid.

'Not a fan of green?' he asked.

'Reminds me of my boyfriend,' Claire hiccupped. 'Old boyfriend,' she corrected herself.

'*Ex*-boyfriend!' Maggie interjected.

'What if it could remind you of your *new* boyfriend?' Alex smirked.

To Claire's booze-soaked brain, his words made little sense, but she liked the way his chestnut eyes sparkled mischievously when he looked at her.

'That was my failed attempt at applying for the job . . .' The song ended, plunging the bar into an ear-ringing quiet just as Alex shouted, '. . . of your boyfriend!'

The crowd watched, awaiting her reaction. Even the bartender paused mid-pour.

Claire's head buzzed. She'd been hoping for a Hollywood-style moment with Neal but wasn't this every bit as good? Even better maybe. A vacation romance – a fling. How adult! The perfect way to banish all thoughts of her ex. She'd be crazy to let this opportunity pass her by.

Handing her martini glass to Mags, Claire pulled Alex into her by the flaps of his jacket pockets. She pressed her mouth to his full lips. He tasted a lot like whiskey and a little bit like magic. Claire finally understood that 'weak in the knees' was more than an expression.

Claps and whoops enveloped them as Alex held her tight, lifting her off the stone floor, the way couples celebrated after they won the grand prize on a game show. When he set her down, she kissed him again.

Why had it taken her so long to realize that happiness had been right there in front of her all this time? She'd only needed to reach out and grab it.

Mags, Claire, Alex, and his pal, who was visiting from Scotland, shared a cab back to the hotel. Alex's friend rode shotgun as they sped through deserted streets. Drunk and laughing like idiots, they'd implored the driver to *please* get back on the right side of the road while he cranked up the radio and ignored them.

When the taxi hit a bump depositing Claire in Alex's lap, he cupped her face with his hands and kissed her. Perhaps it was the cocktails, passing Big Ben as moonlight danced across the Thames, or the surprise of it all, but for the first time in ages, Neal hadn't crossed her mind. Her thoughts were solely on Alex.

As they stumbled out of the cab and into the hotel, Claire was overjoyed to learn that Alex's pal was rooming with another travel buddy. She couldn't wait to have him all to herself.

'Wanna take the stairs?' she asked after the elevator failed to arrive within a minute.

'You're wearing heels and I'm on the ninth floor,' Alex grinned, 'but I'm digging your sense of urgency.'

When the elevator finally came, Mags rode up with them, exiting on the fifth floor.

'Have fun, you two,' she said.

'I'll be back soon . . . ish,' Claire told her, her heart-rate accelerating to near stroke levels at the thought of being alone with Alex.

'I won't wait up.' Mags winked.

The elevator doors had barely closed when Alex looped his hand through Claire's scarf and reeled her into him. Pressed against the panel, her backside illuminated all the buttons, causing the lift to stop on every floor.

As soon as they reached Alex's room, they began undressing. Electric shocks sparked between them, making them gasp, laugh, and shed another layer.

The dress Claire borrowed from Annabelle was so tight, it ripped as she pulled it over her head.

'Whoops,' Alex whispered, kissing her neck, his warm fingers unhooking her bra, stroking her nipples.

He lowered Claire to the bed slowly. She shivered against the cold sheets, eager to feel the weight of him on top of her.

'I've wanted to do this since you hopped on my back,' he moaned.

'Maybe this time I'll hop on your front.' She playfully bit his earlobe and wrapped her legs around his waist.

His hands were in her hair, his tongue everywhere. Claire's entire body hummed. She closed her eyes, trying to imprint the moment on her memory. The experience felt brand new. Neal in bed was like Neal on stage – demanding adoration, hogging the spotlight. More than once she'd caught him looking at himself in the mirrored closet doors in his bedroom.

Alex was the opposite; slow, generous, making sure she was comfortable, satisfied.

They fit together so well, made for each other, like interlocking puzzle pieces.

Everything was perfect – except for Annabelle's dress. Claire would buy her a new one . . . if she ever left Alex's bed.

September 4, 2024

11:14 a.m.

Sabrina would be hounding her again any moment, but Claire couldn't get her mind off Alex. Now that she told him she'd meet him, she was doubting her decision. Was he all she'd built him up to be? She opened the app and skimmed his messages.

In one of the earliest ones they'd exchanged following the reunion, he'd written that he'd have recognized her anywhere, that she hadn't changed a bit.

'No, that's not true,' he corrected himself. 'You're even lovelier than I remembered. And, I've thought of you, Claire. Often.'

Each line made her feel like the star of her own romantic comedy. Of course, she recognized she was a sucker for flattery, in much the same way the elderly were prime targets for phone scams. Lack of attention would do that. After years of fishing for compliments on everything from a new dress to her signature corn muffins, Claire was starving for the kindness and appreciation Alex generously bestowed through cyberspace.

If he'd filled his messages with dirty limericks or insights on the best places to fly-fish, they would've seemed quirky and insightful, because she hadn't spent more than a decade listening to him snore or watching him trim his nasal hair in the half-bathroom with the door open. Naturally, free of those irksome qualities, Alex couldn't help but appear intriguing and infinitely desirable.

To be fair, though, Claire wondered if he'd grate on her nerves if she'd been married to him for the past sixteen years. Surely, he must have some loathsome habits. Would he drive her minivan and fail to mention it was out of gas? Did he place empty cereal boxes back in the cupboard rather than recycle them, causing family-wide disappointment and confusion?

She thought of Bea, 'If I'd ended up with Marty, I'd have landed in the exact same place . . .'

Would Alex's penchant for inspirational phrases become something she mocked on ladies' nights out with her neighbors?

'And then he said, "Even if you're on the right track, you'll get run over if you just sit there!"' She pictured herself laughing as she tried to nail Alex's earnest, upbeat inflection.

Maybe seeing the same person every single day – no matter who it was – was the problem. When she was younger and visited museums with her mother, she'd often wonder if the tour guides still found the Monets and Matisses awe-inspiring, or had their beauty and brilliance worn off, a sad byproduct of familiarity?

But Paul hadn't always been so predictable, had he? Claire wondered if she could truly blame all of this on him. If she were being honest, she had let herself go a bit. Most evenings, she'd had little to talk about other than the boys and their frenetic schedules. And, because Paul liked to keep their bedroom at a chilly sixty-five degrees, Claire slept covered head to toe in a tracksuit and fluffy socks. No wonder things had gone stale.

And yet they'd lasted so much longer than most of their friends. When they watched their wedding video, as they did each April on their anniversary, they were stunned by how many of their guests had called it quits.

As a child, Claire had sat perched at the top of the staircase, eavesdropping on her parents' dinner parties. She'd come to believe that the very definition of true love was the ability to listen to your partner tell the same stories and still laugh at all the right places and not spoil the punchlines out of spite. Now she knew it involved that, and so much more.

Her relationship with Paul had been exciting once. Why did it feel so difficult to recall those days now?

July 19, 2006

6:48 p.m.

The click-clack of fingers tapping against keyboards lulled Claire into a trance. For the past three years, she'd worked for her hometown newspaper, published every Thursday and Sunday. She was bored but grateful to be there after languishing at a few dead-end internships. She hoped to have her own column one day soon, but hadn't worked up the nerve to pitch Larry, the paper's owner.

Each Wednesday evening, Claire proofread pages until her vision blurred. She started with the obits because she believed they deserved a sharp eye. She ended with the classifieds – often using it as an opportunity to look for a better job. Many ads repeated week after week, making it an easy way to end the workday.

As she wrapped up, Claire stumbled upon a classified she hadn't seen before. It read: **Claire Collins! (Yes, YOU!) Meet me in the lobby. NOW. (Please.)**

Tired yet jittery from too much caffeine, Claire initially thought *These caps and parentheses are an absolute nightmare*, before she realized the message was indeed directed at her.

She looked around the newsroom. The view was bleak: dead plants, stained Mr Coffee pots, very few reporters. The paper's staff had been reduced to a skeleton crew because advertising was down thanks to the internet. She imagined it wouldn't be long before she, too, was let go, and when she was, maybe she'd finally write that novel.

She re-read the classified ad again.

Claire Collins! (Yes, YOU!) Meet me in the lobby. NOW. (Please.)

Could Ned, the weird guy who covered high school sports and wore *Napoleon Dynamite* T-shirts, be pranking her? He'd asked her out every week for three months straight before giving up.

Claire spun in her swivel chair. Nope, Ned sat hunched over his desk, gnawing his way through an Italian sub, lettuce decorating his 'Vote for Pedro' tee like pale green embroidery.

She stood hesitantly and moved toward the lobby. She'd hated surprises ever since her parents had brought her younger brother, Kyle, home from the hospital and announced 'Surprise!' amid a flurry of blue balloons and a shrill cry from the wrinkly lump swaddled in her mother's arms.

When she opened the old oak door that led to the lobby, she found Paul, down on one knee, while Ernie, the janitor, mopped around him. *Caution: Wet Floor* signs adorned the faded tiles like bright yellow daffodils. Claire almost laughed thinking Paul had slipped and somehow landed in this precarious figure-skater-at-the-end-of-a-routine pose. Then she spotted the velvet box and red roses on the ground beside him.

'Claire!' Paul exclaimed, his cheeks blooming as scarlet as the flowers. Without breaking eye contact, he grappled to free the ring. Ernie momentarily stopped mopping to take in this spectacle.

'Claire Catherine Collins, will you marry me?' he asked, straight to the point, no big preamble like you'd get on *The Bachelor*.

Though they'd been dating for close to two years, Claire was stunned. Her hands flew to her face, a subconscious act that she hoped hid her shock as a million thoughts flashed through her head: *I'm only twenty-seven! I still haven't been to Greece or written a novel! What about my column? Will I need a punchbowl?*

Even as they flitted across her mind, Claire recognized these as utterly bizarre musings. Compared to her friends and relatives, she was a veritable spinster. Annabelle was already on her second engagement. And, it wasn't like Greece had an embargo against Paul. Surely, he could join her on the black sands of Santorini, couldn't he?

Still, she'd harbored a fantasy about writing that column at the paper – not quite Carrie Bradshaw's *Sex and the City* – OK, exactly like that, only set in the suburbs and with more comfortable and affordable footwear. That dream would end here. Because, let's face it, no one wanted to read about an engaged woman debating the merits of registering for a gravy boat. But deep down Claire knew, even if she remained single and Larry agreed to let her write something like that, the thought that her parents might read it would require it to be G-rated. And who gets a book deal based on *Lady and the Tramp*-like dinner dates and courtships? No one.

Maybe marriage would spark inspiration and provide great material for her novel? Claire knew Jane Austen, one of her literary heroines, would take umbrage with that. But look at Nora Ephron, though *Heartburn* was hardly a fairytale.

The wall clock *tick tick tick*'d, but for Claire, time stood still. Paul remained on one knee.

As much as she loved him, and she really did, some small part of her viewed his proposal as a scene from a movie she wasn't quite prepared to see yet. Was she ready for this next stage of life to begin?

Sweat prickled beneath her rayon blouse; she had trouble breathing thanks to her pencil skirt. The ticking grew louder. She had to give Paul an answer before Ernie began mopping again.

'Yes!' Claire said, the certainty in her voice surprising her.

Ernie dropped his mop and began a slow, awkward clap.

'Phew!' Paul wobbled a bit as he stood and slid the ring on her finger. 'I've been out here for two hours now. You've told me which section of the paper you edit last a thousand times, but I guess I wasn't paying attention.'

They kissed and he handed her the bouquet. While the red roses were lovely, daisies had always been Claire's favorite. She was sure she'd mentioned that at least a thousand times as well.

September 4, 2024

11:25 a.m.

A lifelong connoisseur of literary devices, Claire now wondered if Paul's inattention to detail – to her details, really – could be considered foreshadowing. And if so, didn't that mean she should've known exactly how everything would turn out all along? Swept up in their relationship and thoughts of a future together, she'd willingly overlooked things she couldn't see past now. But what was marriage if not recognizing someone's shortcomings and loving them anyway?

Two hard-boiled eggs chilled in the fridge, but Claire had lost her appetite. She felt like an asshole as she remembered leaving

Parker Westbrook alone at the bus stop and then barking at that random teen.

She hoped he'd been taking a series of selfies and not filming her as she sped away, shouting at him to do 'something useful'.

Are people really calling me a bully?

In the past, this would've sent her into a self-doubt spiral where she'd question the kind of person she'd become. Was she a good mother, daughter, friend, tipper? But as she'd been doing for the past few months, the very second any negativity crept in, she'd think of Alex, and the lighter, more carefree woman she had once been, and feel strong and confident again.

Before bumping into him and beginning their correspondence – and whatever it was about to become – Claire's deepest longings involved the mouthwatering desserts she'd scrolled past on Pinterest. The biggest excitement in her days had been confined to conquering stains and sometimes mistakenly using her Oil of Olay night cream in the morning.

With the exception of the hours she spent with her sons (when she needed to be on high alert to avert potential calamity and possible concussions), she realized she'd practically been sleep-walking through her life.

Just thinking about Alex elicited a full-body quiver that reminded her of the time she'd accidentally plugged in her freestanding mixer with wet fingertips.

Instant messenger jingled. Knowing it would be Sabrina made Claire want to call out sick for the rest of the day.

Sabrina: Claire, I looked at the single mom daycare drop-off piece. Your reported story is back. Why? Hope this is a tech glitch! Please revert.

Claire: Not a tech issue. I think this piece has a lot more originality and heart than one featuring old social media posts from reality stars.

Sabrina: We don't care about 'originality and heart', Claire. We care about traffic.

Claire: I interviewed these women and told them we were honored to share their stories, stories that may help other single moms.

Sabrina: That was before the team came up with a better angle.

Claire rested her head on her dining-room table beside her laptop. Crumbs stuck to her cheek. She was on the verge of slipping back into another 'How did it come to this?' pity loop when she remembered something Alex had said at the reunion.

They'd been standing in the crowded bar among old friends. A tall guy everyone called Sully, who'd roamed their campus with a St Bernard (the most likable thing about him), handed out shots of dark liquid.

Though she wasn't sure where the night would lead, Claire knew she didn't want it to end with Stacey and Annabelle holding back her hair as she vomited into the sewer on the walk to the Hyatt.

'I'm going to pass,' she'd said responsibly.

'Don't be such a baby, Claire,' Sully had shouted. Jägermeister splashed over the sides of the tiny glasses, causing him to lick his wet thumbs, ensuring no precious alcohol went to waste. 'You were always a goody-goody, weren't you?'

'Don't let anyone tell you who you are, Claire,' Alex had said, draping his arm around her shoulder, the warmth and weight of it as welcome as a down blanket on a snowy night. 'Listen to your inner voice,' Alex knocked on his broad chest with his free hand, 'and you'll always live your authentic truth.'

'Jesus, Alex, what the hell? I know you got those fancy-pants degrees, but who do you think you are, Deepak Chopra?' Sully had spat.

'Yeah, Alex, stop pretending you're like Oprah now just because you run a software empire. For one thing, you don't have enough hair, and you don't have your own book club either,' Annabelle had snickered.

'Well, Annabelle, that's two things, really, and if I did have a book club, I'd suggest my members read *How to Not Be a Sheep*,' Alex had responded.

Claire watched as Annabelle and Stacey narrowed their eyes and glared at Alex, making her wish she'd just accepted the shot glass.

'A toast,' Alex continued, removing his arm from her shoulder and raising his drink. 'To Claire not being a sheep!'

'Baaaa!' Sully had emitted an ear-splitting bleat before dropping his beer on the head of the woman next to him, prompting a bouncer to escort him to the door.

Because Claire's head still lay on the dining-room table beside her laptop, the *ping!* of instant messenger was louder and more irritating than usual. She could barely muster the strength to lift her eyes to read Sabrina's next message. Craning her neck slightly, she squinted at the screen.

Sabrina: **Just had a thought: If you can't find enough** *Teen Mom* **posts, throw in some** *Real Housewives*.

Claire gritted her teeth. 'To Claire not being a sheep!' She heard Alex's voice like a foghorn calling out to her across a sea of stupidity. Was this lingo – the whole 'authentic truth' stuff – something he'd learned while getting that MBA in Leadership Development? She found it empowering and felt herself slipping under its jargon-ish spell.

When she'd been hired by MamaRama.com, she thought she'd be writing things like *18 Ways to Make the Most of Your Rotisserie Chicken*, and while she hadn't been thrilled about that, at least it wasn't complete nonsense. At her six-month review, Sabrina told her she needed to 'push back more' and not be afraid to come up with her own take on these 'stories'.

Oh yes, it was time to push back and live her 'authentic truth'. She sat straighter and placed her fingers on the keyboard.

Claire: **Let's back up a second. That wasn't the original assignment, and if the team likes the other idea better, then maybe someone else on the team should write it.**

For a moment Claire thought about adding 'Just pushing back as you suggested, LOL!' to the end of her message. These women loved to write 'LOL'. Was there any other acronym that held the same passive-aggressive appeal? It subtly implied, 'Yes, I'm being rude, but because I'm telling you I'm laughing out loud, how bad can it be, right? And if you don't think it's funny, then clearly you're overly sensitive or a humorless dimwit.'

Claire hit 'send' and waited for Sabrina to hit back with the written equivalent of a body slam.

Dots danced and then disappeared on Claire's screen, indicating Sabrina was typing and then deleting her reply. She couldn't rule out that her editor might fire her on the spot. Finally, the messenger pinged.

Sabrina: **Fine, do it your way, but get it to me by noon.**

Holy crap! It worked!

Why had she not lived her authentic truth all along? Alex was right! She wasn't surprised. He exuded confidence and common sense. Paul would never have given her that advice. Instead, he'd have said, 'Is Sabrina your boss? Well, then you'd better do what she says,' or some other bullshit straight out of 1952.

Claire realized that attitude probably had a lot to do with why he was going nowhere in his job and would soon be replaced by a robot or a twelve-year-old.

Paul never took risks.

Alex made Claire want to run headlong toward them.

September 4, 2024

11:48 a.m.

Her morning assignments complete, Claire sent an instant message to her editors and colleagues: *ROFL AFK BRB!!* (Running Out for Lunch, Away From Keyboard, Be Right Back), followed by a string of smiley face, sandwich, and iced-tea emojis. Using the MamaRama holy trinity – acronyms, exclamation points, and emoticons – would surely buy her extra time if she needed it.

After taking a mental inventory of her wardrobe, Claire decided to run to the mall to hunt for an outfit that would make Alex drop his Scotch in mid-air and undergarments that didn't look like they'd been salvaged from a dumpster.

She grabbed her purse and car keys, and was sliding her feet into sandals when the doorbell rang.

Paul finally changed the battery, Claire made a quick mental note to thank him as she opened the door to find Abby McClaren standing on her welcome mat. She swallowed the urge to scream, 'What now?' and instead said, 'Listen, Abby if it's about Parker West—'

'OMG, Claire! Did you get a dog?' Abby asked.

Claire looked at the plastic bones that littered her porch – pieces of a skeleton, a decoration from last Halloween. Had they really been out there nearly a year?

'Oh, no, the boys were working on an anatomy project,' she lied.

'Not that,' Abby scowled, 'I'm asking because there's a steaming pile of dog crap on your front lawn.'

'Motherfucker,' Claire swore under her breath. Who was doing this and why? It had started rather suddenly. Was it someone new to the neighborhood? Had Alex ever told her where his ex, Jocelyn, had settled? Could she have learned of their connection and begun leaving these mounds of dog poop as her way of cautioning Claire: 'Careful where you step!'

No. That would be nuts. Claire had watched too many *Dateline* episodes and her imagination was getting the better of her. Still, it was gross and unsettling.

Last week, she'd found Paul in the driveway hosing off a loafer when he'd stopped by after work to take Max to soccer practice. Then, on Tuesday, the boys' first day of school, Joe had slipped in a particularly mushy heap of poo and fallen flat on his back. Fortunately, his *Star Wars* backpack had borne the brunt of it. Still, his screams had echoed through the neighborhood when he saw Darth Vader's face obscured by dog feces.

Claire had narrowed down the suspects to a boxer and a golden doodle. Each time she entered and exited her home now, she scanned the street, hoping to catch the filthy beast in the act and unleash some of her pent-up rage on its owner.

Abby pushed her way inside Claire's foyer and sniffed at the air. 'God, Claire, don't take this the wrong way, but it positively reeks in here. You're not abusing laxatives, are you? Because Joan Peterson got hooked on those, and it's a nightmare. Every time she stops by Something's Brewing, she uses the toilet, and my poor mother-in-law goes through an entire can of Glade.'

'Thanks for your concern.' Claire shifted her weight from foot to foot, annoyed that she was wasting valuable time. 'I just made some egg salad.'

Instead of eating the eggs with a sprinkling of Himalayan pink sea salt as that incredibly toned supermodel suggested, Claire, in a celebratory mood from her shocking victory over Sabrina, had mashed them with gobs of mayo. Then she slathered two scoops onto one of Henry's favorite sesame-seed rolls, probably rendering it just as calorie-loaded as the bagel sandwich she really wanted.

'Oh, good! I was going to say, yes, you've put on some weight this summer, but *that* is not the answer,' Abby said.

Claire desperately needed this conversation to end so she could keep moving forward. The pulse in her neck began to throb. She wanted to get in her van, drive to the mall, and possibly find some clarity among the push-up bras. The weight of having to get her ensemble, her excuses, her body hair, which sprouted with the intensity of a chia pet, in place and under control if she decided to meet Alex, rested like a Cadillac Escalade on her forehead.

'Anyway, I was thinking you could quickly write up something for *The Acorn*!' Abby raised her eyebrows hopefully. 'You know, help us humanize this battle against Starbucks.'

'I'm not there anymore,' Claire shrugged. 'Sorry.'

'But you still have contacts, right?'

'Um.' Claire struggled to remember if she knew anyone who'd survived the layoffs after Larry had sold the paper to a larger regional outfit. Even if she had connections who'd agree to publish this sort of thing, she didn't have the time nor the inclination to write a call-to-action piece (for free!) to save the fate of a coffee shop. She needed to focus on her own future.

Abby stared, waiting for an answer, no doubt counting on the awkward silence to guilt Claire into complying. Little did she know that Claire, now more than ever before, was determined to follow her own 'truth' and avoid getting suckered into anything that steered her off-course. She was done being a sheep. She thought about something Alex recently shared on LinkedIn: 'Good leaders *do*; great leaders *delegate*.'

'I think you should write a really heartfelt letter to the editor, enlightening the public about what it means to be part of a small, local family business. Explain that your kids worked there as their first real jobs, and how you and Patrick hope they'll possibly take over one day. Continue the legacy of local, family-owned, small-business pride. Something like that would be so much more powerful.'

'OMG, Claire, that's brilliant, I love it.' Abby placed a hand over her heart. 'I'm practically crying just thinking about how incredibly touching that could be!'

Claire nodded enthusiastically and inched closer to her front door, hoping her neighbor would take the hint and hurry home to get started.

'But, wait, help me write it! Do you have time now? You're so much better at this stuff than I am.' Abby was nothing if not relentless.

'Oh, shoot. I would but the school nurse called. Joe's got a stomach bug and they're sending him home,' Claire lied, hoping she hadn't jinxed herself. It seemed fitting that on this day she'd get hit with a karmic boomerang and one of her kids would actually fall ill as a result of her small fib. 'I should really run.'

Abby squinted at Claire and stepped between her and the door. Would she not let Claire leave her own home?

'You've got . . .' Abby touched the skin beneath Claire's eyes. 'Are those Shrinky Dinks?'

Claire pawed at her face. The under-eye patches had shriveled up to nothing more than gummy bits. She stuck them in her pocket and took a quick selfie, which came out every bit as frightening as the first. Abby looked bewildered.

Claire took an aggressive step forward, forcing Abby back to the porch, and pulled the front door shut behind her.

'Can I at least send you a rough draft? To edit?' Abby called after her. 'Please? Free lattes for life! I promise!'

Claire missed every word. She was already in her van, racing toward the stop sign at the end of the street.

September 4, 2024

11:59 a.m.

Driving to the mall to find the perfect ensemble, Claire imagined pitching articles to her editor: *What to Wear When You're About to Cheat on Your Baby Daddy*, *How to Find the Ideal Undergarments for Your First Extra-Marital Affair in 30 Minutes or Less*, and *99 Thoughts You Experience Before Popping Your Infidelity Cherry*.

Sabrina would eat those up.

Thinking about the possibility of sleeping with Alex (*Tonight!*) while outside the cocoon of her home suddenly made everything feel very real. She desperately needed a friend who'd offer an honest opinion, free of judgement.

Her relationship with Stacey and Annabelle hadn't been the same since the reunion in June. Claire knew things were off because Stacey had stopped sending photos of her twins. Maybe that was the difference between having sons versus daughters. Claire had to bribe and threaten her boys to pose for a holiday card, while

Stacey sent new pics almost daily. New hairstyles, new piercings, neon-polished pedicures. Honestly, Claire was glad they'd stopped. How many times had she wanted to say, 'Did you mean to send this to their grandmother?'

She'd exchanged a few texts with Annabelle, and things definitely seemed strained with her, too.

The trouble began at the end of the evening when they'd reached the last dive bar on their reunion's spontaneous pub crawl.

Claire and Alex had stood together amid a circle of friends, but were pushed apart by waves of middle-aged, would-be alcoholics elbowing their way toward the bar.

How could it be 2 a.m.? she wondered as the first notes of Semisonic's 'Closing Time' reverberated through the packed space. On cue, the lights began to flicker, signaling the old, 'You don't have to go home, but you can't stay here.'

She hadn't been up that late since one of her middle-of-the-night trips to the ER when Joe had croup. She and Paul never stayed awake beyond midnight, not even on New Year's Eve. Where had the time gone? Would Alex come to find her? And if he did, what would he say? She had no idea if they were staying at the same hotel.

As the song ended and the crowd thinned, Claire had swayed through the gauzy veil of alcohol, trying to figure out her next move. She remembered how back in the old days the bar would close out the evening with a slow song. If you were going home with someone it seemed hokey. If you weren't, it felt mocking. 'The Way You Look Tonight' began, and before she knew it, Alex stood before her.

'Hey,' he'd said, 'I don't suppose you'd want to—'

'Claire, I need you!' Annabelle stepped between her and Alex. 'Stacey is sobbing. This was her and Ethan's wedding song. We have to go! Now!' Annabelle grabbed Claire's beer-free hand and began pulling her toward the corner where Stacey, who'd recently finalized her bitter divorce, stood wiping her nose with a pile of soggy cocktail napkins. 'Alex, until next time,' Annabelle yanked Claire forward, leaving her mouth just inches from Alex's. 'Good luck with your book club,' Annabelle added sarcastically.

'Alex, I . . .' Claire started, voice failing her as she wondered what he'd been about to ask before Annabelle interrupted.

'It's OK, Claire, go. I'll find you tomorrow at the barbecue.'

Claire had intended to stay for the alumni barbecue. Though she'd paid for it as well as a second night at the Hyatt, Henry's Little League team had unexpectedly made the playoffs, (despite Claire secretly rooting against them). How could a team that had resembled the *Bad News Bears* for 70 percent of the season rally in the backstretch?

She'd wanted to tell Alex that she wouldn't be there and that it had been wonderful to see him, but with Annabelle tugging her away like a petulant child, she couldn't find the words. And if she had, she didn't want to say them in front of Annabelle. So she simply gave him a quick hug. The heat coming off his rock-hard chest coupled with his unfamiliar scent caused goosebumps to multiply up and down her arms.

After collecting Stacey, Annabelle and Claire kept up a running commentary on how much the campus and neighborhood had changed, hoping to distract their distraught friend, who wept again when they discovered their favorite late-night cheese fry stand had become a nail salon.

'I wish Maggie were here with us,' Claire said, as the trio cut across campus toward their hotel. She missed the college roommate she seldom saw more acutely since returning to the place where they'd shared so many memories.

Maggie, Claire's roommate all four years, had a delightful ditziness about her that people found either endearing or infuriating. One of Claire's favorite Maggie stories involved a night when they'd bumped into one of their dorm-mates, Valerie, at an off-campus party. She'd been holding hands with a big, goofy guy who wouldn't shut up about his love for Yuengling Lager. Thinking she was being helpful, Maggie had pulled Val aside and whispered, 'Honey, you're beer-goggling! Ditch this loser. You'll thank me tomorrow.'

'That's my boyfriend!' Val had snarled. 'He came all the way from Delaware to see me!'

'Oh, sorry. He's totally cute,' Maggie had backpedaled. 'Let me grab you guys each a fresh drink!'

Back then, with her curly auburn hair, and smattering of freckles, Maggie resembled Broadway's lovable Orphan Annie. Maggie's current existence, however, bore no similarity to a 'hard-knock life'. Now blonde, she'd married a stock trader, Pete, who grew more successful with each passing year – at least according to Maggie's social media. They lived in some fancy Connecticut suburb, where magazines routinely showcased their backyard in glossy spreads. A famous rapper, Lil' Something-or-Other, wanted to throw his latest release party there, according to one of Maggie's posts. It broke her heart to turn him down, but she felt certain 'his all-star posse' would violate local noise ordinances.

'Seriously, guys, don't you miss her?' Claire asked Stacey and Annabelle again.

'Let me see?' Stacey stopped walking as if to give this question serious thought. 'Do I miss Maggie? Do I miss the Maggie who offered to help Professor Ross shop for a more supportive bra? Yes. Do I miss the Maggie who can't stop blowing up my Insta feed with reminders about how she's closing in on having visited every island in Greece? That Maggie? Um, no.'

It was true, the Maggie they'd loved was gone, replaced by a pseudo-influencer hellbent on proving to the world that her life was perfect. In fact, Maggie couldn't attend the reunion because the mayor of her posh enclave was due to arrive Saturday morning for a ribbon-cutting at the gym franchise Pete bought her as a birthday gift.

When she'd first told Stacey, Annabelle, and Claire he'd purchased a studio for her, they'd envisioned a cozy, light-filled artist's space. But she'd meant a two-thousand-square-foot rectangle, outfitted for a fitness fad involving straps suspended from the ceiling and small trampolines. When Claire had watched the video Mags shared on Instagram, her first thought was, 'I'd wet my pants.' Paul, watching from over her shoulder had muttered, 'I hope she's got great insurance.'

It all seemed wildly out of character. While they were in college, Maggie often discouraged the group from walking to parties that took place more than three blocks away. She'd told them Pete had gotten her into it, and now she was addicted to this exercise cult. 'You have no idea the clarity you get from just hanging out upside down.'

And it agreed with her. From the photos Maggie posted all over social media, she appeared to be well on her way to bench-pressing a Subaru.

'I know it sounds like jealousy, or maybe it's the tequila talking, but I actually think I kind of hate her,' Annabelle had said.

'What's the deal with that studio – areola fitness? Is she hoping to audition for Cirque du Soleil?'

'It's aerial,' Claire corrected, laughing while Stacey blew her nose into her bell sleeve and shifted the conversation to her own situation.

'You know, I thought coming back would make me feel better, but it's the opposite. The last time I was here, I was young, beautiful, my entire life ahead of me. Why was I in such a rush? I could've gone in a thousand different directions, and look! Look how I've ended up! I have nothing other than a shitty condo and twins who hate me because I didn't feel like sticking it out while their father screws his assistant.'

What could you say to that? Stacey had gone quiet, and Claire hoped the worst of this heartbreaking display was behind them. It wasn't.

'And you, Claire!' Stacey's sadness switched to rage. 'You're just like Ethan now. I saw Alex's arm around you and your hand on his thigh.'

'I . . .' Claire's first instinct had been to deny it, but then she remembered she had placed her hand on Alex's leg to stop herself from slipping off a barstool. And, my goodness, it was thick and strong as a tree limb.

'You were practically in his lap! Throwing yourself at him. You don't appreciate Paul,' Stacey had hissed.

'What are you talking about? You two never missed a chance to tell me what a dud Paul is – how I "settled", remember?'

Claire and Paul had been dating for about a month when Stacey's wedding invitation had arrived. Though she'd asked him to be her 'plus one', Claire had cautioned, 'My friends aren't very nice.'

'If they're not very nice, why are they your friends?' Paul had asked logically.

In that moment, Claire wondered if that said more about her than about them. She didn't want to tell him what she really meant. They'd compare him to Neal, the life of every party, and he'd inevitably fall short. Even without contrasting him to her old boyfriend, it seemed like every descriptor Claire had shared about Paul ultimately worked against him.

When she'd told her friends how they'd met, explaining that he was a nice guy who'd offered her a coupon at Bed Bath & Beyond, they'd asked if he was a senior citizen, and before she could answer, advised her to prepare for a decade of early bird specials.

When she'd said he worked with computers, they'd been intrigued, thinking she'd landed the next Mark Zuckerberg. After she'd confessed that he was less into social networking and more into calculating risk, even Claire had to admit he sounded kind of dull.

'We've always liked Paul,' Annabelle said half-heartedly, undoubtedly recognizing that her judgement wouldn't be deemed credible. Right before the reunion, she'd broken off her third engagement when she discovered her newest fiancé was in massive debt due to a series of bad investments in the exotic pet breeding industry.

'Well, congratulations, Claire! It looks like you're the winner,' Stacey had slurred as they stumbled toward the Hyatt. 'You're the only one who's in a relationship. Until you screw it up – anyway.'

'Whoa, now, wait a sec.' Annabelle stopped walking. 'Just because Claire got a little tipsy and maybe a bit handsy with an ex in a bar, that doesn't mean her marriage is doomed.'

'You already sowed your wild oats senior year after Neal left, Claire, remember?' said Stacey, refusing to let up.

'Stacey, that's not fair,' Annabelle interjected. 'If Claire is having a sexual reawakening we, as her friends, should support that.'

'Listen, Paul and I . . .' Claire had been waiting until the reunion weekend to tell them about the separation. It seemed easier to get it over with while they were all together. But she hadn't wanted to dampen the mood when they'd first arrived. The walk back to the hotel would've been the perfect opportunity to open up and yet she'd stopped herself.

Compared to her friends' relationships, Claire's grievances seemed trivial. So what if Paul had left her at the airport in the middle of the night? She was a grown woman capable of getting home on her own. Was it a crime that he failed to fix a doorbell or that he never backed her up when she attempted to limit the boys' screen time? He wasn't having sex with a co-worker like Stacey's ex, nor was he on the verge of bankruptcy because he'd been convinced chinchillas were poised to become the new Labradoodles, as Annabelle's former fiancé had believed.

It made Claire wonder if she'd been exceedingly harsh in banishing Paul. Did she expect too much from him? And what if she was partially to blame? There were times when she needed his help, but because it would've taken longer to explain what she wanted, she ended up doing everything herself. Maybe she was more like her mother than she'd realized.

Alex seemed so take-charge, so vibrant. She thought about the way his eyes, warm and twinkling, stayed laser-focused on her as she spoke. It tripped a switch inside her; a dormant fuse crackled to life. Once she'd felt it, she wanted to experience it again. And so she'd spent most of the evening with him.

Claire looked at her friends and longed to share these conflicting thoughts and feelings. But seeing them swaying, jaundiced beneath the glow of the streetlight, convinced her it wasn't the right time.

Hoping to end the conversation, she'd said, 'Look, it was nice to see Alex again, and you can't blame me for being flattered by a little attention. You know what it's like when you've been married for ages. It can get a little, well, boring.'

'Boring is fine, Claire,' Stacey snapped. 'I wish I had boring back. You think it's fun and glamorous to be single again? It's not. It's hard and awful. Everyone just wants to check you out and then trade you in for a newer, more interesting model. I'm not an iPhone; I'm a person. With feelings.' She started crying again. They'd walked the rest of the way in silence.

When they'd arrived back at the hotel, Claire sensed an alliance had formed between Stacey and Annabelle. Feeling like an outsider because her marriage was, to their knowledge, intact, Claire volunteered to sleep on the pull-out couch, allowing her friends to take the two queens.

Tossing and turning on a mattress thinner than an Eggo waffle, Claire thought about the conversation she'd had with Alex when they'd stepped outside for their first cigarette.

'How long ago was your divorce?' Claire had asked, beer making her bolder. She exhaled a plume of smoke toward the ground and gazed down at the diamond that hadn't left her finger since Paul placed it there in the lobby of the newspaper building.

If she took it off and her mother or her friends noticed, she'd have to explain why.

'A little over two years ago,' Alex said without a trace of bitterness.

'Oh, I'm sorry,' Claire had said, more as a reflex than because she truly meant it.

'Don't be.' He'd shaken his head. 'It's for the best. About a year into our relationship, I accepted a promotion that required me to move abroad. So, she gave me an ultimatum: Either we get married or we break up. Not an ideal way to begin, but we got married, had three great kids. Now we're divorced.' He shrugged, taking a long drag on his cigarette. 'No hard feelings.'

'Wow, that's so refreshing to hear,' Claire had said, thinking of all the terrible divorce stories that circulated through her neighborhood and among her friends.

'Yeah, my ex, Jocelyn, is a wonderful mom, and I try to be there as much as I can when I'm not traveling. Do I wish it had worked out? Of course, but we're making the best of it.'

He'd sounded so positive and reasonable, Claire wondered if his former wife felt the same way.

'Who knows?' He smiled. 'Maybe we'll meet here again in five years and you'll be divorced? I'm not wishing it on you. I'm just sayin' . . .' He stubbed out his cigarette and winked again.

The moment Alex had said that, and later, as Claire lay awake on the pull-out couch at the Hyatt, the very idea of permanently ending her marriage to Paul seemed crazy.

But now, in early September, as she searched for a decent parking spot at the mall with the sole intention of buying naughty knickers that she hoped would make Alex swoon, everything felt different.

She could no longer remember what had made her so confident her marriage would survive another five years, that she and Paul would emerge safely on the other side of their trial separation.

Claire's birthday was fast approaching, making her wistful. She'd turn forty-seven on Sunday. Would Paul even remember? Two years ago, he hadn't . . . until Henry asked for a ride to the grocery store to 'buy Mom's birthday cake'.

After she'd blown out the candles, Joe began chanting, 'Presents! Presents! Presents!'

'Yay! Presents!' Claire had clapped as her husband's smile vanished.

'Sorry, I-I,' he'd stammered. 'I didn't know we were exchanging.'

Exchanging? It wasn't Christmas; it was her birthday. The same date every year.

Claire hadn't wanted or needed anything, really. And she certainly didn't expect diamond earrings like the ones Patrick McClaren gave Abby at the party he'd thrown for her fiftieth. Still, something – a bathrobe, even a sturdy umbrella – might've been nice.

At the time, Paul tried to soften the blow by offering a consolatory, 'Listen, how about this weekend, I'll get up with the kids, and you can sleep in? How about that?'

'You mean, you'll parent your own kids? Yeah, how about that?' Claire snickered.

After a second piece of store-bought, *Cars*-themed pudding cake, Claire spent the rest of her birthday sulking and watching *Daniel Tiger* with Joe.

Alex would never have forgotten her birthday.

In mid-August, Claire was putting the finishing touches on a quiz: *Which Golden Girl You're Most Likely to Become Based on Your Handbag* when Alex sent her a late-night message – one that stopped her heart. Twice.

Guess who I was out with tonight? he began, causing Claire's stomach to turn as if she'd just eaten bad salmon. There it was – the message she'd been dreading, the one in which he'd tell her that he'd met 'someone special' and thank her for being happy for him and such a good 'friend'. Her cheeks burned, her armpits pumped sweat like the Fountains of Bellagio. She'd grabbed the table for support and read on.

Jason! The bartender from my days as a valet.

Claire exhaled with relief. Alex had worked at a fancy hotel near their college. She was glad to hear he still kept in touch with the friends he'd made there.

He and Lara split. He's taking it pretty hard. But he'll be fine. I told him, hey, you never know when you might bump into someone from your past, and, suddenly, your future looks a hell of a lot brighter. I still think about that dress you wore to their wedding, Claire, I felt like the luckiest guy in the room.

Claire had forgotten that day until that moment. She'd borrowed a royal blue silk slip dress from Annabelle, whose closet resembled a high-end boutique even at age twenty-one.

Claire wrote back to Alex within seconds.

Of course, I remember that day! You drank only cocktails with people's names in them – Bloody Mary, Harvey Wallbanger, Brandy Alexander. Things got decidedly wilder once you settled on Johnnie Walker. I can still picture you doing the Macarena with those white-haired ladies. They all thought I was the luckiest girl in the room.

Flirty, but not too much, Claire had assured herself as she tapped 'send'.

If Alex could remember a dress I wore two decades ago, he definitely wouldn't forget my birthday, Claire reasoned as she looped around the mall parking lot.

'If I live to be ninety, more than half my life is already over,' she said aloud. The words seemed to echo inside her silent minivan. Would she allow more years to pass without savoring them? The last decade had flown by amid a whirl of grocery shopping, potty training, and reading emails from her sons' schools. She hadn't written a novel, and now her mother's diagnosis made her keenly aware of how precious each moment truly was. But would she even know how to return to a more fulfilling path? Yes, she believed she could, with Alex as her navigator.

Still, the idea of being with Alex (*Tonight!*) felt like crossing over into a world from which there was no return.

Just as Claire debated turning the van around and heading back home, she found a parking spot right near the entrance. How often did that happen? Almost never. It would be foolish to waste it.

It felt like a sign.

September 4, 2024

12:12 p.m.

As Claire hurried toward the mall, a landscaping crew tastefully arranged cornstalks, pumpkins, and gourds around the entrance. It was September fourth, only the third day of school, and already people were prepping for Halloween. The whole world seemed to agree: 'The present is utterly disappointing; let's fast forward to something more appealing.'

Not that she blamed anyone. But today Claire wanted time to slow down – not only because she needed every second to weigh her options for that evening, but also in a larger sense.

Her in-laws would return the first weekend in October, and Paul would either move back home or find a new place. How he'd afford that, she had no clue. Of course, he could continue to live at his parents' house. In Claire's opinion, that was the least desirable option. With Paul's mom, Florence, waiting on her only child as if he were Lady Mary from *Downton Abbey*, Paul would become more helpless than he was when Claire first asked him to move out.

Then it would be Halloween, followed by Thanksgiving, with Christmas close behind. Every year she and Paul hosted a New Year's Day open house, gathering family, friends, and neighbors for brunch and cocktails. She imagined pitching Sabrina: *Holidays With Your Ex: All the Dos and Don'ts That'll Save You From Murdering Your Former Partner in Front of Your Nearest & Dearest.*

If she and Paul split for good, they'd need to figure out who'd spend which occasions with the boys. She wondered how the children would handle that. Since the separation began, their lives hadn't been terribly disrupted. After spending the weekend with Paul at his parents' house, Max would muse, 'How can it still smell like old people if the old people are in Maine?' Henry would complain about missing his favorite cooking shows because Fred and Florence refused to pay for anything beyond basic cable while they were out of town. Only Joe suffered the strain of being shuttled back and forth.

One night as Claire tucked him in, he'd looped his arms around her and refused to let her go. 'I miss you when I'm at Grams' with Daddy, and I miss Daddy when I'm here with you,' he'd whimpered.

It would only grow harder as the boys got older and didn't want their lives and schedules divided. Right now, her children's biggest complaints centered around the fact that she made them write thank you notes, play musical instruments, and go to a museum once a year. If they reached adulthood with only those gripes, they'd have had a pretty nice childhood. Should she risk messing it up because she wanted to feel alive again? Because wasn't that what this was about? Her own vanity and desire to feel appreciated? Beautiful? To experience a soaring sense of excitement? Alex reminded her all that was possible again. But at what price?

Recalling how Stacey had treated her like an adulteress when she hadn't yet done anything remotely scandalous left Claire feeling irritated and off-balance. The morning after Stacey's reunion night meltdown, she, Claire, and Annabelle discovered that the retro diner they'd loved as students had been converted into a Dunkin' Donuts-Baskin-Robbins. Knowing that Claire had to rush back home to catch Henry's game, they'd eaten bagels standing at a sticky countertop. Stacey had apologized to Claire for her blistering criticism, or as Stacey put it, 'being a Lil Miss Judge-y Pants' the night before.

'I'm just saying, appreciate what you have, Claire. If you're going through a rough patch, fix it. Fight for your marriage,' she'd said in between blowing on her coffee and rubbing her temples.

Because they were all hungover, Stacey might as well have been reciting nursery rhymes. Claire couldn't process any of it.

'You know what this Alex thing reminds me of?' Stacey continued. 'It's just like when I blew my first alimony check on my Audi A5 convertible. I thought it was going to make my life so much more exciting. But you know what? After a month, the novelty wore off, and what was I left with? Bigger car payments and a bump in my insurance rates. And, oddly enough, I missed my old car. Even though it was just a boring Nissan Altima, I knew it inside and out. I longed for the familiarity. I'm telling you, Claire, treasure what you have, no matter how dull you think it is, because it's ugly out here and new isn't always better.'

Stacey's words looped through Claire's head as she drifted past kiosks of sunglasses and fluffy slippers. What if she ended her marriage and things didn't work out with Alex either? Stacey wasn't wrong; it was ugly out there.

Back in June, several nights before the reunion, Claire's friend Kristie, who was divorced and aggressively dating, had been stood up by a guy she'd met online and was drinking alone at a restaurant within walking distance of Claire's home.

When Kristie had called, her speech already slurry, she'd begged Claire to meet her for 'one quick cocktail'.

'C'mon, Claire, please! I got a sitter and eyelash extensions for this!' she'd whined.

Claire glanced around her home. Paul sat on the patio, sorting through the mail, separating junk from bills, and watching Max and Henry toss a football. It was his night to have dinner with the boys. Sometimes, he'd take them out for pizza, but Henry had insisted on roasting a chicken. When Paul came over for these midweek dinners, Claire usually went grocery shopping or walked around the mall to kill time. But on that particular evening she had no plans. It was also one of those rare days when she'd already showered, which meant it wouldn't take too long to pull herself together.

'OK, give me twenty minutes.' Claire's mouth suddenly watered at the thought of drinking a chilled glass of white wine in an attractive setting. It was nearly summer. The school year was wrapping up and Claire could almost taste vacation in the air – not that she had one planned beyond the quick reunion getaway, but still.

'Wait, Claire!' Kristie squealed.

'Yeah?'

'Really make an effort, OK? No yoga pants. I need a full-on wing-woman tonight.'

Claire's body went rigid before drooping in a mix of pity and exhaustion. She also felt a flicker of annoyance for not remembering it was never 'one quick cocktail' with Kristie. 'Wing-woman' implied Kristie was on a mission.

'In that case, give me a few extra minutes to pluck my beard,' Claire joked, but Kristie, calling out for another Pinot Grigio, wasn't listening.

Claire plodded upstairs to her bedroom, irked that just when women felt like putting in the least amount of effort, the most was required. Kristie's 'no yoga pants' made her jaw clench. Claire had debated confiding in her friend about the state of her marriage, but realized if she did, Kristie would expect her to fill the role of 'wing-woman' on a weekly basis. With that in mind, she'd decided to keep the separation news to herself.

Entering her bedroom, she spied a rumpled pile of shorts and T-shirts on the floor beside her nightstand. Her drawers and closet didn't hold anything more attractive. All she had was the outfit she'd purchased to wear to the reunion. She'd wanted the black pants and silvery halter top to be fresh and clean for Friday night, but why not give them a test run?

Claire cut the tags off her new ensemble, looked in her full-length mirror, and wondered if the boys, who were downstairs finishing Henry's chicken and buttery green beans, would notice that for once she looked put-together and not like someone headed to a sleep study.

'Mom! I told you, I don't eat vines!' Joe began his nightly vegetable protest as soon as he heard her heels click on the steps.

'Joe, stop! These aren't vines! They're haricot verts!' Henry corrected.

Claire entered the dining room, prepared to give him the same lecture about rickets and scurvy that her mother had issued nightly, when Henry, who'd always been more like an adult man in a little boy costume, emitted a wolf-whistle followed by, 'Who's that sexy mama?'

'Gross, fool, that's *your* mama!' Max hurled a skinny string bean at his brother.

'I know she's my mom, but I can still appreciate a fine-looking lady, can't I?'

'No more sneaking off to the basement to watch *South Park* or *Real Housewives* or wherever this is coming from, mister.' Claire pointed at Henry.

'It's June. Isn't it a little warm for pants?' asked Paul, barely looking up from slicing a dinner roll.

Claire, who'd hoped for a compliment from her husband rather than her twelve-year-old, didn't want to confess that few other things fit and that she'd been too lazy that morning to shave her legs. Rather than answer, she simply kissed each of her sons on the forehead, grabbed her purse, and said, 'Don't wait up.'

At the restaurant Claire spotted Kristie, deep in conversation, seated at the bar with her back to the door.

'Maybe her date has shown up after all,' Claire thought, feeling relieved that perhaps this really would be 'one quick cocktail'. All day she'd struggled with the nagging feeling that she'd forgotten something.

She slid onto the barstool to Kristie's left, ordered a white wine, and waited for her friend to realize she'd arrived. When five minutes had passed, she tapped Kristie on the shoulder and said, 'Hey.'

'Claire!' Kristie shouted. 'Meet Bob, he owns a car dealership in Morristown.'

Claire had a hard time looking away from Kristie's new eyelashes, which were as dark and abundant as Miss Piggy's.

'Hi, Bob.' Claire forced herself to stop staring and extended her hand. 'Nice to meet you.'

'I *work* at a car dealership,' corrected the man, who appeared closer to Claire's dad's age than to hers or Kristie's.

'Think big, Bob! You'll get there!' Kristie punched him playfully on the arm as she took a slug of Pinot Grigio. 'Claire is an author and a mom of three. She should be working on a novel, but she keeps getting suckered into volunteering for bake sales. Though that's how we met, actually.'

Kristie's daughter, Leah, and Max had gone to preschool together. Stupidly, Claire had agreed to chair the autumn harvest bake sale, which coincided with the fall carnival. It was her first year at the school, so she had no idea she needed about twenty times the amount of baked goods she'd solicited from fellow parents. Because Kristie worked full-time as a pharmaceutical sales rep, her nanny brought Leah to school (with cranky toddler Oliver dangling from her hip) each day, so Claire hadn't met Kristie until the evening of the fundraiser. Seeing Claire standing amid a sad sampling of sweets, Kristie rushed to the grocery store. With her crying kids in tow, she purchased dozens of cupcakes, cookies, and muffins, saving Claire from being ostracized by the school's overachieving parent group.

'You are an angel,' Claire had gushed. 'How can I ever thank you?'

'My husband told me this morning that he'd like a d-i-v-o-r-c-e. So, please, picking up this kiddie crack is the least of my problems.' Kristie had a throaty laugh Claire instantly admired. 'Buy me a drink sometime and we'll call it even.'

They'd been friends ever since.

Bob couldn't have cared less about Claire's writing, nor her foolishness when it came to bake sales. He was too busy attempting to steal a glimpse inside Kristie's blouse.

'Is this your date?' Claire tried to do her best ventriloquist impersonation in case Bob took his eyes off Kristie's chest long enough to read her lips.

'No, I just waved him over after I saw him get out of a Lincoln Navigator alone.' Kristie nodded in the direction of the valet parking area, visible thanks to the bar's wall of windows. 'I'm thinking about leasing one and wanted his opinion.'

'Ladies, my wife's here. Nice talking with you.' Bob gave Kristie's ample bosom one last appreciative glance before waddling off toward the hostess station.

'Shoot! See that? All the good ones are taken!' Kristie turned her attention toward Claire for a moment before flagging down the bartender.

'Wait, that was a good one?' The wine, sluicing through Claire's bloodstream, was already having its truth-serum effect. 'He seemed more like an extra from *Dirty Grandpa* to me.'

'Claire, stop, you have no idea what it's like out here,' Kristie snapped. 'Sure, they all sound great on their profile pages, but then you meet them in person and it turns out their pictures were taken when Ronald Reagan was newly elected, or they're the size of garden gnomes or . . .'

Claire thought about Joe (one of the smallest in his grade!), who right then was probably hiding his green beans under the tablecloth or flushing them down the toilet. She made a mental note to try harder to get him to eat well so women wouldn't end up making fun of him in bars later in life. She'd recently signed him up for classes at Kung Fu 4 U to try to boost his confidence, but he'd been less than enthused about the activity. She'd put Paul in charge of ordering the uniform – or gi, as they called it. She just hoped he didn't screw it up.

'Or they want you to give them a hand job in their cars in the parking lot of the TGI Fridays where you just had to pay for your half of the potato skins.' Kristie took a gulp from her newest glass of Pinot. 'So, hey, my lashes! What do you think?' Kristie batted her eyelids and then took a long look at Claire. 'You'd be a great candidate for these. I'll give you the number of my aesthetician. If you go, mention my name, I'll save ten percent on my next visit.'

Before Claire could respond, Kristie spun her barstool in the other direction and introduced herself to the guy who'd just sat down on her right. Claire cringed, knowing her friend would open with her favorite line, 'Hey, I'm Kristie. I'm a drug dealer. What's your story?'

If only Kristie channeled the energy she expended on dating into another cause, she could end world hunger or save endangered species.

Another forty-five minutes passed while Kristie chatted up the man beside her as Claire stared at the episode of *Jeopardy!* that played above the bar, half-heartedly checking her email.

She was about to tell Kristie she was leaving when two young men sat down beside her and introduced themselves. Theo and Brody – if those were even their real names – told her they were in town for the summer to run soccer camps on a local college campus. It seemed odd that two baby-faced athletes would select this upscale lounge, attached to a high-end dining establishment, rather than a sports bar. But Claire had to admit, the choices were slim in the suburbs. Believing her 'wing-woman' had lured in a pair of decent prospects, Kristie quickly swiveled back and introduced herself.

'We're celebrating Claire's birthday!' she squealed. 'She turns fifty tomorrow! Doesn't she look fabulous?'

'Shit, dude, she's older than your mom!' Theo elbowed Brody. (Or maybe it was the other way around; Claire didn't think it mattered anyway.) 'Still, ma'am, if you don't mind my saying, you look pretty smokin' for forty-nine.'

'This calls for shots,' exclaimed Brody, fist-bumping his buddy and dropping what Claire assumed was his parents' Amex card on the bar. He snapped his fingers at the bartender and Claire cringed.

'I'm going to kill you,' she murmured to Kristie. 'I am not doing shots with anyone who calls me "ma'am" and is young enough to be my child. Plus, I'm only forty-six!'

'Listen, it's my month to pay for Leah's horseback riding lessons. I'm completely tapped out. If they're willing to pay for us, let them! Besides, you'll be fifty before too long.' She squeezed Claire's forearm. 'Get used to it.'

Claire knew that when Kristie was surrounded by wine and men, reasoning with her was as futile as asking the boys to remember to lower the toilet seat. She glanced around the bar and watched as couples flirted, laughed, clinked glasses, and shared appetizers that looked almost too pretty to eat.

She thought about Paul not even offering her a simple, 'You look nice tonight,' and threw back the shot of Cinnamon Toast Crunch the soccer coaches declared their favorite. Theo told the bartender to pour them another round while Kristie ran her hands through Brody's unruly hair and asked him if he'd ever want a Brazilian blowout. Anticipating a serious misunderstanding, Claire excused herself after tossing back the second shot and chasing the fiery taste with more white wine.

In the ladies' room, she washed her hands and wondered if this was how most of Kristie's nights out went.

'Claire!' A familiar voice bounced off the subway tile. 'Fancy meeting you here!' Judy Thompson, middle school PTA president, emerged from a stall and theatrically embraced Claire, air kissing both cheeks.

Claire could only ever think of her as 'JudyThompson-MiddleSchoolPTAPresident', because that's how she introduced herself, as if her identity and sole purpose stemmed from her fundraising abilities.

'Thank you *so, so much* for volunteering to bake those cupcakes!' she shouted amid the whirl and echo of flushing toilets.

'Mmmm! Cupcakes!' said Judy's sidekick, Francine Whitman, popping out of another stall.

'If you could drop them off by nine a.m. sharp tomorrow, that would be amazeballs!' Judy said.

'What cupcakes?' asked Claire, her words muffled by an automatic hand dryer.

'Thanks again!' Judy waved, as she and Francine swanned out of the bathroom. 'You're the best!'

Claire pulled out her phone. Sure enough, a text from SignUp Genius had just arrived, reminding her she'd volunteered to drop off four dozen cupcakes for an end-of-the-year picnic the following morning.

She exited the restroom, prepared to tell Kristie she was leaving, and found her friend attempting to convince Brody to grow dreadlocks if he was truly against straightening. Theo smiled as Claire approached.

'What are you doing here?' she asked him.

'Oh man, ma'am, you're deep when you're wasted. It's kinda hot.' Theo put each of his baby hands on Claire's shoulders. 'Birthdays can make you really philosophical. I get it. What are any of us doing here, right?'

'No, no.' Claire lowered his arms. 'I mean, what are you doing *here*? Why this bar?'

'Oh, yeah, so this older coach from our camp – he's like twenty-six – he told us this is where the desperate older women hang out.' He jerked his head toward Kristie. 'Dude was spot-on.'

Kristie giggled as she patted the crotch of the barely legal Brody. 'You *are not* wearing a cup!'

Claire pulled Kristie's hand away, unlocked her phone, located the Uber app, and ordered her friend a car. If she selected the 'pool' option, it would be there in just two minutes, but Claire couldn't take the chance of Kristie trying to hook up with a fellow passenger, so she chose the single ride.

'Kristie, your car is seven minutes away. I'll pick you up and drive you back here in the morning.' Claire placed forty dollars on the bar and hoped it covered the wine she and Kristie ordered before the coaches began buying.

Kristie reeled back as if Claire had slapped her, but grabbed her purse and thrust a business card into Brody's hand.

'Call me!' she demanded, sliding off the barstool and losing a heel.

'Oh, no way! Dude, Birthday Girl is a total cock-blocker!' Brody said to his buddy as Claire put her arm around her pal and ushered her toward the sidewalk to wait for the car.

With Kristie on her way home, Claire stumbled back to her house and dropped her keys twice on the front porch before Paul opened the door.

'You're awake?' she said, surprised.

'Sorry to disappoint you.' He stepped aside to let her wobble into the living room.

'No, I just thought you'd be napping.'

'Yankees game went into extra innings. It was a good one.'

The smell of Henry's roasted chicken hit Claire in the face and she didn't know if she wanted to vomit or pick the carcass clean with her bare hands.

'So, did anyone say you looked stunning tonight?' Paul asked.

'You mean other than our twelve-year-old?' Claire laughed and swayed as she attempted to kick off her sandals.

Paul steadied her and held her for a moment. Their bare forearms touched and Claire shivered, though the night air was particularly warm for June. When was the last time he'd been this attentive?

'Listen, we should make some time to go out – just you and me,' he'd said. 'What are you doing Friday night, Sexy Mama?'

'It's my college reunion weekend, remember?' The thought of additional drinking and making small talk in a loud bar made her head spin.

'That's right; I forgot,' Paul said. 'Well, maybe the following Friday?'

'If you really want to do something with me, you can stay a while longer and ice my cupcakes.' Claire unhooked her strapless bra, slid it out from beneath her halter, and tossed it on the couch.

'If that's a euphemism for something sexual,' Paul grinned. 'I'm in.'

* * *

Together, they stood in the kitchen, Paul filling the muffin tins with paper liners while Claire cracked eggs, too woozy to care if any shells fell in the batter.

'It was brutal out there,' she groaned, collapsing on the couch after shoving the cupcakes in the oven. 'Promise me we'll fix this – us.'

'Tell me what to do, Claire. I want to come home,' Paul had said, but Claire didn't hear him. She was already snoring.

Just as she couldn't ask Stacey or Annabelle what to do about Alex, there was no way Claire could go to Kristie for advice now. The morning after their night at the bar, Kristie had pulled up in front of Claire's house.

Certain her friend had stopped by to thank her for ensuring she got home safely, Claire walked up to the car. Kristie lowered the window.

'Hey,' Claire said. 'How are you feeling? My head is pounding. I would've picked you up and driven you back to get your car.'

'I took an Uber. I seem to be doing that a lot lately.' Kristie jammed her sunglasses atop her tangle of blonde curls and returned her hands to the ten-and-two position on the steering wheel. 'Claire, I'll cut to the chase. You had no right to send me home last night. I was having fun. You're not my mom. I'm forty-three years old, and if I want to stay out drinking and meet new people, that's my choice. Leah and Oliver were with their father. What I do in my free time is up to me.'

'I'm sorry.' Claire's cheeks burned. 'I-I just wanted you to be safe and wake up at home without any regrets. You say you'd like to get married again. I didn't think you had twenty-two-year-old soccer coaches in mind.'

Kristie recoiled.

'I'm sorry,' Claire tried again. 'You know what I mean. I—'

'Maybe I just wanted to have a little fun. Even if it's only a dumb summer fling, I'd like to feel good about myself for a change,' Kristie said. Though she'd sounded furious just seconds earlier, Claire could see her friend's eyes brimming with tears.

'I'm sorry,' Claire apologized again, though she still didn't believe she was in the wrong. 'Come inside. I'll make us some coffee.'

'I'm late for work.' Kristie replaced her sunglasses, rolled up her window, and pulled away without another word.

Now, of course, Claire understood what Kristie meant. After all, here she was, a still-married mom of three, randy as a rabbit, ready to pounce at the slightest hint of interest.

So, was there really something magical about Alex or would anyone suffice? Was the way she felt about him now a function of being attracted to him all those years ago? Many of Maggie's recent Facebook posts were about muscle memory. The heart was a muscle. Did it recall that he was a good, smart guy who brought out a fun side of her? Or was the pull she felt toward him merely because of how he made her feel about herself? And if that were the case, then, really, couldn't he be anyone? What if all she needed was a therapist or a life coach? But she probably wouldn't fantasize about those professionals undressing her in a hotel room.

These were things Claire and Maggie could've discussed for hours. She missed her former roommate, sometimes unbearably, but lately it felt as if they'd gone in such different directions, they'd never be able to recapture that connection.

Plus, these were big questions, ones that could only be answered by someone with decades of wisdom. Claire thought of her mother. She usually confided in her mom about everything. Everything except sex. She thought back to 1992, the year *The Bridges of Madison County* came out. It was her mom's generation's *Fifty Shades of Grey*. Every woman at the town pool fanned herself with a copy. Claire recalled her mother standing in her childhood bedroom, the back of her hand pressed to her forehead, as if just thinking about the romance novel caused her to swoon.

'Whoa, Nelly!' her mom had said, placing the book on Claire's dresser before heading back downstairs.

'Ew! Gross!' Claire muttered under her breath before opening the tale of the lonely housewife and the photographer who reminds her of the passion she's been missing.

When the film adaptation was released a few summers later, Claire and her mom went to see it together.

'Personally, I'd pictured Robert Redford in that role, but Clint Eastwood was fine, too,' her mother had said on the way back to the car, mopping her brow from the steamy storyline, the balmy June heat, and what Claire now realized were probably hot flashes.

Young and snarky, Claire had wanted to tell her mother that both men probably had erectile dysfunction and smelled like flannel. Not good, sexy-lumberjack flannel, either. More like unwashed-old-person-with-dandruff flannel. But she didn't want to spoil their night out.

Shit! She still hadn't called her mother! As if on cue, Claire's cell phone rang. Digging it out of her purse as she walked through the mall, Claire saw the word 'Mom' flash on the screen. If she let it go to voicemail, Eleanor would only call back in twenty minutes. Plus, keeping the phone pressed to her ear would be a great way to avoid conversation if she bumped into anyone she knew.

'Hey, Mom, sorry I haven't gotten back to you yet, I—'

'Claire? Honey, did you get my message? I left one hours ago.'

'Yes, sorry, I'm just . . . Are you OK?'

'I'm perfectly fine, honey. Listen, do you have brown sugar for the baked beans or should I pick some up?'

'Um, let me look.' Claire jiggled her purse, hoping her mother would believe she was rifling through her pantry as she rode the escalator that deposited her in front of Victoria's Secret.

'It's OK, hon, I'm going to stop at the store anyway to buy some more biscuits. I don't think five will be enough for your hungry brood!'

To her mother, food conveyed love, and with that, Claire felt certain her mom would continue force-feeding her family until her grandsons qualified to appear on *My 600-lb Life*.

Claire's neck ached from keeping the phone pressed between her ear and shoulder as she tried to find a bra in her size. It was astonishing how, since turning forty, she injured herself doing routine tasks. Maybe she could find a Groupon for a personal trainer.

'Sounds good, Mom. Thanks!'

'Is Coupon working late and meeting you at the school? If he's coming home first, I'll buy more chops,' her mom continued as Claire pictured additional crusty roasting pans piling up in her already crowded sink.

'Um, I don't know what's happening,' Claire said. *Not a lie.*

'And if you and Coupon want to go out for a drink after back-to-school night, go! I certainly don't need to rush home to your father.'

Her mother had said that frequently in recent years, noting that she had no reason to 'rush home'. Claire didn't want to think of her parents getting frisky like those lovey-dovey old couples in Viagra and eHarmony commercials, but still. It made her sad. And scared – not that her parents' marriage was on the brink of failure, but that she could very easily see herself saying the same thing before too long if she and Paul stuck it out.

Also, maybe it was because she was on the verge of torpedoing the 'forsaking all others' part of their wedding vows, but Claire suddenly bristled at her mother's use of the nickname 'Coupon'. Sure, Paul would probably never find out, but he was the father of her children. Didn't he deserve more respect? Claire was about to bring this up when her mother asked, 'Has anyone gotten in touch about that playroom makeover you won yet? It's been months now!'

'Not yet, but I'm sure—'

'Claire, I really don't like these people not keeping their word! Do you want me to contact Skippy Tompkins? I know he's a divorce lawyer, but maybe he could draft a threatening letter that would scare MamaDrama into finally giving you the prize you deserve!'

'It's MamaRama,' Claire rolled her eyes, 'and I don't think that's necessary, but thanks for the offer.'

'You're too nice, Claire. People take advantage of that. Your family room looks like the inside of one of those boardwalk claw machines!' Eleanor chuckled. 'Even proper shelving would be an improvement. Get that makeover!'

Claire sighed and held up an extra-large pair of panties that would be tight on a miniature schnauzer.

'OK, let me run!' her mother said. 'See you tonight!'

September 4, 2024

12:32 p.m.

Before running into Alex at the reunion, Claire would have said she was closer to buying adult diapers than lingerie. But here she was browsing lacy undergarments and attempting to straddle that fine line between sexy and trying-too-hard cringey.

She stood in front of the full-length mirror, and thanked God and the store manager for placing her in a fitting room with dim lighting. The detailing on the lilac bra she'd selected made her nipples itch. There was no way she could sit and sip a cocktail without scratching at her chest like an orangutan.

Claire was reluctant to give the panties a go. Who else might've tried them on? It would be just her luck to contract crabs before she'd even slept with a man who might as well be a total stranger in terms of his sexual history. A lot could happen in twenty-five years. Plus, she didn't want to turn around and see her own behind, dimpled as a golf ball, in the lacy thong that matched this pricker bush of a bra.

She looked in the mirror. The underwire's lavender hue seemed to bring out the reddish-purple half-moons that hung beneath her eyes. *Shit!* She needed to get back home and test more under-eye patches, though she wasn't convinced they'd camouflage her lack of sleep. She and Max had gone to bed at close to midnight the previous evening, after spending three hours crafting a Revolutionary War diorama.

'Who gives homework this complicated on the second day of school?' Claire had asked.

'It's because of Mrs Watkins,' Max said, while fashioning a forest with flat-leaf parsley.

'Who?'

'The mom who started the Environmental Committee. She goes to Board of Ed meetings and asks that teachers give us more homework in middle school so we're well-prepared for high school so we get into better colleges so your property values remain solid.'

Claire stared in disbelief. These kids were more informed than she'd ever been as a child – or possibly even as an adult.

'Geez, Mom, don't you keep up with local news?' Max had asked exasperatedly.

No wonder eighth graders raided their parents' liquor cabinets and popped pills like Skittles.

She'd fought the urge to pour a glass of wine after forcing herself to cut white fur off the ear of Frosty, Joe's stuffed polar bear, to fashion George Washington's wig.

Max had insisted on squeezing out a puddle of blueberry Go-Gurt to serve as the Delaware River. Claire allowed it, secretly hoping it drew thousands of ants to the classroom. *Then who'd learn a lesson about giving homework so early in the year?* she'd grinned maniacally.

Based on her reflection in the fitting-room mirror, Claire realized that even after a shower, some self-tanning lotion, and an insane amount of concealer, there was no way she could pass for even a poor man's Gisele Bündchen – unless the supermodel and former Victoria's Secret angel hadn't slept in a month, grazed on a steady diet of donut holes, and been dragged behind a garbage truck.

She was gathering the courage to try on a red corset when her phone began playing the *Jaws* theme song – her cue that Joe's school nurse was calling. Much like when that deadly shark reared its head on Amity Island, if you were on Crystal Sprayberry's radar, things were about to get ugly.

Frantically, Claire swiped at her screen. *Damnit!* This is what she got for lying to Abby about having a sick child. 'Hello, hello?'

'May I speak with Claire Casey?'

'This is she.' Claire attempted to unhook the pricey push-up bra before it broke a rib.

'Mrs Casey, are you aware that your son Joe has head lice?'

'What?'

'Mrs Casey, if this is a bad connection, I suggest you call back on a landline because we need to have a serious conversation.'

'No, I can hear you, I just mean, "what?" as in, how can he have head lice?'

'Did you not get the memo? It's running rampant through your son's classroom. We sent a notice home yesterday.'

Of course Joe hadn't given it to her. He refused to bring anything back or forth until his new backpack arrived. Even before his beloved Darth Vader book bag had become encrusted with dog feces, Joe frequently failed to give her things in a timely fashion. Cards he'd made for Mother's Day sat in his knapsack until Father's Day. Last winter, she and Paul had been convinced an animal had died in their minivan's undercarriage. But it turned out Joe had left a half-eaten tuna sandwich inside his lunchbox and tucked it beneath the van's third row during the holiday break.

'We asked that all parents get a lice comb and do a thorough head-check before sending their child to school today,' Crystal continued.

Parents. 'Did you call Joe's father about this?' Claire asked.

Silence.

'What?' the nurse asked, stretching the word to two syllables.

'Joe's dad – he's listed as the primary contact on the emergency forms.'

Claire knew the answer before Crystal's feeble, 'Well, um, no. We don't like to bother the dads. But, Mrs Casey, that's not the point.' The nurse's condescending tone returned. 'The point is, Joe has lice.'

Claire caught a glimpse of herself in the mirror. Frown lines made her look like someone on the 'before' side of a Botox ad. Would Crystal Sprayberry deem Claire the world's worst mother if she asked, 'So, is it a little lice or a lot of lice?'

'I never got the memo.' Her mind raced as she tried to figure out how she'd deal with this on top of everything else. 'Are you absolutely certain you have the right student? Have you seen actual bugs in his hair?'

Normally, Claire wouldn't be so bold, but Crystal had a history of making mistakes. Last fall, Claire had gone flying out of a mammogram and driven to school with her bra poking up from her handbag after Crystal called to announce that Henry had chicken pox. In reality, those red dots were nothing more than mosquito bites her son had gotten from shooting hoops near standing water.

But this explained why Joe had been scratching his head with the intensity of a capuchin monkey at breakfast and the bus stop. Just thinking about it made Claire's scalp itch in sympathy.

She continued, keeping her voice low, 'I mean, are you positively, one hundred percent sure? I only ask because I'm in a very important meeting in the middle of a jam-packed day.'

The words were barely out of her mouth when a sales associate, shouting to be heard above the blaring pop music, knocked on Claire's door and bellowed, 'You OK in there? Let me know if you need a bigger size! Those panties are hot as fuck but they run small!'

Claire buried her face in her free hand. Did Crystal catch that? And, if so, how much time would pass before she told every adult in the building that Claire had sent her child to school with head lice so she could fritter away the afternoon trying on thongs?

'This never happens when you buy your underpants at the grocery store!' Claire silently berated herself.

'Well, needless to say, Joe – your Joe, Joseph Casey – is extremely uncomfortable. He's here in my office. Please come pick him up immediately. Also, if you really didn't receive the memo, then you probably aren't aware that the rules regarding infestations have changed. You'll need to walk Joe into school tomorrow and wait while I comb through his hair before he's allowed back in the classroom.'

Claire gave the phone the middle finger and calmly said, 'I understand. I'll be there as soon as I can.'

September 4, 2024

12:59 p.m.

Claire left the mall with a simple black bra and panty set. While it would never be described as 'seductive', it was certainly more attractive than anything she currently owned.

Walking back to her car, afternoon blown completely off-course, Claire tried to plan her next move.

She needed to pick up a lice removal kit, but bringing Joe into CVS with her would be excruciating. If she did, they'd have to stop at the toy car display for at least ten minutes. Though he had dozens of plastic and metal vehicles littering each level of their home, Joe loved those multi-tiered spinning car towers found at pharmacies. Once he finished begging for a new taxi or postal truck, Joe would insist on testing out the blood pressure machine for the millionth time and then spend the rest of the afternoon worrying about his health. *No.* She couldn't handle that on top of everything else. She would go alone. Crystal could occupy Joe and his nits a few minutes longer.

Before hitting the store, Claire decided to swing by the house to drop off her new underwear. If she didn't, she could see Joe trying it on in the backseat while she drove. She pictured the panties and remembered the salesgirl's words 'hot as fuck'. She hated that phrase. Sabrina constantly tried to get her to use 'AF' at the end of every headline. In her editor's opinion, few things couldn't be described this way. Ankle booties were 'cool as fuck', a baby sling made from organic cotton was both 'responsible and adorable as fuck', a new Starbucks drink was 'delicious as fuck'. *Starbucks!* Claire thought she'd heard Abby yelling something about a rough draft as she'd gunned it in reverse and sped out of her driveway. The memory left her scared to check her email. Surely, an over-the-top letter to the editor waited in her inbox, along with a plea from Abby to make it more compelling.

Thinking about editing, Claire's mind flitted to her job. She'd been gone for more than an hour, when typically no one at MamaRama took even ten minutes for lunch. To heighten the illusion that none of these women ever even thought about food, many meetings were scheduled between noon and two. Was Claire the only one whose stomach growled as if she'd endured a month-long hunger strike? Why didn't anyone speak up? Again, she thought about Alex and the sheep. She'd send Sabrina a quick email stating that she had a family emergency – lice or lust? Both were applicable.

As she pulled into her driveway, Claire caught sight of the mound of dog poop Abby had pointed out. More determined than ever to catch the offending pooch, she wondered if she had time to set up Max and Henry's Spy Gear surveillance camera. It was probably out of batteries. Anytime she needed a child's toy, like a flashlight or a walkie-talkie, it didn't work. But somehow, in the middle of the night, a large plastic dinosaur or monster truck would roar to life, scaring the shit out of her and Paul, another one of the great unexplained but universal parenting phenomena.

As it was, Claire had been hearing odd buzzing, beeps, and even barks from the back of the minivan for weeks. Had Joe stashed some dying toys back there just to troll her? She'd been meaning to climb back to the third row and hunt around for the source, but forgot again as soon as the noises stopped.

Claire bolted through the front door, determined to run upstairs, stash her new undergarments in the far recesses of her dresser, and get out of the house as quickly as possible, when her home phone rang.

If this is my mother calling to discuss biscuits and beans again, I just can't, Claire mused on the verge of a meltdown. She tried to understand what the caller ID voice said, but it always came out a garbled variation on 'Walla Walla, Washington'.

What if Crystal somehow knew Claire was taking her sweet time and was phoning to tell her she was a negligent mother? Could it be Alex calling to ask her point blank if she was meeting him tonight? Her throat went dry thinking about his deep voice.

The day had been so chaotic, she hadn't checked to see if he'd written back to her. She hoped his reply read something like, *Fantastic! I'm counting the minutes until we're together.* Alex never did things halfway.

Did he have any clue that his email had sent her into a tailspin? If she did meet him, what would she do about Joe, back-to-school-night, Abby's meeting, and the marketing team's farewell?

Maybe the right thing – the adult thing – to do was to cancel. She was already in over her head. But if she bowed out, what would she even write? She composed a few mental drafts:

Alex,

Of course I'd love to see you but my youngest was sent home with head lice and I have to spend the evening ridding my home and family of parasitic insects . . .

That was spectacularly unattractive. She started again.

Alex,

I've thought about you and an offer like this all summer, but I just realized it's back-to-school night and I really should be there!

Ditching him for a stupefyingly dull school function would be the ultimate insult. She could never send that.

If she wrote anything, she wanted it to be this:

Alex,

Of course, I'll be there. I haven't stopped thinking about you since the moment you held my hand in yours when we ran across the street, dashing from bar to bar, back in June.

It was true, she'd been fixated on the feel of his hands, thick and supple yet rugged as a catcher's mitt. How often she'd imagined them pulling her toward him, on the small of her back, caressing her—

'Hello?' Claire answered the phone without looking at the caller ID.

'Claire? This is Marjorie Watkins.'

That name sounded vaguely familiar. Claire could picture it at the end of an email. But within what context?

'I'm the head of the Environmental Committee,' Marjorie continued.

'How can I help you, Marjorie?' Claire ventured, filling the growing silence.

'Well, Claire, it's been brought to my attention that your Joe has just consumed his third lunch this week that was completely filled with litter.'

Claire remembered the litter-less lunch initiative and realized Marjorie was referring to the generic Ziploc baggies that held her son's sandwich, pretzels, grapes, and chocolate chip cookies, yet she couldn't resist having a little fun.

'Wait, are you saying that someone is bullying my child by putting other people's rubbish inside his lunchbox? Oh my God, this is awful. Does the principal know? I'm furious! Thank you for bringing this to my attention!'

'No, Claire. That's not what I'm saying at all,' sighed Marjorie, clearly annoyed that she needed to explain her pet project after sending a dozen emails outlining it throughout the summer. 'I'm talking about the fact that over the course of three days you've used at least a dozen plastic baggies in Joe's lunch alone. I imagine you have other children, and I shudder to think about the way you're allowing them to besmirch the planet with their carbon footprints as well.'

Claire didn't know if she should laugh or cry. Marjorie certainly had an enviable command of language. Yet the demands parents placed on each other grew exponentially crazier each day. It filled Claire with despair – to the point that she was finally beginning to understand the appeal of homeschooling.

'Claire? Are you there? Don't you agree that it's very important to set a good example? Don't you care about this planet, Claire?' Marjorie shouted.

Claire's mind spun back to a commercial from her childhood – the one with the Native American gentleman shedding a lone tear as he stood amid a pile of litter. That 'Keep America Beautiful' public service announcement always made her stomach ache, rendering it impossible for her to go back to enjoying a mindless episode of *Gilligan's Island* while crunching her way through a box of Apple Jacks.

Part of Claire wanted to say, 'I'm so sorry, Marjorie! Of course, I care about the planet. How could I be such a thoughtless asshole?' But the larger part wanted to say, 'If you think that forcing people to stop using plastic baggies is going to be enough to save this planet, you're even loopier than I thought.'

But what she managed to passive-aggressively say was, 'Well, Marjorie, I'd be lying if I didn't confess that I'm more than a bit jealous of the amount of free time you have to devote to these causes. Now, if you'll excuse me, this is the part of the day when I typically go out back and light plastics on fire. Goodbye.'

Claire hung up, giddy with the exhilaration that came from speaking one's mind, no matter how crazy she might sound.

September 4, 2024

1:19 p.m.

As she roamed the aisles of CVS in search of a lice removal kit, Claire wondered what else she needed. She called up a mental image of her fridge. They were out of milk, bread, and eggs. Eggs. Birth control! For all she knew, Alex could be the Hugh Hefner of the greater Philadelphia area. She'd need protection.

But perhaps she was being presumptuous. What if Alex merely wanted to reminisce about bygone days, have a drink, and share a few cigarettes with an old friend? It was becoming increasingly difficult to find anyone who smoked. Claire couldn't understand this vaping craze. What a pack of assholes these people looked like, sucking on something that resembled a light-up kazoo and smelled like bubble gum. Go Big Tobacco or go home, she wanted to tell them.

What if Alex was on his way to break it to her that he'd embarked on a whirlwind summer romance with a woman who had far less baggage and lived closer to his trendy Manayunk bachelor pad? She'd Googled his luxury apartment, with its stunning river views, and imagined him surrounded by young and flexible yoga instructors. She envisioned a lithe, raven-haired beauty with a small nose ring, who didn't pee a little each time she sneezed. Her name would be 'Sky' or 'Indie' and she'd spiralize vegetables for the nutritious dinners she'd serve him each evening before they engaged in hours of tantric sex.

Claire had recently written an article, *Divorce Statistics That Are Shocking AF*, and it turned out three years was the amount of time it took the average person to remarry. Alex had been divorced two and a half; he was entering the sweet spot. What if he'd proposed and his new fiancée had discovered their messages, and he was coming to the area to tell Claire that they had to stop this – whatever *this* was – at once. *That would be mortifying.* Should she spare herself the potential embarrassment by sending him a 'Sorry, can't make it!' email and put an end to this fantasy once and for all? She felt as indecisive as a squirrel caught in the middle of a two-lane road.

She reached for the least expensive lice removal kit and skimmed the directions, which promised her son could be successfully de-loused in three easy steps. That was another thing: If she went, was she obligated to tell Alex about the lice and suggest that they make love while wearing shower caps? Could you even call it making love? Or was it purely primal? Was she, in fact, actually saving him money that he'd otherwise spend on a sex worker?

Claire's mind spun in a dozen directions as she tried to focus on the kit's instructions. She practically needed a magnifying glass to read the ingredients as she tried to discern how something that promised to kill the critters 'on contact' could also be 'non-toxic'.

Poor Joe, Claire thought, subconsciously scratching her own scalp, as if comforting her son by proxy.

Alex was graying at the temples, but he still had more hair than most guys their age. *He shouldn't have to resort to paying for sex.* Claire's instincts told her what they had was real. She had no reason to doubt him. He'd sent at least one email that caused her to believe she was the only one. A message that, unlike most of their playful but innocent back-and-forth, carried significantly more meaning.

When Claire had confessed to Alex that her job at MamaRama was a terrible fit, she began mocking her position in her messages, sharing her disbelief that the company held a 'Come to Work Wearing Your PJs!!' day and ranting about how she'd been forced to watch *Sister Wives* and then write detailed recaps of the show.

I have to get out of this, she'd typed, half-joking. I need to write a best-selling novel, or better yet, a series. Help me think of the next big thing – you know, teenage vampires, boy wizards, nice girls who get swept up in S&M-style romances . . .

Taking her plight to heart, Alex had spent a week beginning each message with a pitch for a book that Claire should write.

The FDA attempts to kill a teenage farm boy who refuses to grow genetically modified fruits and vegetables. It's up to his girlfriend, who, by the way, is the MVP of the all-gender varsity wrestling team, to save him.

Aliens abduct cyberbullies and leave them all on whatever is the coldest planet (with Pluto out of the race, I'm guessing Neptune, but fact-check me on that) where they're forced to either fight to the death or work together to survive.

Claire had seriously entertained that one as she imagined *Hunger Games* and *Star Trek* fans devouring it. But it was his last proposal that made her breath catch.

A middle-aged divorced dad and software salesman reconnects with the woman he's wondered about for decades. Will he be able to woo her with the promise of a happily-ever-after filled with corporate jargon, cocktails, and cigarettes? He hopes so because when he thinks about her – and he thinks of little else – he can see a future there. A bright one.

When Claire had read it, she'd spilled her pomegranate tea down the front of her white bathrobe, making it look as if her heart had burst inside her chest. It sort of had. Because, suddenly, she could see it too. A fresh start. A do-over. What did they call it in books or her mother's beloved Hallmark channel movies? 'A second-chance romance,' she'd whispered the words, her knees weak and wobbly.

Yes, she'd definitely buy condoms. Making her way toward the pharmacy area in the back of the store, Claire threw a few packages of dental floss in her basket and thought about Paul. He'd always been excellent about making sure the boys brushed their teeth before bed. Paul also handled the mountain of insurance paperwork that followed every dental exam and now Max's orthodonture visits as well. Even when the reimbursement checks inadvertently ended up at the dentist's office, Paul diligently tracked them down.

Seeing the packages of floss, all that waxy white twine, took Claire back to a few weeks earlier. It was Paul's night with the boys, and he and Henry had barbecued together while Claire went to the movies to escape the August heat.

Before heading to bed, Claire decided to check the backyard for the usual things Paul left behind whenever he grilled: plates, a spatula, slices of cheese. She flicked the switch that turned on the floodlight above the patio. Suddenly, the landscape glimmered. Strands of twinkling white lights ran along the fence, sparkling over the shed, and creeping up the trunk of the oak tree to glitter in its branches. The effect was dazzling. So lovely and unexpected.

'Wow,' she whispered.

Joe and Henry rushed up behind her.

'Do you like it? Do you like it?' they demanded.

'I love it!' She opened the French doors and they stepped onto the patio to admire the transformation of their ordinary yard into this magical garden. 'How did you do it?'

'Dad bought the lights,' Joe said.

'It was his idea,' added Henry, 'but we helped.'

'I climbed the ladder and only fell twice!' Joe high-fived his brother.

'How'd that turn out?' Henry asked, mimicking Alice Masters.

'Pretty darn perfect!' The boys shouted in unison.

Once they went to bed, Claire called Paul to thank him. She prepared a message in her head, expecting his phone to be dead and the call to go to voicemail. Instead, he picked up.

'Hey,' Claire said.

'Hey,' Paul repeated.

She took a deep breath. She couldn't recall the last time he'd done anything that had left her feeling this impressed or grateful. Her cynical side wondered if he'd found inspiration peering into Alice Masters's yard. Claire had begun following the domestic diva on social media and she had to admit the woman was beyond talented.

Claire cleared her throat and began. 'So, thank you. The lights look incredible. What a fun surprise.'

'Well, I saw your slideshow: *15 Ways to Brighten Your Backyard on a Budget.*'

'Really?' Claire asked, momentarily flattered. 'You read it?'

She was about to thank him again when he said, 'I found it a lot more useful than *25 Baby Names to Avoid Unless You Want to Raise a Future Felon.*'

Claire's mouth turned dry, and her cheerful mood darkened recalling that stupid post. For days, she'd fielded expletive-filled comments from irate readers whose children's names made the list. She'd known that slideshow was a horrible idea, but Sabrina insisted it would get 'mad traffic', which it did because angry mothers shared it and called her things that made her shut her laptop in shame. Not even HotDogLuvR had rushed to her defense.

Paul probably thought he was being funny, but to her, it was a painful reminder of how each day her career sank to a new low.

'Listen, Paul, no one's more embarrassed than I am that I have to write this crap, but in case you've forgotten, I took this job because you thought you were losing yours, and one of us had to do something.'

Disappointment at how her life was turning out made her voice crack, further humiliating her.

'I haven't forgotten, Claire, I've—'

'And I'm worried about my mom. She's in complete denial about what her future might look like and, while I'd like to be with her, helping her, I'm writing these stupid—'

'Alice and I have been working on a project,' Paul interrupted, 'and I—'

A hum filled Claire's head. Was he listening to her at all? She was in no mood to hear about some 'project' he'd undertaken with another woman.

She remembered something Alex had posted not long ago. *If you don't like what's being said, end the conversation.* Most of the time Claire thought Alex was brilliant, but occasionally she suspected he was merely paraphrasing *Mad Men*'s Don Draper. Either way, she ended the call with a chilly 'I have to go, Paul. Have a nice night.'

Then she flicked the switch beside the door, plunging the backyard into darkness once again.

Claire slipped a box of condoms into her basket beside all that floss. Her phone pinged, preventing her from lingering on how this purchase pushed her one step closer to ending her marriage.

As if it were a live grenade, gingerly she pulled her cell from her purse, certain it was nurse Crystal with a slightly more polite version of 'Where the fuck are you?!' Instead, she spotted an email from Sabrina. *Sabrina!* Claire looked at the time on her phone: 1:32 p.m. She'd left for lunch almost two hours ago. She'd meant to send her boss an email, but that call from Marjorie ranting about litter completely derailed her.

Claire took a deep breath and squinted at the cracked screen.

> From: Sabrina Wilson
> To: Claire Casey
> Sept. 4
> 1:31 p.m.
> Subject: Gone rogue?
> Claire, unless the CMS and instant messenger are lying, you've been offline for 102 minutes. Hoping you are OK?!? Assuming that you are, the team has come up with a new slideshow idea: Celebrities Who've Gone Gray & Regretted It. Check all the socials and embed photos. Please include and link to those Color Me Fab at-home dye kits. They're one of our newest advertisers so this couldn't be more perf! Playfully suggest that these women look hideous and should buy these kits ASAP.

Claire wanted to tell Sabrina where she could stick those kits. But instead, she wrote:

> From: Claire Casey
> To: Sabrina Wilson
> Sept. 4
> 1:34 p.m.
> Subject: Bugs!!
> So sorry. Dealing with a lice crisis – my eight-year-old, not me – back online soon!

At any other job, Claire never would have been so unprofessional as to blame her child for her disappearance, but she'd realized early on that at MamaRama complaining about your offspring was a form of female bonding. As she expected, her email pinged seconds after she'd sent her message.

> From: Sabrina Wilson
> To: Claire Casey
> Sept. 4
> 1:35 p.m.
> Subject: Poor You!
> OMG! Claire, what a nightmare! Seriously, isn't that supposed to be like mega-contagious? Maybe when you're rid of this infestation you could write a gut-wrenchingly honest post like, All the Ways I Felt Like an Awful Mom After My Son Was Diagnosed with Head Lice. That would totally resonate! So (only if you can!), take some notes on all the feelings you're experiencing this afternoon while you're dealing. Good luck and Godspeed! (OH! Maybe you could keep your hair tucked inside a wool hat at tonight's farewell happy hour? Most people tend to be creeped out by the very mention of lice.)

Previously, Claire would've been offended by Sabrina's candor and wished head lice on her editor's entire family, including her innocent bald newborn. Instead, Claire rejoiced that Joe's condition bought her some much-needed free time.

Unfortunately, Sabrina's comment about gray hair forced her to recall those pesky white wires that stood up in the middle of her own head. Claire, who could barely polish her toenails without making a toddler-style mess, doubted her hair-dying abilities. But from a quick scan of the Color Me Fab box, the process sounded fairly straightforward. Comb it on and voilà! you could say goodbye to your grays in just ten minutes, the instructions all but guaranteed.

Tossing Bottle Blonde No. 6 into her basket, Claire headed to the pharmacy register at the back of the store where she was less likely to see anyone she knew. As she emptied her basket, Claire attempted to bury the condoms and lice kit beneath Altoids and gum. She was about to pile on a *People* magazine when she heard a familiar voice.

'Mrs Casey?' It was Sister Mary Agnes Flaherty, head of the Sunday School program at their parish.

'Oh, Sister Mary Agnes.' Heat traveled up Claire's neck and

cheeks until her face burned a freshly slapped fuchsia. 'Hi! H-H-How are you?'

'That's, um,' Sister Mary Agnes cleared her throat, 'an interesting assortment of purchases you're making there.' She nodded toward Claire's ridiculous line-up.

Unwilling to be mom- and slut-shamed in the same conversation, Claire kept her head high and said, 'Ah, yes. The Boy Scouts are collecting these for hurricane victims. They specifically asked for floss, prophylactics, and lice removal kits. The mints and gum are just a little something extra I thought might be a nice treat.'

Sister Mary Agnes frowned and fiddled with the crucifix dangling from a silver chain that hung around her neck.

Claire already believed she was going straight to hell on account of the impure thoughts she'd entertained about Alex all summer long. Now she could add 'lying to a nun' to her list of sins.

'The Scouts requested these items?' Springing onto the scene like a goddamn jack-in-the-box, Judy Thompson, middle school PTA president, popped out from behind a display of cheap reading glasses, startling both Claire and Sister Mary Agnes.

'Yes. Didn't you get the email?' Claire, unable to maintain eye contact and purple with embarrassment, attempted to throw her motley purchases into her purse, but the cashier insisted on dropping them into a plastic bag one item at a time, with the deliberate and infuriating slowness of someone paid by the hour.

'No, I don't believe I did,' said Judy, eyes darting from Claire to her cell phone, her thumb scrolling furiously.

'Check your spam folder!' Claire called over her shoulder as she grabbed the shopping bag and ran for the exit, silently praying she didn't bump into another soul she knew.

September 4, 2024

1:47 p.m.

Safely inside the cocoon of her van, Claire separated her purchases. She shoved the condoms in the glovebox and the gum and mints into her purse. The floss, lice kit, and hair dye she left in the plastic bag on the passenger seat. She put the car in reverse as beeps and buzzes sounded in the third row again. If she had more time, she'd have parked and dug around to find the source of those irritating noises. But she'd already left poor Joe with the nurse far longer than she'd intended. She hoped he hadn't clawed his scalp raw by the time she arrived. She imagined a new title for a memoir: *Claire Casey's Never-Ending Apology Tour*.

As she pulled up to the elementary school, she wasn't surprised to find mothers there already, waiting in their cars. Some chatted on cell phones; others sorted through junk mail. Though the dismissal bell didn't ring until 3:05 p.m., these women – the same ones who never missed a single body sculpting or spin class (not even on Christmas Eve) – spent upwards of an hour in their vehicles to avoid walking an extra block. Even on this, a gorgeous September afternoon.

Claire parked around the corner and quickly hid the lice kit beneath the seat. If a mother or even a curious nanny spied it, Joe would be regarded as Patient Zero and all future birthday party invitations would cease.

Claire hurried toward the brick schoolhouse and pressed the buzzer.

'Hello?' crackled through the speaker.

'This is Claire Casey. My son Joe is in the nurse's office.'

The door emitted its angry, elongated *zap* and Claire gave it a yank. As she entered the stuffy building, the security guard made a point of staring down at his watch. Yes, she was beyond late, but she was here now. Wasn't that all that mattered?

Claire knocked softly on the nurse's partially open door and hoped Joe wasn't sharing a couch with any of the barfers.

'Mommy!' he yelled, and raced into Claire's outstretched arms.

Instinctively, Claire kissed the top of her son's head before remembering what had brought her there. She subtly swiped the back of her hand across her mouth in case lice eggs could travel that quickly and were already germinating inside her gums.

Each time she saw one of her sons in the middle of the day outside their home, Claire was struck by an intense rush of love that nearly knocked her off her feet. They were so precious, how did she ever let them leave the house? They were experiencing things she'd never know about, having feelings they chose not to share with her.

A second wave hit, this time a sudden tsunami of loss that almost toppled her. They were all getting too big too fast. When Max had been a baby, she'd wheeled him all over town in his navy jogging stroller and anyone over sixty would take the opportunity to impart unsolicited wisdom: 'Enjoy every minute!' 'The days are long, but the years are short!' 'It goes so fast! You'll see!' and her least favorite, 'You blink, and he'll be the one pushing you!'

Claire had wanted to tie these busybodies to the handlebars of her enormous stroller and bring them home with her. Let them attempt to build model airplanes out of Play-Doh as Max said less-than-encouraging things like, 'You're doing it wrong! The wings are too small!' and 'Where's the landing gear?' Claire would oversee it all. 'Still want to tell me to savor every second?' she'd cackle demonically.

Now she realized they'd been right. All of them. Max, a full-fledged teen, barely spoke to her in complete sentences anymore. Surely, Henry and Joe would follow suit in just a few short years. The boys were growing up and away from her and there was nothing she could do but stand there and watch it happen.

Since the separation began in May, the boys stayed with Paul at his parents' house every other weekend. Though Claire initially spent Friday evenings basking in the sublime stillness of having her entire home to herself, that elation shifted to a disorienting loneliness by Saturday afternoon.

She'd asked Alex how he'd gotten through those early days.

'Nurture yourself and your interests,' he'd written, and forwarded links to writing retreats. 'Do something just for you, Claire. You deserve it.'

What a novel way of thinking – putting herself first. Yet she was woefully out of practice. She took his advice to heart and signed up for a surfing lesson, attended a poetry reading, and visited the Guggenheim Museum. Walking that glorious spiral rotunda, she savored the fact that she could linger as long as she liked, inspired by all the artists who found a way to pursue their passions.

But when she returned to her quiet home and shuffled past the boys' empty bedrooms, she wished they were there, even if it meant she'd need to step in and break up fights over socks and video games. Her toilet seats remained in the lowered position, yet it felt like a hollow victory. If she and Paul called it quits for good, she'd see so much less of her children. Her heart and mind almost couldn't process it.

In that moment, hugging her lice-infested baby in the nurse's office, Claire couldn't imagine letting any of them go – possibly not even Paul. She pictured him laughing at her impersonation of Crystal Sprayberry, who frowned and fretted as if tasked with managing a wartime field hospital.

'Mrs Casey, here's the memo you *claim* you didn't get,' the nurse stood behind a small desk, one hand holding the letter, the other planted on her hip.

Claire's momentary swooning over Joe evaporated as she wondered how many other notices he'd neglected to deliver. How soon would they, too, boomerang back to bite her?

'Thank you.' She accepted the paper, too tired to say anything else.

As she and Joe made their way back to the car, Claire fought the urge to peek through her son's hair to see just how bad it was. Though the mothers and au pairs in their vans and SUVs pretended to be engrossed in their novels, knitting, and meditation, Claire knew they were as intuitive as CIA operatives. If she so much as tousled Joe's curls, their eyes would train on them with sniper-like precision. So, when Joe lifted his arm to scratch his head, Claire instinctively snatched his hand in hers and swung their locked arms as if they were the most carefree pair in the world, simply out for a midday stroll.

Inside the van, Joe, always her most demanding child, begged for a chocolate milkshake.

'Let's see how long it takes to wash your hair, OK?' Claire stared at the clock. 2:01 p.m. Where the hell had this day gone?

Now that they were on their way home, Claire came to terms with the task at hand. She pictured herself combing through her son's hair and eradicating the bugs nesting there. Her stomach lurched. She was glad she hadn't showered yet.

'Please, Mom, please! It's all I really want!' Joe whined. 'Just a milkshake. That's all!'

Claire bit her lip to avoid screaming, 'Cool it, pal, you have lice not leprosy!'

Paul was much more patient with the children. She wanted to believe it was because he spent less time with them, but she knew that wasn't the case. She remembered all the nights he'd rocked them back to sleep when they awoke teething or feverish. In fact, it was his kindness that had drawn Claire to him.

On one of their early dates, a waiter carrying an enormous tray of dirty dishes back to the kitchen had tripped on a ripple in the carpet and dumped a half-eaten order of linguini with clam sauce squarely in Paul's lap. It landed with such a splash, Claire was certain they must've been on a hidden camera show. The waiter, who was new and clearly distraught, apologized profusely while gaping at Paul's soaked crotch, realizing that any attempt to wipe up the spill would only make matters more uncomfortable for everyone. The manager appeared seconds later, and other patrons, turning away from their own conversations, stared in rapt attention, expecting a fight or, at the very least, some forceful expletives from the now-drenched customer.

'It's fine! I'm fine!' Paul had assured everyone. 'It wasn't even hot. I'm not burned.'

The waiter and his boss seemed stunned that Paul handled it so well, they insisted on bringing them more wine, repeating, 'Dinner's on the house!'

'More like, dinner's in his lap!' said one of their fellow diners, who laughed and pointed at Paul's garlic-and-oil-stained khakis, where parsley flakes had fallen in shamrock patterns. The whole thing was kind of comical and Claire did her best to hide her smile behind her napkin.

'I'll probably have some stray cats following me home,' Paul joked. 'But seriously, I used to wait tables during college. It happens.'

Claire had marveled at his sense of calm and generosity of spirit. If the same thing had happened to her father, he would've been polite to the waiter but then ranted the whole way home, threatening to never dine out again. This, in turn, would've sent her mother into a funk as she envisioned never getting a night off from cooking her husband's usual – a meat and two sides – for the rest of her life. They'd then spend the next three to five days not speaking to each other until something happened – an appliance broke, a phone solicitor called during *Jeopardy!*, Claire or Kyle came home with a failing test grade – and once again they'd be united by a common enemy.

Though she'd only known Paul for about a month at the time, watching him handle the linguini situation with such grace stirred something inside her. Like one of Oprah's 'Aha' moments, she was struck by a sudden thought: Could Paul possibly be 'the one'? He was kind and adorable in a Paul Rudd sort of way. How nice it would be to go through life with someone so even-tempered. He'd make a lovely husband, father, a good provider; hell, he traveled with extra Bed Bath & Beyond coupons. She looked at him, covered in clam sauce, and saw her future unfurl, a feeling, warm and delicious as a loaf of garlic bread, nearly overtook her.

They'd planned to catch a movie after dinner and Paul had been willing to go, knowing how much Claire had been looking forward to seeing Kate Hudson in *How to Lose a Guy in 10 Days*. Claire insisted they return to his apartment where he could change out of his wet and pungent clothing.

It was her first time at his place. She was impressed by how adult and well-kept it appeared. He even had plants – and they were alive. A guitar stood in the corner. 'You play?' Claire had asked.

'Nope. My roommate left it behind,' Paul said.

'Good,' Claire thought. She was so done with the wannabe rockstar type.

'Make yourself at home.' Paul handed her a glass of white wine. 'I'm going to hop in the shower and, hopefully, leave the fish market funk behind.'

When Claire heard the water turn on, it gave her an idea. She wandered into his bedroom, where a queen-sized bed (nicely made) sat beneath a bay window. His apartment was on the fourth floor. She closed the blinds. Next, she slipped off her shoes, pulled her dress over her head, unhooked her bra, removed her underpants, folded everything and left it in an orderly pile on a leather chair in the corner. Claire couldn't recall a time she'd initiated sex. But something about Paul's laid-back vibe made her want him that much more.

She'd turned the bathroom doorknob, relieved it wasn't locked. But that also meant there was no turning back. She opened the stall shower door, entered, and stood beneath the pounding spray, facing him.

'Well, hello!' Paul said, and kissed her in a way that made her feel at once lightheaded and fantastic.

They'd had sex three times that night. (Over the last few years, they were lucky if they did it that many times a month.) Tender but not hesitant, sure of himself but not rough, hungry but not savage, Claire found herself suddenly invested in the guy she'd originally thought of as a sweet diversion from the usual egomaniacs she dated.

For weeks after that night, each time Claire caught even the faintest whiff of garlic, she experienced a pleasant tingle throughout her body – a sensation she quickly realized was love.

September 4, 2024

2:01 p.m.

'If you loved me, you'd get me a milkshake!'

Joe's wail jolted Claire back to reality and made her suddenly aware that they'd been at a stop sign for who knows how long.

'What?' she asked absently.

'Mom! You're ignoring me!' Joe shouted.

'Sorry, sorry,' she said, through clenched teeth, attempting to channel Paul's patience.

'I want a milkshake!' Joe was near tears and using both of his little hands to scratch his head.

Screw it, she'd never be as patient as Paul. But she had other good qualities, Claire told herself. She was a good bowler and a strong speller. Surely, those counted for something.

'Joe, honey, you have bugs in your hair, you're not dying. Pull yourself together.'

'Yes, I am, Mom. I heard Ms Sprayberry talking on the phone and she said, "If I catch lice from these kids, I'll die." Then she told me that lice are insects that are slowly sucking my blood and trying to eat my scalp. I don't know how much time I have left. Please, Mom, just one milkshake.'

'Jesus Christ, half the adults in that school should be neutered,' Claire almost said aloud. 'Oh, Joe, baby, you're not going to die. You know what it's like? Remember when Uncle Kyle's dog, Ginger Spice, had fleas? It's like that. I bought a special shampoo for you, and you're going to be just fine.'

'When Ginger Spice had fleas, Uncle Kyle gave her lots of treats. I remember. Why can't I get a milkshake?'

Full-blown sobbing now, Joe's shoulders heaved. Had he been wearing a long-sleeved shirt, surely he would've wiped his nose on his arm, but because it was a warm September day, he wore only a tee. He opened the glovebox in search of a tissue or, at the very least, a napkin from a fast-food joint. Heavy from the van's manual and the wad of Bed Bath & Beyond coupons Paul stored there long after the retailer had gone bankrupt, the compartment door swung down quickly, dumping the box of condoms, in all its shiny black and gold glory, into her son's open hands.

Damnit! Joe, under eighty pounds, wasn't supposed to be riding shotgun. Claire was so distracted she hadn't even noticed. He knew better but constantly wanted to be as grown-up as Henry and Max.

'Hey, what's this?' Joe said, holding the box. The words 'Large-Size' and 'Lubricated' appeared in bold capital letters as they sailed past women pushing strollers and walking golden doodles.

'Oh, that's a present I bought for Mrs McClaren,' she lied, grabbing the box and sticking it under her seat. 'But *shh*! Don't tell anyone! It's a surprise!'

Who was this monster she'd become?

Hungry for redemption, Claire gently pinched his cheek. 'You know what, pal? I think we might have time for that milkshake after all.'

September 4, 2024

2:04 p.m.

Claire and Joe idled at the Burger King drive-thru for what seemed like two days.

'Geez Louise, is this guy milking the cow?' Claire huffed. 'Let's get on with it!'

If only she'd stopped at the grocery store like a proper parent instead of going underwear shopping and acting like a lovesick fool, she could've made a milkshake at home. As it was, she was tempted to climb through the miniature window and take over the process.

Hearing a ping, she realized she hadn't checked her email in ages. She pulled out her phone. It was dead. That was odd. The sound must've come from whichever gadget was languishing in the third row.

'Joe, what was that noise?'

'I hope it's the milkshake machine!' He smiled hopefully, all sadness and fear of dying magically erased by the promise of whipped cream and a cherry. Oh, yes, these kids knew just how to play her.

Claire plugged in her phone charger and waited for her cell to glow back to life. She was afraid to check for new messages. Knowing Sabrina, she'd probably written to ask Claire to take high-resolution photos of Joe's insect-laden scalp as well as before-and-after delousing pics to include in the piece, which she felt certain her editor would title, *All the Ways My Son's Lice Outbreak Made Me Realize I'm a Bad Mom*.

She'd accomplished nothing today. She didn't own a stitch of clothing she liked. Her eyebrows, not to mention multiple other body parts, needed to be shaved, waxed, or plucked. She had no alibi to give Paul, Abby, or Sabrina if she blew off each of them to get liquored up in a trendy lounge overlooking the Hudson River. More than five hours had passed since she'd read Alex's message and still, she didn't know what she'd do.

She rested the phone screen-side down in her lap and stared out the windshield. On the main street, just yards from her van, horns blared, and brakes screeched. She instinctively thrust her arm across Joe's chest. Traffic skidded to a halt.

'Hey, asshole! Learn to signal,' screamed the driver who'd swerved and stopped just inches before impact.

'Fuck you!' The other driver shouted back, causing Joe to grin at his mother as he savored the thrill of hearing 'the f word' yelled so brazenly.

Claire thought of her father who'd taught her and Kyle to drive. In between shouting about getting too close to mailboxes or tailgating, he coined a phrase that, later, he considered the ultimate metaphor.

'Just because somebody's got his blinker on, that doesn't necessarily mean he's gonna make the turn!' Her dad repeated this whenever they'd arrive at a stop sign and Claire would start to pull out, trusting that the approaching driver intended to go in the direction their signal indicated.

In the years that followed, Claire's father recycled variations on that expression: 'Just because so-and-so has a PhD, that doesn't mean he's got any common sense!' Claire's mother adopted it too. 'Your cousin Sarah may have gotten engaged, but that's no guarantee they'll make it down the aisle.'

Claire and Kyle, who rarely agreed on anything, would roll their eyes at one another.

Now she understood what her father meant. Just because someone indicated they planned to do one thing, that didn't necessarily mean they'd go through with it. Maybe things didn't have to move so quickly with Alex. Perhaps they could enjoy each other's company and she could tell Paul she had to skip back-to-school night to meet an old college friend who just happened to be in town on business. *Not a lie.*

After they'd broken the ice over a single cocktail, Claire would persuade Alex to take the ferry to Manhattan. Once there, they'd stroll The High Line. Alex had probably never been, and oh, how she adored the unexpected and stunning oasis – a public park that bloomed on the site of a historic elevated freight rail line on the city's west side. They'd wander toward Chelsea and she'd take him to a rooftop bar for another drink and a bite to eat. He'd probably have cigarettes. She salivated at the thought of an errant fleck of tobacco on her tongue. How adult it all sounded. Unless it involved baseball, ice cream, or roller-coasters, Claire couldn't get the boys to go anywhere with her. Paul, too, had been reluctant to join her whenever she'd suggest taking a day trip to a new destination. 'That sounds exhausting,' had been his perennial excuse.

She longed for the days when her sons were little and didn't argue. She could pop them and sandwich bags filled with Goldfish crackers into the stroller and walk for hours. They'd go to the zoo, museums, botanical gardens. But once they grew older, her boys realized that if they made an outing particularly hellish, she'd stop asking and let them stay home, face-down in their gadgets. And so they went out of their way in their attempts to pet lions, touch Picassos, and stomp tulips. As they'd hoped, she'd given up, and, subsequently, they – and she – went nowhere. Claire pictured herself in the future: a lonely old woman walking around a shit-brown reservoir pushing a double stroller loaded with chihuahuas. It was a bleak image.

Let Paul go to back-to-school night, meet the teachers, pay the PTA dues, sit on bleachers in the stifling gym, and learn about this year's health class curriculum. Claire always attended the concerts, school-wide puppet shows, and book fairs. Surely, Paul could step up and handle this on his own. Knowing her husband, she could email him casually to say she'd gotten a last-minute invitation, and he wouldn't ask for any further details.

For the past few years, she'd viewed his lack of interest as a personal slight. Now, the one time she hoped he didn't press her to explain her plans, she wondered if it was simply trust. Trust that she was about to – or may have already – betrayed. Because really, even if she didn't allow the spark she felt for Alex to ignite into a full-fledged fire (one that might burn so hot it would require half the Hudson River to extinguish), wasn't the emotional connection, and the fact that she'd thought about him non-stop for weeks, months, just as bad as anything physical?

A ping sounded from somewhere in the van. She turned over her phone in her lap and checked the app.

Alex had sent a message. Claire's pulse accelerated; her wrists went weak. Could she read her would-be lover's words with her son sitting beside her, making him complicit in the ongoing betrayal of his father? She looked over. Joe was tying his shoelaces together.

Realizing she could probably burst into flames without her child noticing, Claire took a deep breath and clicked.

So sorry to do this . . .

Her heart stopped. *So sorry to do* what? Had the cracked screen caused her to misread his words? Was he about to say he'd sent his previous message to the wrong woman? She squeezed the steering wheel and braced for the worst before reading on.

Having a bit of a family crisis. Nothing major. My son got into an altercation this morning. His mom is freaking out, and I might have to cancel. I'm so sorry, Claire, you have no idea how much I want to see you.

Claire let the phone drop into her lap and pressed her hands to her face. She blinked back tears, proof she'd been looking forward to meeting him more than she wanted to admit. Her disappointment was palpable – a gut punch that completely threw her off-balance, a full-body shudder like missing a step in a staircase. The thought of seeing him again had consumed her. Now, in less than a hundred words, it was over.

Trying to look on the bright side, she *had* gotten new underwear. Small consolation.

Another horn blared, this time from behind.

'Get it, Mom! Get it!' Joe shouted.

'Ma'am!' a Burger King employee was attempting to shove a chocolate milkshake through her half-open window.

Claire shook herself back into the moment and handed Joe his drink.

'Where's the "thank you", mister?' she asked as her son blew the straw's paper wrapper at the windshield and giggled.

They'd barely pulled on to the main road when he whined, 'I don't like it! I want strawberry. Can we go back?'

'No! We can't go back. We have to get home and wash your hair. Why'd you pick chocolate anyway?' Claire knew why – because Max and Henry always chose it. She reached for the frosty concoction. 'Here, give it to me. I'll finish it.'

She sucked through the straw with the greedy fervor of someone who'd spent weeks stranded in a desert. The shock of Alex's message, coupled with the drink's icy cold sweetness, caused a near-instant brain-freeze. Claire didn't care. She only hoped the shake didn't wreak havoc on her insides. The day's events had already left her dizzyingly nauseous.

April 30, 1999

7:02 p.m.

The scent of shrimp scampi made Claire dizzy with longing. Even though the restaurant was only a few blocks from campus, Alex had driven them to Captain Ahab's Crab Shanty in his Miata with the top down. Mags was right, it was a cool car.

Since returning from London, they'd gone out a bunch of times. Claire had even accompanied Alex to his co-worker's wedding. He'd been a wonderful date – introducing her to everyone and providing colorful details about their backstories, refreshing her drink, twirling her around the dance floor. When he introduced Claire, he added, 'America's next great literary voice.' She'd let him read a few of her poems and short stories and he'd been so encouraging and complimentary, it made her dreams seem possible.

She no longer checked the mailbox for a postcard from Neal. She'd stopped looking for him in the corners of dark bars where his band had played. After he left, the group morphed into a Ric Ocasek tribute band, the Getaway Cars. Though Claire didn't care to see her ex again, she'd have given her prized Discman to watch Neal's reaction if he witnessed how far the band had fallen without him.

Inside Captain Ahab's, she and Alex sat in a booth half holding hands, half thumb wrestling across the red-and-white checkered tablecloth, mocking the chianti bottles' little wicker basket bottoms.

'So, any nibbles?' Alex asked.

'Sure,' Claire said. 'How about fried calamari?'

Alex laughed. 'No, I meant any nibbles on those résumés you sent?' He'd helped her revise her cover letter and convinced her to expand her job search beyond newspapers to include editorial assistant positions at magazines and publishing houses.

'No,' she sighed. 'I mean, I had a couple of phone interviews, but they didn't turn into anything.' Claire picked up the menu and hid her face between its sticky, laminated pages. She tried not to think about her future on weekends.

When the waiter came to take their order, Claire asked for the crab cake special.

'Scratch that!' Alex said. 'We'd both like the veal Parmesan.'

'Um, no.' Claire looked from the waiter to her date. 'We're at Captain Ahab's Crab Shanty, we can't get veal!'

Alex closed his menu decisively. 'I'd still like the veal,' he told the waiter.

Claire didn't consider herself an animal activist, but she wanted to ask Alex if he had any idea how those calves were treated. Her brother, Kyle, had dated a vegan, Mary Ellen, who often gave spontaneous lectures about animal rights.

But knowing how unbearably depressing they found it when Mary Ellen started up about the living conditions of farm animals, Claire kept her mouth shut.

'Cage-free means nothing. Nothing!' Mary Ellen would admonish them as Claire's mom served one of her signature soufflés.

'Then don't eat it,' Claire's dad would mumble under his breath, her heart instantly swelling with love for her father.

As they waited for their meals, Alex asked, 'What about grad school? Maybe get your MFA?'

'I don't know,' Claire deflected, 'you don't need a master's degree to write a novel. I've already started one.' *Not a lie.* She had a strong opening sentence and some mediocre dialogue.

'You have?' Alex's brown eyes widened. 'That's amazing. You never mentioned – what's it about?'

Claire's cheeks flushed with deceit. 'Well, the main character is this young woman who's kind of at a crossroads . . . you know, trying to figure stuff out.'

'What stuff?'

'Life, I guess.'

'That's pretty vague.' Alex buttered a roll without breaking eye contact. 'So, is this a memoir?'

'No!' Claire insisted defensively. 'It's a novel.'

'But more like autofiction, right?'

Claire was saved further embarrassment by their waiter's arrival. But as she stared at the plump crab cakes surrounded by coleslaw and corn salad, she lost her appetite. What was she going to do after graduation? She felt as stuck as the giant plastic lobsters that dangled overhead, trapped forever in brown frayed netting.

In between bites, Alex chatted happily about the job he'd secured at a software company. They offered a generous 401k package (Claire had no idea what that meant but she nodded anyway) and tuition reimbursement so he could pursue his MBA.

'That's awesome,' Claire said numbly, a panic steadily seizing her chest.

Neal's new group, the Soul Proprietors, were gigging all over LA. Mags, Stacey, and Annabelle had jobs lined up. Alex would probably secure a corner office within the next decade. She had nothing.

'You barely touched your crab cakes,' Alex aimed his fork at the fried beige lumps, 'mind if I . . .'

'Go for it.' She pushed her plate toward him.

They were supposed to see a band (not the Getaway Cars) after dinner, but when she complained of a stomachache, Alex offered to drive her home and she was grateful.

As he pulled up in front of the house on North Harrington Street, she couldn't open the door fast enough.

'Thanks,' she mumbled, kissing him quickly on the cheek.

'If you ever want to role-play sometime . . .'

Claire made a face.

'I mean, I'll be the interviewer, you be the interviewee. Maybe I can see where you're going wrong.'

'Yeah, I'd love that,' Claire groaned sarcastically and slammed the car door.

When she stepped inside the house, Maggie was sitting on the couch watching an episode of *The West Wing* she'd taped.

'Your hair!' Mags pointed at Claire's head then aimed the remote at the television to pause her show. 'Tell me you did not just have sex in that tiny car! Actually, tell me everything!'

'No. Alex put the top down – after putting *me* down.' Claire flopped onto the sectional.

'What? I'll murder him! What did he say?'

'He asked me about jobs and what I'm doing after graduation.'

'And?' Mags twirled one of her red ringlets around her index finger and cracked her gum. 'What else?'

'Well, that was kind of it – but he did try to order for me!' As the words poured out, Claire heard how ridiculous she sounded. 'It's just . . . everyone has plans and what do I have?'

'Hey,' Mags squeezed Claire's calf, 'this just gives you more time to write that novel.'

Claire cringed. 'I don't know, Mags, I don't have any ideas, any cool experiences. What do I have to say about anything?'

'Look, your boyfriend broke your heart but you've rebounded. You're job-hunting but haven't had any luck – yet! You're about to move back home with nothing more than a stack of poems and a diploma from a – let's be honest – pretty mediocre university. I'd say that's plenty of material!'

Claire choked out a sob.

'Sorry,' Mags grimaced. 'Is this not helping?'

When Alex called the next day and the ones that followed, Claire let his calls go to voicemail and refused to return any of them. After a week, he left a note in her mailbox asking if he'd offended her in some way.

She still hadn't gotten any 'nibbles' from employers, and she certainly didn't feel like talking about that or the fake novel she'd mentioned to shut down his career-related questions. She knew he was just trying to be helpful. Maybe she'd overreacted?

Claire debated calling him. It was almost graduation. Their time together was limited anyway. It was probably smarter to let things fizzle.

September 4, 2024

2:16 p.m.

'Don't even think about it, mister!' Claire said as Joe headed straight for the Xbox.

Upon entering the house, her sons exhibited a gravitational pull toward video games, but Joe had no time for carjacking virtual strangers or blowing up aliens now.

'Go upstairs, put your clothes in this plastic bag, I'll be right there. We have to get your brothers soon,' she reminded him, fighting the urge to collapse on the couch.

If she stayed upright, she could bury her sorrow and fill the void created by Alex's cancellation with the mundane tasks the rest of her day demanded. Of course, now that their plans were off, seeing Alex again was all she could think about. She shook her head as if to clear away images of the way he'd looked at her at the reunion, the warmth in his eyes stirring something in the base of her stomach. Those butterflies were back, or maybe that was the shake she'd sucked down in record time.

Joe handed over the box of hair dye, grabbed the lice kit, and stomped up the steps. Claire knew she should follow him before he did something inexplicably Joe-like and rubbed his head against everyone's pillowcases to see if this situation was as highly contagious as Ms Sprayberry suggested. But she wanted to check her messages first. Only ten minutes had passed, but maybe Alex's situation had changed?

After logging into her laptop, a pop-up flashed: a Facebook message from Maggie. It's Over. Call me!

Shit! Claire assumed the aerial fitness craze had come to its inevitable end, shuttering Maggie's business mere months after its grand opening celebration. Sad but not surprising. How long could people pretend to enjoy dangling upside down like bats or bouncing on mini trampolines like toddlers at a birthday party? Toned limbs were nice, but at what cost?

Maggie will land on her feet, Claire told herself as she debated ignoring her old roommate's message. But after re-reading it, *It's over* could mean many things, and Claire's curiosity got the better of her.

What's over? Claire hurriedly typed back.

Dots bounced in a gray bubble. Maggie was responding in real-time.

Oh, only everything! Calling you now!

No! No! No! Claire wanted to type back. She had no time to take on anyone else's drama when she already had so much of her own. But Maggie rarely reached out. Maybe, after she found out what happened and successfully talked Mags down from her crisis, Claire could subtly mention that Alex Larson had asked her to meet for a drink – in a hotel bar – and then canceled, leaving her confused and semi-heartbroken.

First she'd need to explain that she and Paul had separated – hardly a conversation she could contain to the length of time it took lice shampoo to absorb. Still, Claire desperately needed advice – a fresh perspective. But could she trust the wisdom of someone who'd sworn off complex carbs and was clearly dealing with problems of her own?

Claire's home phone rang.

'Joe, I'll be right there. Run a bath, OK? But don't get your hair wet!' she yelled upstairs, hoping Joe heard her and wasn't creating a mural with shaving cream Paul left behind.

'Mags, what's up? You OK?' asked Claire, opening the Color Me Fab box.

Skimming the directions, she walked over to the entryway mirror, and began combing the caramel-colored potion through her graying roots. Even if she wasn't meeting Alex, why not give her hair a quick touch-up? Surely, that would lift her spirits.

'C.C., thank God!' Maggie exhaled. 'And no! I'm not OK. I've been living a lie. For at least a year.'

For months, whenever Claire pictured her friend, she pictured her mid-lunge, a medicine ball poised above her head like that Atlas statue in Rockefeller Center. But now, hearing Maggie's voice, she envisioned her lying on her back, pulling one of her red ringlets between her fingers and studying it for split ends, the way she'd done when they lived together.

'What happened?' Claire hoped she'd take the hint and cut right to the chase.

'Pete's been sleeping with his assistant,' she said. 'I should've known. How many late-night business meetings can one man have? I'm such a dummy.'

'Oh, Mags, I'm so sorry, and you are not a dummy,' Claire consoled her. 'This could, *this does*, happen to a lot of people. Look at Stacey.'

'He only bought me the studio as a parting gift!' Maggie fumed. She seemed to be in the 'anger' stage of grief, whereas Stacey was squarely in the 'depression' phase. 'He said he wanted to "set me up" so I could support myself. I'm totally getting left behind here, C.C. I'm Garfunkel.'

On Sunday afternoons during their college years, stuffed from brunch, Maggie and Claire would lie at opposite ends of their L-shaped couch, and listen to Paul Simon's *Graceland* straight through. They'd wonder how Art Garfunkel handled Paul's success following their split. Then, they'd move on to *Rhythm of the Saints*.

'There's not a single track I want to skip on either of those,' Maggie would say when the CDs ended. 'Poor Garfunkel. This must be killing him.'

The roommates would sigh, send sympathy vibes to Art, and drift off to sleep, napping until someone knocked on their door to borrow a sweater or invite them to dinner. Those were simpler times, Claire thought wistfully.

'Mags, you are not Garfunkel in this situation.'

'Seriously, if I stopped straightening my hair, I'd even look like Art Garfunkel!'

Hair! Claire stopped pacing around her living room and peered into the mirror. She couldn't be certain, but an orange hue seemed to be spreading outward from her roots. How long had the dye been on? She'd forgotten to look at the clock when she first applied it.

Maggie said something, but Claire was distracted by the sound of running water. She hoped Joe would turn off the faucet before the tub overflowed. She pictured the stain on the kitchen ceiling. Was it pulsating? *I don't have the time to deal with a small-scale flood*, she thought as Maggie began to cry.

'Have you been drinking?' Claire asked tentatively.

'I've taken a Xanax and maybe had a splash or two of Riesling.' Maggie hiccupped. 'But that's so light and fruity; it's like apple juice, really.'

'You're home, right? You're not driving or picking up Amelia and Daphne?' Claire felt a stab of sadness. She had no idea what her former best friend's day-to-day life was like anymore. Did she drive a carpool? What activities were her adorable daughters involved in? What did she order at Starbucks? How had their lives, once so happily entwined, grown so far apart?

Why do we go to so much trouble to build up friendships for our children without tending our own? Claire wondered if there was an essay or feature article in there somewhere. Maybe she could get a therapist to weigh in on the importance of maintaining relationships despite all of life's outrageous demands. She grabbed a pen and scribbled 'No friends?' on her hand so she wouldn't forget to pitch this idea to Sabrina later.

'C.C.,' Mags moaned. 'I haven't touched pasta – not even one goddamn elbow macaroni – in a year. For this? I can't compete. I've seen this girl. And she's a girl – barely out of college. She looks like Kristen Bell, like *Veronica Mars*-era. I want to hit her in the face with a kettlebell. And it's probably my fault. I brought the kids in to visit Pete, took one look at his former assistant, pointed at her belly, and said, "Shouldn't be long now!" You know where I'm going with this.'

Claire cringed, knowing exactly what her blunder-prone friend would say next.

'She wasn't pregnant! And, Pete, asshole that he is, burst out laughing. She gave her notice that afternoon, and next thing, he replaces her with Miss Teen Manhattan. My world is imploding.' She hiccupped again. 'It's so cliché, it's embarrassing. I mean, how did I not see it coming?'

This was the second friend whose husband had left her for an assistant – did this qualify as an epidemic? Claire suddenly felt grateful that all of Paul's co-workers resembled the characters from *The Big Bang Theory*. The fact that her first emotion was relief made her wonder if maybe, for all her complaints, Claire still had much stronger feelings for her husband than she'd allow herself to admit.

Would she fly into a panic if she discovered that Paul didn't want to come home? What if he preferred to move next door to his parents and spend the rest of his days sipping Alice Masters's moonshine, or whatever she was fermenting in her basement, and arranging her quilting squares? What project was he working on with her anyway? The thought caused Claire's teeth to grind. Surely, if her marriage were over and there was no love there, she wouldn't care.

She recalled her early days at the newspaper. Joyce, the deputy editor, was an older woman who, when Claire reflected on it now, was probably only forty-two at the time. One snowy afternoon, Joyce told everyone in the break room about a woman flirting with her husband at a New Year's Eve party. Claire had expected Joyce to be outraged. But instead, she'd smiled and said, 'After she touched his arm for the third time, I said, "You know what, honey, you're so interested in this guy, you can have him! Take him home with you. Enjoy fishing his balled-up socks and underpants out from under your bed. Watch him leave the room and ignore your relatives on Thanksgiving. Oh, and maybe while you've got him, you could teach him how to change a lightbulb." Well, you should've seen her face. I haven't laughed that hard in years. My New Year's resolution is to say whatever the fuck I want. It just feels so damn good.' Joyce slapped her thigh for emphasis. Then she looked at Claire. 'Try it, kid. It's liberating as hell.'

Before that conversation, Claire had feared Joyce, who often got on her case for not using more powerful verbs. After that, she'd admired her. A month later, Joyce left her husband, rented a small apartment, and began writing historical fiction. She said as soon as she realized she didn't care if someone else was interested in her husband, it was time to leave.

'He's leaving me, C.C., and I should've seen it coming,' Maggie whimpered. 'Last year, after Christmas, I'm going over our credit card statement, and I see this charge from a jeweler. I'm not kidding, it was something crazy like six grand. So, naturally, I thought it was a mistake, credit fraud, whatever. But before I filed a dispute with Amex, I sent Pete an email asking him about it. He called right away. I should've known something was up because he never calls – like not even when I left him a message to say there was a motherfucking black bear in our hot tub.

'So, he tells me he bought me a diamond and sapphire bracelet, but he left it in his desk and the CEO's cokehead nephew swiped it. He convinced me there was nothing we could do about it. It wasn't insured. No witnesses. We had to eat the loss. And you know what I got for Christmas? Slippers! Slippers from L.L.Bean. Yes, they were lined with genuine Australian lambswool, but so what? That's a gift you bring your nana in her nursing home. It's not something you give your wife! The mother of your children! Unless, of course, there's a diamond and sapphire bracelet tucked inside the toe portion.'

After pausing to blow her nose, Mags sniffed, 'You know it's true what Oscar Wilde said, "Never love anyone who treats you like you're ordinary."'

'Oof, that's brilliant,' Claire said, surprised that her roommate, a finance major, was quoting the Irish poet and playwright. 'What's that from?'

'Originally? I don't know but it was at the beginning of *The Guncle*. My book club just finished it. You'd really love it.' Maggie began to cry again.

'Oh, Mags, I'm so sorry.' Claire bit her bottom lip. There was no way she could cut the call short now.

'I'd believed him. I only just called the jeweler now. I lied and told him it was our anniversary and I wanted to be sure to wear the gift my husband bought me last Christmas, but I couldn't remember which piece it was. It was a diamond-studded choker. A choker? I want to strangle him.'

'So, wait, that's how you caught him?' Claire felt bad trying to rush the story out of Maggie, but she needed to shampoo Joe's hair and get the dye off her own, which seemed to be shifting from orange to pink before her very eyes.

'No!' Maggie sounded disgusted. 'I didn't catch him, which is even more infuriating. This morning, he gets off the Peloton, sweating like Guy Fieri at a pig roast, and announces, "I'm done."'

'And, like an idiot, I think he means with his spinning. But, duh, no, he means he's done with *me*. He's moving out. He said he'd wanted to leave in June but decided to do the right thing and wait until the girls were back in school. Then he gets in the shower as if he didn't just take an enormous shit all over our lives, and that's when I called the jeweler. And when Pete came out of the bathroom, I confronted him. He spilled the whole thing. He looked relieved, actually. Happy, even! And why shouldn't he be? He's free to go start his second act now.

'When men have a midlife crisis, they get sports cars and mistresses. What do women get? Ads for supplements to reduce belly fat. New wrinkle creams. Memes about hot flashes. If we've got money, maybe Botox and bunion surgery?' Maggie let out a wry laugh. 'Well, fuck that, C.C. I want more. He's not gonna get off cheap. I'm hiring a shark of a lawyer and taking this smug asshole for everything.'

'Mags, you shouldn't be alone right now. Where are your friends?'

'What friends?' Maggie blew her nose.

Claire pictured the gorgeous blonde and raven-haired women from Maggie's Facebook posts. 'The women from your book club or Bunko group? The ones from your studio?'

'Those women aren't my friends. They're just people I hang out with. They use me for my pool. You've seen the pics. It's a fucking oasis!' Maggie ranted. 'Plus, if I'm single, I'll be deemed a pariah – they'll think I'm after their husbands. I've seen how it goes. As if anyone wants these bloated Vineyard Vines-wearing pricks. You're all I've got, C.C. Stacey and Annabelle hate me.

They never "like" any of my Facebook posts. Stacey might've unfriended me after she and Ethan split. And, I'm sorry, but I get why Ethan left. Stacey's such a downer, always sending me Lyme disease warnings just because I live in Connecticut. And what is up with all these pics of the twins? They're cute but I have my own kids. I'm not their grandmother, thank you very much.'

'I know, it's weird, right?' Claire glanced at her watch. They'd gotten off track. Whole minutes ticked by quick as seconds.

'We were supposed to go to Corfu for Thanksgiving,' Maggie went on. 'And we were talking about finally getting a place of our own on the Vineyard. I'm telling you right now, I'll be damned if I'm spending the holidays in Queens with my parents.'

Claire wanted to tell her longtime pal these statements were the reason people unfriended her.

'Mom!' Joe yelled. 'The water's cold! Where are you?'

'Shit, Mags, I'm sorry, but I have to go. Joe is home with head lice, and I have to pick his nits then get Max and Henry.'

'Yuck,' Maggie said. 'Listen, I was just thinking, remember when we went to London senior year for spring break?'

Claire's stomach dropped. Did Maggie know she'd reconnected with Alex – that that very morning she'd been thinking about the night she'd spent in Alex's hotel room? His scruffy beard had left her cheeks red, her lips bee-stung and raw from kissing until dawn. Throughout the excursion they'd taken to Oxford later that day, Claire had found herself touching her chapped skin and smiling, despite her eyes burning from lack of sleep.

If she concentrated, she could almost conjure his scent: vanilla and smoke.

'I was thinking, we should go on another trip,' Maggie said. 'Just the two of us. Really cut loose.'

'Totally,' Claire agreed.

'Remember how you hooked up with that guy? Alex Larson?'

'Yeah,' Claire gulped.

'Was he at the reunion? I saw you connected with him on LinkedIn a couple months ago. What's the deal with that?'

What was the deal? Claire, heart soft and damaged as a small, bruised plum, longed to tell her friend everything. But there wasn't time. And what if Maggie thought she was the Pete in this situation – a would-be home wrecker? It didn't matter anyway. She remembered Alex's most recent email. *So sorry to do this . . .*

'So sorry, Mags, I really have to go. I'll call you tomorrow. Love you!'

September 4, 2024

2:32 p.m.

'Jesus, Mom, what took you so long?' Joe harrumphed, attempting to tie a towel around his waist. 'And what did you do to your hair? Is that the lice medicine? I don't want pink hair!'

'Joe, we don't say, "Jesus" like that,' Claire scolded, terrified to look in the bathroom mirror.

'Max does!' Joe stomped his foot.

'Well, I'll have a talk with him about that. Now, let's get a look at this head, shall we?'

Joe, believing she meant *his* head, craned his neck toward his mother while Claire turned cautiously to look at herself in the mirror. Her roots appeared to be a rusty pink, but she hoped maybe she was merely suffering from a stress-induced retinal issue. Swiftly, she knelt beside the tub and rinsed the dye out as fast as she could while Joe watched in silent confusion.

Running a brush through her wet hair, there was no denying it, Claire appeared to be wearing a mauve yarmulke. 'What the hell was I thinking?' she muttered. Claire knew she wasn't good at tasks like this. That was the whole reason she handed over two hundred dollars every three months to a young woman named Lana, who hid her brown-gray roots and restored her golden halo. Why hadn't she called and asked for an emergency appointment? Such a thing had to exist in today's world, right? Maybe it was a good thing that Alex had canceled, or else she'd have to try to pull off a headscarf like the fashionable and elegant Erykah Badu.

'What about *my* head, Mommy?' Joe whined.

'Right, sorry!' Claire turned away from the mirror. 'I tried to touch up my roots, but it didn't go so well.'

She hoped Joe might say something comforting like, 'I think pink suits you,' knowing that was about as unlikely as hearing her son suddenly speak in iambic pentameter.

'I'll say it didn't go so well!' Joe giggled. 'Jesus!'

Too tired to admonish him again, Claire tried to focus on her son and put her hair and her call with Maggie out of her mind – at least temporarily. She'd skimmed a somewhat reassuring article that declared lice shampoo perfectly safe and head-shaving unnecessary. Ushering Joe toward the closed toilet seat, Claire gave him a washcloth to cover his eyes and got to work applying the solution to his scalp.

She could see the oval-shaped orbs clinging to the hair shafts. They were white, which, according to what she'd read, meant they'd hatched. She twitched with revulsion, filled with a newfound respect for anyone brave enough to enter the pest control business.

'The one time Crystal Sprayberry is right about something, it has to be today,' she whispered and affixed a new set of under-eye patches to her face.

While they waited the ten minutes required for the potion to work its magic, Claire fetched *Froggy Builds a Tree House* from Joe's nightstand. Perched on the edge of the tub, she'd barely opened the book when he plucked it from her hands.

Instead of struggling to sound out each word, Joe read effortlessly, his small fingers gliding across the pages until he happily declared, 'The end!'

'Joe!' Claire beamed. 'That was amazing. Has someone been working with you at school?'

'No.' He shook his head. 'Dad has. He let me go in Grams's attic and bring down all the books from when he was a kid. Then we read together. We're running out so he said he'll take me to get my own library card soon.'

'Wow.' In June, Joe's first-grade teacher had sent an email recommending they hire a reading tutor. Claire had forwarded it to Paul to ask his thoughts. He'd written back, 'I'll handle it.' She didn't know he really had. Paul had always been a patient instructor. She remembered how, in the early days of their marriage, he'd tried to help her with her golf swing. She'd been hopeless – even at putting.

The thought of him working with Joe sent a warm feeling

through her. She wished she could've seen them, heads bent toward one another.

She smiled even as she separated the layers of Joe's hair only to uncover more poppy-seed-like nits.

'This is nice,' Joe said.

'What is, honey?' Claire asked, trying not to let her disgust for the insidious critters creep into her voice.

'This. Hanging out. Just us.' Her son turned up his sweet face to look at her. With his bright blue eyes, he looked so much like Paul, sometimes she almost imagined someone had shrunk her husband.

'It *is* nice,' Claire said, walloped by the gut-wrenching guilt only preoccupied mothers experience. Did it take a case of head lice for Claire to give her son the one-on-one attention he needed? Maybe she had more to write in Sabrina's 'negligent mom' essay than she'd initially realized. She would make more time for him.

She glanced at the small clock above the toilet. They needed to leave in three minutes to pick up Max and Henry. After Joe took a fast shower, Claire grabbed a clean towel, hoping she'd removed all the bugs and eggs. She felt oddly comforted by the fact that she'd have to repeat the process in seven to ten days, according to the box. She'd have more time then, she assured herself.

She wrapped the towel around Joe's head, turban-style, the way her mom had done for her when she was little and fresh out of the tub. Claire had loved to float through the rooms in her terry-cloth bathrobe, pretending she was a Moroccan princess.

'You *are fun*!' Joe exclaimed, straining on tiptoes to admire his new look in the mirror.

The way he emphasized the words *are* and *fun* seemed to imply that someone had said Claire was the opposite. She imagined Max and Henry turning her baby against her after she insisted they go to sleep before 9:30 p.m. and banned electronic devices from their bedrooms.

Curious, she said, 'Oh, thanks, sweetie. Hey, did somebody say I wasn't fun?'

'Yeah,' Joe called, racing down the stairs, no doubt hoping he could steal a few minutes on the beloved Xbox. 'Dad did.'

September 4, 2024

2:50 p.m.

Claire's face tingled as she packed away the lice kit and straightened up the bathroom. The tile floor, with its dingy gray grout, reflected her failed attempts at housekeeping. But really, she'd reached the point where her attitude was more 'why bother?' than inspired. Occasionally, she'd sit with a cup of coffee and allow herself to slip into the delusion that watching a home-flipping show on HGTV might motivate her. (It never did.)

The toilet-paper holder had broken; only one arm of it remained attached to the wall. It extended out as if wanting to shake your hand while you did your business. Fixing it required a single screw, but waiting for Paul to find that bit of hardware and then make the necessary repairs was as ridiculous as expecting him to recreate the Eiffel Tower out of twigs in their backyard.

Channeling her frustration, Claire had started her own little game which she called 'How Long Will It Take?' as in 'How long will it take for Paul to replace that holder?' The answer was six months and counting. Her sons, who knew how to use their arms to open the refrigerator door a dozen times an hour, were incapable of moving the empty cardboard toilet-paper rollers to the wastebasket. Five cylinders littered her bathroom floor. How many more would it take before anyone else noticed?

This wasn't the only room where she played 'How Long Will It Take?' A recessed light above the kitchen sink had been out for more than three weeks last winter before Claire dragged over a dining-room chair and changed it herself. The battery in the clock that hung in the dining room had died a year ago, which meant every meal, whether she served it at dawn or dusk, occurred at exactly two fifteen. When Claire first invented this pastime, she envisioned telling Paul about it some day and laughing at how long it had taken for him to even notice. She'd foolishly hoped that by that point everything would be restored to order.

Now, with only Claire at the helm of the household, it all fell to her, and the game lost its appeal. Of course, the boys could help, but making the ask, listening to them whine, and then having to nag them to get moving was often more difficult than doing the job herself.

In one of their exchanges, Alex told her his sons had chores when they stayed at his house. But he didn't call them that. No, they were 'covert operations', which lent the otherwise dull tasks an air of authority and mystery. One child might be 'commissioned' to take out the trash, and this 'job' would be timed so he did it stealthily and soundlessly – Alex's ingenious way of eliminating procrastinating and complaining.

Another washed the dishes while his brother dried them. Their challenge? Do it without getting a drop of water on the floor or breaking anything. Alex rewarded them with fly-fishing gear, golf balls, or trips to the driving range. So far it had worked, he'd said. The concept sounded kind of brilliant, but at the same time Claire was tired of gimmicks and the whole, 'Here's a sticker and a pat on the back for doing what you should be doing in the first place!'

Alex. Her stomach dropped and she let out a long sigh. Removing head lice and giving herself a hideous dye job had distracted her temporarily. But now that she thought about his message, she realized she'd been so stunned, she hadn't even replied. Where had she left her phone? How would she respond? *No problem. Hope your son is OK! Next time maybe?*

And what if he *did* suggest another time? She'd have to go through this whole mad cycle all over again. Maybe it was better to not respond. At least not yet.

'Mom!' Joe shrieked from the living room. 'Do I have time to play Minecraft?'

'Not right now, pal,' Claire yelled. As she raced down the stairs, she tripped on Max's flip-flops, turning her ankle and yelping *Motherfucker!* under her breath. 'Let's go! We're already late!'

Joe, head swathed in a bath towel, bolted for the door, sidestepping the lunchbox he'd dropped on the floor when they'd arrived home, used sandwich bags and a dirty napkin snarled in its zipper.

September 4, 2024

2:54 p.m.

Claire's phone chimed as she buckled her seatbelt. She glanced at the message and smiled. Each of Bea's texts began the same way:

Siri, text Claire. Claire, it's Bea,

This one was no different.

Siri, text Claire. Claire, it's Bea, Stop by when you can. New developments.

Oh no. Had something gone wrong at the orthopedist? Or did Bea mean literal new developments – as in an over-fifty-five community she actually liked?

'Mom!' Joe shouted. 'You said I couldn't play Xbox because we're late but now you're just sitting there.'

He was right. She'd reply to Bea later.

But as they cruised down the block, the older woman leapt from the bench, her usual spot on Julie's front lawn, and hurried toward Claire's minivan.

'Claire!' She waved. 'I found him!'

Oh no, had Bea accidentally lost Julie's puggle, Walter, again? Claire slowed and pulled over.

Winded but grinning like she'd won the lottery, Bea panted, 'I found him!'

'Who?' Claire asked.

'Marty! Marty Devlin!'

'Stop! How?'

'I had time to kill in the Uber, so I did a little Googling and it turns out he's been in New Jersey – Montclair – the whole time.' She dropped her voice and wiggled her eyebrows. 'And he's a widower.' She waved her phone. 'I called him!'

'You called him? Nobody makes phone calls anymore.' *Thank God*, Claire nearly added.

'I know, dear, it's a lost art, a bit like cursive. He remembered me, said he could picture me doing cartwheels in the sand!' Bea's cheeks blushed seashell pink. 'I was a gymnast – for a hot minute, as my grandsons would say.' Beside the open window, Bea chuckled and patted Claire's arm. 'It was so good to hear his voice, Claire. For a moment, I was sixteen again. I could almost taste the Red Vines.'

'I'm so happy.' Claire meant it, even as her chest constricted thinking about how Alex had canceled.

'He wants us to get together. Soon!'

'*Mom!*' Joe bellowed from the backseat.

'I'll let you go, dear.' Bea stepped back and studied Claire. 'It's the funniest thing, maybe it's the light or my cataracts playing tricks on me, but it looks like a flamingo landed on your head.'

September 4, 2024

3:01 p.m.

'Do not sit near Joe!' Claire implored as Max and Henry climbed into the van.

'Mom!' Max shouted. Typically, her oldest son spent the ride home fixated on his phone and mumbling one-word answers to her questions about his day. But this afternoon he was practically levitating through the van's sunroof.

'Yes?' Claire braced herself.

'Mom!' Max repeated in the same hysterical tone he used when he'd gotten a bad grade on a test and attempted to convince her it was the teacher's fault. She wasn't sure how much more bullshit she could stomach today.

'Geez, Mom, you look like a Bratz doll!' Henry said. 'What happened to your hair?'

'I'm trying something new.' Claire recalled a quote Alex posted over the summer: *Inhale confidence. Exhale doubt.*

Alex. What was he doing right then? Did the thought of not seeing her tonight make him feel lost and hopeless too? Or, had he typed the message, hit 'send', and moved on with his day?

Kristie had shared plenty of online dating horror stories with Claire. Men who initially seemed smitten with her found younger, childless women and canceled at the last minute. Sometimes they ended the relationship out of the blue via text. Had Alex been offered better plans and used his son as an excuse? No, she couldn't imagine that. If she let herself, she could still feel the warmth of his hand on the small of her back as he ushered her inside Ted's Olde Town Tavern. There was a connection there, longing; bodies remembering one another from what felt like another lifetime.

'Anyway,' Max continued while eyeing his mother's head in disbelief, 'Harper Westbrook came up to me crying before last period and said that you tried to abduct her brother at the bus stop today and then bullied him when he wouldn't get in the van. She said that Iris Watkins texted her sister, Sage, and said that you called him a baby! How crazy is that?'

'Oh, no, Max, it's totally true; I saw it,' Henry said, excitedly scrolling through his phone. 'It's everywhere. Hold on a sec. I'll find it. It's hilarious. Someone distorted Mom's voice so she roars, "Come on. Get in!" like a T-Rex,' Henry growled, doing his best dinosaur impression. 'It's awesome! Here, look!' He thrust his cell phone between the driver and passenger seats, holding it aloft with the pride of an athlete carrying the Olympic torch.

Afraid to take her eyes off the road, Claire continued staring straight ahead as she heard herself on video murmur, 'Geez, what a baby.'

'That's amazing!' Max hooted, slapping the dashboard, more animated than she'd seen him in months.

'I know, right?' Henry said. 'At first, I didn't believe it. I told the guys at my lunch table – even Smith Westbrook, Parker's brother – that it couldn't be Mom because she hates driving other kids around. But then I saw it!'

Claire sighed. It was true. She *did* hate chauffeuring other people's children around their congested town. Even though she certainly wasn't driving anything fancy like a tricked-out Range Rover or a fully loaded Porsche Cayenne, she couldn't bear all the debris these kids left behind. Max's preschool friend had once tucked small triangles of Laughing Cow cheeses between her third-row seats because he didn't feel like eating them. They'd melted inside their foil wrappers and Paul had spent at least forty-five minutes scraping spicy pepper jack off the upholstery one Saturday morning many years ago. Then, there was the time Darby Williams, a neighbor, barfed voluminously after competing in a ketchup-eating contest at lunch. He'd lost, but based on the amount of vomit he left in Claire's cup holders, he'd put up a valiant effort.

Sure, every once in a while, she overheard a funny anecdote. Back in May, she'd learned that Susie, her former power-walking buddy, brought her iPad into the bathroom with her 'while she takes a poop'.

'She's totally addicted to Candy Crush,' Susie's son, Wyatt, told them on the way home from the library chess club he and Henry attended.

But for the most part, driving kids around offered nothing but headaches.

'Bullying is serious stuff, Mom,' Max said delightedly.

'I offered him a ride to school; I wasn't—'

'Mom!' Henry squealed. 'You might be on the news tonight!'

Tonight! Though she felt like driving into a tree, Claire continued down Main Street, grateful she'd grown up in an era where her every foible and misstep wasn't documented and hashtagged. These poor kids. Yes, they could have food delivered at two a.m. and get walking directions to Saskatchewan in fewer than a half-dozen keystrokes, but at what cost? Would her viral video have any repercussions beyond cracking up her sons? Time would tell. She needed – no, deserved – a break from all of it. Could she write to Alex and tell him she'd meet him at the hotel no matter what time he finished handling his family crisis? Or did that fall into the 'desperate' category?

'Wait, what's wrong with Joe?' Henry asked. 'Why can't we sit near him?'

'Hello!' Joe piped up from the third row. 'I'm right here! Why don't you ask me?'

Claire glanced in the rearview mirror at her youngest. Joe looked like an irritable fortune teller with his head still wrapped in the makeshift bath-towel turban. They did tend to talk about him as if he weren't even there.

'OK, Joe,' Henry said patiently, 'What's wrong with you?'

'None of your business!' Joe shouted and crossed his arms in a huff.

'Boys, please stop. My head is about to explode.' Claire took one hand off the wheel to rub her right temple, which bore orange dye dots she hoped she could pass off as freckles in the event that they lasted forever.

'It's the guilt,' Henry said.

'The what?' Claire's face started to itch and sweat.

'The guilt,' Joe repeated. 'You know, 'cause you bullied that kid at my bus stop.'

'Oh, yes, that guilt,' Claire said, relieved that was all her sons meant.

September 4, 2024

3:06 p.m.

Claire did her best to slow down and not turn the corner on two wheels, but Thursdays were tight. She needed to fix the boys a quick snack and drop Max at soccer practice by 3:45 p.m. Invariably, they spent a solid ten minutes searching for missing cleats and shin guards. Then Joe's martial arts required them to arrive at the dojo by 3:50 p.m. She wanted to let him quit because the last few times she'd observed the class, he'd stood with his hands shoved in his pockets for most of the forty-five-minute session. It did not seem like a natural fit. Still, she enjoyed having an excuse to say the word 'dojo'.

Because each session averaged approximately forty-two dollars and there were no make-ups for missed classes, Claire emphatically told Joe his lice was 'cured' but strongly suggested he not mention it to Sensei Ralph.

Henry wanted to get to the library, where the debate club would host its inaugural meeting, before four o'clock, so he could check out which kids might join before committing.

'The nerd herd will be there, duh,' Max advised him, uncharitably.

As Claire sped toward their home, crafting an afternoon activity drop-off route in her head that accounted for school bus traffic and crossing guards, Henry said, 'Aw, look at that cute pup!'

'He's a cutie, all right,' said Claire, adding, 'we're still never getting one,' under her breath. The very thought of adding another living thing to the veritable petri dish that was her home almost made her LOL, as her co-workers loved to write.

'Mom, why did you just assume that dog's gender?' Henry asked.

'Because I can see his testicles, Henry,' Claire said.

'How do you know that dog doesn't identify as non-binary?'

Testicles. Why had she had such a clear view of that dog's privates? Because he was taking a shit on her lawn!

Claire didn't want to jump the gun, but she was pretty sure she'd caught her culprit (and it *was* the golden doodle!) in the act. She floored it into the driveway, slammed the gear shift into park, handed Max her keys, and whispered, 'Take these and your brothers and wait inside the house.'

Before accusing the owner of leaving these horsefly-attracting, steaming piles of excrement on her property, Claire needed to watch and wait to see if the woman really did just walk away without scooping the poop.

Sure enough, as the dog kicked his paws in a half-assed attempt to cover his tracks, the owner, focused solely on her phone, gave his leash a yank, indicating their stroll should continue.

'Not so fast, motherfucker!' Claire murmured while shooting out of the van like a lone SWAT team member despite her ankle throbbing from her flip-flop stumble.

The dog and the negligent woman at the other end of the leash headed toward the corner.

'Hey! Hey! Get back here!' Claire shouted, and jog-limped straight over to the furry little shitter.

The owner, barely looking up from her phone, turned around as Claire pointed at the stinking brown swirls of doodie. 'Where's your bag?'

When the woman shrugged and gave a little smirk, Claire, on the verge of hysteria, shouted, 'I said, "Where's your bag?"'

'Didn't bring one,' said the woman, who was younger than Claire expected, and definitely not Alex's ex-wife, which was a relief.

The woman glowering at Claire appeared to be in her early twenties. *Wasn't this generation supposed to care about the environment?*

'Well, that's disgusting,' she said finally. 'Someone is going to step in that filth. In fact, my husband did last week! And my son's favorite Darth Vader backpack was ruined because of you!' Claire knew she sounded completely unhinged but she couldn't walk it back now.

'Look, you seem like you'd be chill 'cause you've got pink hair, but you're actually being totally hostile and, like, really aggressive right now.' The woman pointed at the spot on Claire's hand where Claire had scribbled her adult friendship essay idea while talking to Mags. 'No wonder you have "No friends",' the woman snorted. 'Back off or I'm calling the police.' She began jabbing at her phone.

'Go ahead and call them,' Claire growled. 'You're in violation of City Health Ordinance 002013-044.'

The woman's fingers froze. While Paul had been hosing down his loafers in the driveway one week earlier, Claire had done a Google search and found the code. She'd hastily put together flyers citing the health code violation and added clip-art renderings of a dog, a camera, poop emojis, and a pair of eyes above the words: If you leave your dog's poop on our property, we'll return it!

She'd wanted to post signs on telephone and utility poles up and down the street. But Paul, always one to shy away from confrontation, begged her not to do it.

'Some of your favorite neighbors have dogs, Claire,' he'd said rationally when he saw her approach with her printouts and duct tape.

How could he be so level-headed when he'd just wasted ten minutes wiping his wet shoes on a pile of freshly fallen leaves?

'This makes it seem like you're accusing them,' he continued. 'Why don't you just calm down, and wait to see if it happens again? Maybe this was a one-time thing.'

Claire hated when Paul tried to placate her, and she despised it even more when he chose to be reasonable at the very moment she wanted to Amazon Prime herself a flamethrower. She'd always had a bit of a temper, but since having the boys she'd worked hard to keep it in check.

Then Joe, her baby, her sweet, innocent Joe-Joe, had slipped in the vulgar mound of excrement on his first day of school. After assuring her son that she'd buy him a new backpack and scour his sneakers, she'd blamed Paul for not allowing her to carry out her poster plan.

This was her moment to avenge those wrongs. Claire took a second to glance at the front porch. Max and Joe stood riveted as if ringside at a boxing match. Meanwhile, Henry buried his face in his hands.

'Go home. Get a bag. Come back here and clean up this stinking pile of feces. And if you or your dog ever dare set foot on my property again, I'm going to have you arrested!' Claire barked, not knowing if that last threat was possible but loving how it sounded.

Before the woman could react, Claire turned around and stormed up her porch, wincing as her ankle pain escalated.

'You are a total badass today, Mom! Wow!' Max high-fived her.

This was the first unsolicited compliment she'd received from him in two years; she couldn't let him see that her knees were knocking with fear. She wondered if her rage would startle her boys into finally putting down those toilet seats. Would it inspire Joe, who fist-bumped her and repeated, 'Wow. Total badass!' to finally take his hands out of his pockets and pay attention at the dojo?

Henry, who often suffered from a condition Claire had come to think of as 'too much Paul in him', simply shook his head and said, 'That lady is going to come back and burn our house to the ground.'

September 4, 2024

3:09 p.m.

'Max, grab your cleats! Henry, put that mozzarella back! You do not have time to make a panini! Joe, find your gi and your obi and let's get moving!'

If Claire had a nickel for each time she'd need to repeat those commands during the next thirty minutes, she'd be rich enough to retire.

In the kitchen, a light flashed on the base of her home phone. Two new messages. Claire lifted the receiver cautiously. *This day has taken more odd turns than a Fellini film*, she thought, before punching in the code to access her voicemail.

'Hi, honey! It's your mom. Sorry to bother you, I know how busy you are!' Claire always suspected a hint of sarcasm in her mother's voice when she said that. Eleanor believed today's mothers purposely overbooked themselves so they could complain about it. 'Your father was just on the computer playing solitaire and we started having a disagreement about where the reigning *Jeopardy!* champion is from – I say Arkansas, he says Arizona.

'Anyhoo, your father went out onto the web to get the answer and up popped this video of a mom screaming at a child from her minivan and it looks just like you! Dad says it's "trending" or "viral" – whatever that means. If only I knew how to take a photo with this darn phone, I'd send it to you. The resemblance is uncanny, Claire, really, except that I know you would never yell at a child. That's not how I raised you! And I know you'd never try to abduct a boy. You can barely keep up with the ones you've got!' Her mother laughed. 'OK, I'll see you soon. I'm hoping to be there by five thirty, or five forty-five. Six p.m. at the latest. Any news on that playroom makeover? I hope so! Oh, and I was right, the champ is from Arkansas! See you tonight!'

Wow, so this bus-stop bully business really was a thing, Claire mused. Each day confirmed that the world had somehow become overrun with people who'd look at, share, and comment on things that weren't true, things that made no sense, things that reduced another person to a sad and not-so-funny joke, rather than actually stop and focus on their own lives.

Claire wished more people could be like HotDogLuvR, who'd recently left the comment: *I hope you're pursuing a passion project, Ms Casey. Too much talent to waste!*

Inspired by her unlikely friendship with Bea, Claire had (finally!) begun a new project – a speculative work tentatively titled *Another Time*. In it, a middle-aged woman with an estate sale business and a failing marriage befriends an elderly widow whose son is forcing her to sell her home and move into an assisted living facility. While cleaning out the basement, they discover a time machine built by the widow's late scientist husband. Believing their lives haven't turned out as they'd hoped, the women decide to test the machine and try to change their trajectories. But when they arrive in the past, they discover they're actually the same person at different stages of life. Working together, they must determine if they should rewrite history or accept things as they are.

The Time Traveler's Wife meets *Three Tall Women*, this project was a big departure from Claire's other work. Marcy, her agent, would probably hate it, but Claire was having fun dusting the cobwebs off her creative side, typing at night after the boys went to bed and on the weekends they spent with their dad.

Whenever self-doubt crept in, she thought of Alex reciting lines from *A Panda for Amanda* at the reunion. He'd shared something on LinkedIn: *Dreams don't have expiration dates.* She took a screenshot of that quote and re-read it as needed.

In late August, she'd sent Marcy her pitch and thirty pages. Each time new messages appeared on her cell or home phone, she prayed it was Marcy calling to rave.

Claire deleted her mother's message and braced for the next one.

'Claire, this is Florence. Your mother-in-law.'

She always started off that way, as if the world were teeming with women named Florence who also left messages on their line.

'I wanted to tell you that Fred and I are coming home early – this weekend, actually. I tried to get in touch with Paul but he never keeps that phone charged. Maybe you could buy him a new charger? The other reason I'm calling is because before we left town, Fred installed one of those video doorbells, and he just figured out how to use it. Anyway, we've been watching this man come and go. Fred thought it was a squatter. He was all set to call the police and I said, "Wait! That's Paul!"

'We're just hoping everything is OK with you two. I told Paul when you got married not to expect much in terms of cooking and housework because you seemed so set on having a career. But I know you try, Claire, in your own way.' Florence lowered her voice. 'In case this helps . . . Fred and I have been watching *Outlander* together. There are some love scenes that are quite provocative and, well, it's spiced things up for us in the bedroom, if you know what I mean. I just thought maybe . . .'

'Boys!' Claire slammed the phone back into the wall-mounted charger. 'Fix your own snacks. I need a minute.'

September 4, 2024

3:42 p.m.

Without a minute to spare, Claire barreled into the soccer field parking lot, hitting two potholes at once before rocking to a sudden stop as Judy Thompson, middle school PTA president, jumped in front of her minivan.

Judy motioned furiously for Claire to roll down her window.

Sweaty from getting the boys prepared for their activities, she groaned as she turned down the AC and lowered her window.

'Claire! Boy, am I glad to see you! New 'do? I like it. Very Madonna 2007.'

Upon further inspection, Claire noticed that Judy held a clipboard behind her back, which instantly made her wish she'd run her over instead of pumping the brakes.

'Hey, Judy.' Claire braced herself and put the van in park. 'What's up?'

'I'm looking for someone to bake eight dozen cupcakes for the end-of-the-season soccer banquet,' Judy said. 'Of course, two dozen should be gluten-free, another two dairy-free, and all nut-free – obviously.'

Claire, wanting to be both an asshole and a real journalist again, longed to ask Judy for the data behind those figures. Had she conducted food intolerance surveys? How recent was this information? But her real question focused on the date. It was only September fourth. *Soccer began less than a week ago. Why is she planning a November banquet now?*

Judy frowned, clearly confused that Claire hadn't jumped at the chance to bake. She held up her clipboard and, rolling her eyes in an I-can't-believe-you're-going-to-make-me-ask! way, said, 'So? Can you do it?'

'No.' Claire shook her head. Normally, she'd have launched into a litany of excuses – too busy with her job, her aging parents, a fictional home renovation – but she thought of something Alex had posted: *'No' is a complete sentence. Saying 'yes' to something, means saying 'no' to something else. Time is your most precious commodity. Value it.*

Alex. Would they continue to message? His words, his attention – they sparked something in Claire, reminding her of the bolder, more interesting person she was once. She didn't want to lose that part of herself when it was only just re-emerging.

'I'm sorry, what?' Judy scowled. 'The coach's whistle is so loud I don't think I heard you.'

'I said, "No",' Claire repeated, shifting the van into drive. 'Max, grab your water bottle, I'll be back around five.'

'Badass!' Max whispered in her ear as he leaned over and kissed her cheek.

Sometimes Claire felt as if she had failed her family, like when her children contracted head lice or she made them co-conspirators in destroying the planet with their plastic lunch bags. But other times, like at that very moment, she believed things might turn out just fine.

As Max slammed the door and trotted toward the field, Claire glanced in the rearview mirror. Either the afternoon sun was giving her a particularly rosy glow or she was having an allergic reaction to the under-eye patches or possibly the hair dye.

'I'm still trying to find that email from the Scouts about the hurricane supplies!' Judy called, waving her clipboard as Claire sped away.

A swirl of dust and gravel danced in her wake.

September 4, 2024

4:03 p.m.

After dropping off Max and Henry at their respective activities and getting Joe to karate in his uniform and almost on time, Claire collapsed on a bench inside Kung Fu 4 U. The sun beat through the glass window; its warmth spread across her back like the open palm of an old friend. She leaned into it and exhaled as if she'd spent the day holding her breath.

Claire knew that rather than sit there, she should drive home, shower, send Sabrina an outline for the lice essay or listicle or whatever her demanding editor decided it should be. Once she finished that, she'd figure out how she'd spend the evening. She was staring down a trio of lackluster choices: back-to-school night, the Something's Brewing town council meeting, or the MamaRama happy hour. She didn't want to do anything other than sit for a moment amid the temporary stillness of the dojo as the children lined up and waited for direction.

Direction. That was what she needed. Where was she going? What was she going to do? Not just tonight, but with her life? Exhaustion descended upon her, swift and intense, as if she'd swallowed a fist-full of Ambien.

Sensei Ralph encouraged his students to leave their cares at the door and focus. Claire wished she could do the same as she rested her head against the wall of glass and closed her eyes.

Learning that Paul had told Joe that she was no longer 'fun' stung more than Claire would've expected. After all, she was the one who stayed up all night to bake cakes shaped like R2-D2 and monster trucks to make the boys' birthdays memorable. Much like Bea, she was the parent who rode the precariously assembled carnival rides at street fairs with the boys, while Paul stood off to the side holding her purse and clutching his stomach at the very thought of his feet leaving the ground. If she wasn't fun anymore, maybe it was because her family had sucked it out of her with their near-constant demands and she'd allowed it.

And where had all this doing-the-right-thing stuff gotten her? Slumped inside a karate studio indulging in a pity party, that's where.

Claire squared her shoulders and pulled out her phone. She swiped idly before eventually opening her email. And there it was – a message that jolted her out of her afternoon stupor.

Claire, sorry for all the back and forth. Crisis averted. My ex is troubleshooting. (She's a remarkable parent.)

At the reunion, when Alex had told Claire that his ex was a wonderful mom, it sounded so mature, so evolved. Now, she found it grating. It was enough that this woman had a thriving career, Claire didn't need to hear about her superior parenting skills – especially not when she'd just bribed Joe with the promise of extra dessert not to say 'lice' inside the dojo. And that was after she'd threatened a dog walker while her sons watched.

So . . . I'm in, if you're in! 7 p.m. in the bar? Cannot wait!!

Her heart did a backflip. The pins-and-needles sensation in her face tingled down her neck, traveling lower until her whole body seemed to vibrate. Was it excitement, or did she need Benadryl to combat whichever chemicals in those under-eye patches or hair dye were making her feel like she'd been stung by a Portuguese man o' war?

The date was back on – slated to begin in less than three hours. Could she pull herself together in time? And could she overlook Alex's flagrant use of exclamation points which made their meeting seem less romantic and more like teenagers planning a visit to a theme park? Yet her spirits soared at the thought of seeing him again. Of course, that's what she wanted. She'd nearly shed tears in a Burger King drive-thru when he'd canceled, for Pete's sake. This was a no-brainer, as Paul would say.

Paul. She'd planned to use this downtime inside the dojo to call and tell him that his parents were going at it like rabbits thanks to a TV series. She imagined him groaning in horror then laughing and swearing he'd never be able to look at them again – but he'd have to see them because they were coming home. *This weekend!* Florence's 'bedroom' talk had distracted Claire from the real headline. If her in-laws returned, where would Paul go next? She wasn't ready to solve that.

But she couldn't talk to Paul now – not with Alex making her pulse pound. She distracted herself by returning to her inbox where two new messages waited.

> From: Kyle Collins
> To: Claire Casey
> Sept. 4
> 4:12 p.m.
> Subject: Birthday?
> Claire, when I first started this email it was to ask: Is Coupon in or out of the fantasy league? Well, you're off the hook. He just wrote back and reminded me that your birthday's Sunday. Listen, if we're having some big fancy dinner with Mom and Dad, let's make it an early one. Giants are playing. Kickoff's at 8:30 p.m. Also, LMK what you want. How about a gift card that I can email you? Like what about Home Depot? I know shit is always breaking at your house and I'm swamped at work.

Claire snorted with derision. *What an asshole*, she thought. And her mother wondered why they couldn't get along.

Her birthday. Paul *had* remembered. Still, she'd be kidding herself if she thought he'd plan anything special to mark the occasion – if the past few years were any indication.

Back when she and Paul were first dating, he'd surprised her with concert tickets, reservations at a favorite restaurant, and a new piece of jewelry for her birthday. Now, when he remembered, she'd be lucky to get supermarket flowers and homemade cards spearheaded by Henry.

Her phone pinged, and like the Pavlovian dog she'd become, she checked it. It was Abby. **Did you get my email????** she texted. Claire made a mental note to revisit the notion of spending her birthday the way she wanted to this year (like maybe alone and not at an all-day soccer tournament) and then, because she couldn't stop herself, she checked the message.

> From: Abigail McClaren
> To: Claire Casey
> Sept. 4
> 4:25 p.m.
> Subject: The (Star)'Bucks Stops Here
> Claire, where have you been? I thought you said you'd help me!? Please read the attachment! I think it's good, but I know you can tweak it and really make it perf! TIA for your help with this! See you tonight! Don't be late. And please wear something that makes you look professional in case I need you to give a testimonial about what the coffee shop has meant to you.
> XO Abs

Claire lost track of the number of times she'd rolled her eyes while reading. Joe's class would wrap up any second, but Claire couldn't help it, she was curious. She opened Abby's letter to the editor and startled at the random capitalizations, bolded words, and varying fonts that made it appear more like a ransom note.

Reading it reminded her of how much she'd loathed proofing the local paper each week. No one would print this anyway. Still, she sent her neighbor a response to prevent her from calling to discuss it further, which felt inevitable.

> From: Claire Casey
> To: Abigail McClaren
> Sept. 4
> 4:35 p.m.
> Re: The (Star)'Bucks Stops Here
> Wow, Abs, solid effort on this first draft. Let's talk more about it later. Picking up Joe from karate now.

Claire's email pinged seconds after hitting send.

From: Abigail McClaren
To: Claire Casey
Sept. 4
4:36 p.m.
Re: The (Star)'Bucks Stops Here
Thanks! Can you edit it and bring me a printout I can read at tonight's meeting? Just found out it's too late to submit it to the paper. I wish you'd let me know that earlier. You seem very preoccupied lately.

And didn't you say Joe had a stomach bug? That was a hella fast recovery!

Shit! Shit! Shit! thought Claire. *If I can't even remember a white lie a few hours after I tell it, how will I ever lead a double life?*

September 4, 2024

4:40 p.m.

'"Life is a succession of lessons which must be lived to be understood",' said Sensei Ralph, hands in prayer pose. 'Another cool-ass Ralph said that. Ralph Waldo Emerson.'

Claire tossed her phone back into her handbag and tried to stay present as Sensei Ralph began what she'd come to think of as his own slapdash version of a benediction. The instructor ended each session with some inspirational mumbo jumbo she doubted the students understood.

While he swayed there, eyes closed, it struck Claire that she'd probably never get used to seeing him, the man who used to deliver their pizzas every Friday night, leading a martial arts class in what looked like white pajamas.

Against all odds, Ralph had struck it moderately rich when he'd won a few hundred thousand dollars by having four numbers and the Powerball. For at least six months, he'd been a local celebrity. The notion to plunk down most of it on a Kung Fu 4 U franchise came to him in a dream, he'd told Claire when she'd enrolled Joe in early June.

'Before we say sayonara, we must have a serious conversation.' Ralph opened his eyes. 'We know that inappropriate behavior – especially in the dojo – cannot be tolerated. So, it's with a heavy heart that I must bring up a difficult topic. Someone among us has been acting impulsively and not demonstrating the depth of character that we strive to attain.'

Joe's eyes met hers in the mirror. He looked petrified. Claire, too, could feel the blood draining from her swollen, whoopee cushion of a face. Where was Ralph going with this? Couldn't he just let them get on with their bowing and be on their way? She still had to pick up Max and Henry. She wanted to grab Joe, tuck him under her arm like a football, and run with him to the van, but she knew Ralph would regard this as the ultimate diss.

'In life, you will face numerous temptations,' he continued. 'Many will lead you down the wrong path. You must resist. Take the long view. Be stronger than the pull of whatever it is you want in that moment.'

Could Sensei Ralph, a guy who'd reeked of weed and struggled to make change when he'd delivered their pizzas, somehow have acquired psychic abilities? Because it felt as if he were speaking directly to Claire. In fact, he even seemed to be looking at her. To avoid his eyes, she cast her gaze toward her feet. She'd once had lovely, feminine ankles. Now they were swollen and red, her sandal straps biting into her puffy, blotchy skin. Her heels were rough as horses' hooves. She should've gone next door for a pedicure during Joe's lesson. *Why am I so bad at practicing the 'art of self-care' that Sabrina is always yammering about?* she admonished herself.

'But, know this, if you've made poor choices, or you're about to make another, there is still time to change direction.' Ralph's voice took on a deep, resonant timbre. 'We all make mistakes in life, but it's our job to learn from them, not repeat them, and, when we can, correct them. To have control over yourself and your actions, you need to stay vigilant. You need to generate this control from within.'

Claire grimaced as she remembered how she'd snatched Joe's milkshake and snarfed it down like a wrestler hoping to jump into a higher weight class. In her mind, self-control had gone the way of pantyhose and high heels. They were things of the past that, at least in her world, probably wouldn't make a comeback.

'I'm afraid someone in our dojo has forgotten the importance of self-control.'

For what seemed like the billionth time that day, Claire felt as if others had the ability to read her thoughts.

'We see something we want, and we're tempted. But is going after it the right decision? Or are we giving in to our weaker impulses? You must stoke your inner furnace with good thoughts and an iron will when faced with these wrong desires.'

Sensei Ralph stared directly at Claire as he said this, peering into her soul. She shrunk back, bonking her head on the window. Joe, too, found his mother's face in the mirror's reflection. He looked slightly green. Maybe he was coming down with a stomach bug after all.

September 4, 2024

4:48 p.m.

Why had Paul purchased karate pants with pockets for Joe when a major part of kung fu required the use of your arms? Claire wondered as Joe wandered toward her, fists balled deep in those pockets. This was exactly why she took on most tasks herself.

'Ready, buddy?' she asked.

'Mm-hmm.' Joe wouldn't meet her gaze.

They offered Sensei Ralph sheepish waves as they slunk out of the dojo.

Once in the parking lot, Claire wanted to sprint toward her van, but Joe ambled along sluggishly.

'Joe, c'mon, get in, buckle up.' Claire dropped into the driver's seat and started the engine.

Joe closed the door behind him and began sobbing.

'Oh no, buddy, did you hit your head again?' Claire asked.

'No,' Joe whimpered.

'What is it then?' Claire was losing patience. Maybe if she could get a better job, they could afford a young, energetic nanny who wouldn't be so snappish because she had the luxury of leaving at the end of the day. She looked at her son in the rearview mirror and summoned her inner Carol Brady. 'What is it, sweetheart?'

'C'mere.' He motioned for her to join him in the third row.

'Joe, sweetie, we don't have a lot of time here. We have to get Max and Henry and I have to get back home. Just tell me why you're upset.'

'You have to come here so I can show you,' he whined, wiping his nose on the sleeve of his gi.

'Dammit,' Claire swore under her breath. If she ever made it out that evening, she'd drink like a college kid on spring break. Claire turned off the engine and climbed through to the van's third row.

'What, Joe? What is it?'

Slowly, he opened one of the side compartments. When he was in kindergarten, Claire used to give Joe pennies to store there so he could toss them into the fountain at the mall. Considering his outburst, she anticipated seeing a bumble bee or maybe a moldy chicken nugget in his secret hiding spot. What she didn't expect was a small mountain of electronics. A pile of iPhones, Samsung Galaxies, an iPad mini, and what appeared to be a hearing aid, overflowed from the rectangular holder. Claire stared dumbly at the source of all that random beeping.

'Jesus, Joe, whose are these?' she asked.

'Mom, we don't say, "Jesus" like that,' Joe said through his tears. 'They belong to the kids in my karate class. Or their parents, I guess. Some of these are pretty expensive, I think.'

'That's right, Joe, they are.' A buzz filled Claire's head and she thought she might need to lie across the third row of her van and never get up again.

It wasn't fair. When people talked about parenting, they lamented the early morning wakeups, the sleepless nights. They expressed their fears of toddlers falling down stairs, sticking fingers in outlets, never outgrowing bedwetting. Then they fast-forwarded straight to worries about teens driving or trying to get high school seniors into a college whose sticker wasn't too embarrassing to slap on the back windshield of their Suburban.

'What about all the years in between!' Claire wanted to scream. 'What about when your second grader turns out to be a petty thief? Where's the *how-to* book for that?'

Claire thought about her mother, who was probably on her way to their home, gliding down the winding lanes with her overflowing grocery bags, ready to prepare a lavish meal, a smile on her face, listening to a Mary Higgins Clark audiobook. Damn her for making motherhood look so easy! Claire often felt like this whole parenthood business had been an enormous bait-and-switch. Her mom always knew the right thing to do, and she'd done her best to instill that in her daughter. But since late June, Claire's moral compass had become depolarized. Rarely did her mother appear conflicted about how to handle anything. Even when it came to her illness, her mom remained calm and unflustered. Claire needed to muster the same sense of bravado now. She knew this was one of those damned teachable moments that typically blindsided you and forced you to rise to the occasion.

'Joe, why?' Claire sank into one of the seats in the van's second row, hoping that his explanation would help her figure out how to proceed. 'What made you take all these? You know this is stealing, right? And stealing is wrong.'

Had Claire neglected to impart this very basic message? And if she had, shouldn't Sister Mary Agnes Flaherty have picked up the slack at Sunday school? The parish charged nearly two hundred dollars a year for these sporadic fifty-minute religious education classes. Couldn't they at least cover the Ten Commandments for that kind of money?

Claire found herself developing a newfound appreciation for Sensei Ralph, whose lecture now made perfect sense and, clearly, had struck a nerve with her pint-sized pilferer. Maybe forty-two dollars a session wasn't much at all considering he was doing a better job parenting than Claire and imparting more ethical wisdom than Sister Mary Agnes.

'I know it's wrong,' Joe snorted to stop his runny nose and prevent more tears. 'But you and Dad have phones and Max and Henry have phones. I'm the only one who doesn't have one and everyone ignores me while they're on their phones. It's not fair. I didn't want to wait till middle school. So I took one. But it had a passcode. So I took another and the battery died. I kept taking more. I couldn't stop. It was weird, Mom. It was kind of fun at first because I got to be sneaky, like Dad when he sprays whipped cream into his mouth when he thinks no one is looking. But then I took too many and Sensei Ralph knows it's me. I can feel it. He's waiting for me to do the right thing. But I don't know how.'

'Well, we have to go in there and give them all back, honey. You also have to apologize to all the kids you took them from because they probably got in a lot of trouble with their parents.'

'OK,' Joe said, buckling his seatbelt. 'Let's do it next week.'

Claire couldn't blame him for wanting to put it off. She looked at her phone: 4:54 p.m. Max would be standing around the soccer field wondering where she was. She wished this could wait. Or, as an additional punishment, she wanted to point Joe toward the studio and let him handle it all by himself while she got that much-needed pedicure.

She knew that wasn't possible, and thought of something her mom used to say, mingling the wisdom of Dr Martin Luther King Jr. with her own.

'You know what Nana always told me?' Claire placed a hand on Joe's tear-stained cheek. 'She'd say, "Remember, the time is always right to do the right thing, and it's never too late to right a wrong." So, let's take care of it now, Joe-Joe, OK?'

'OK.' Joe sighed. 'But I'm scared of Sensei Ralph. Will you come with me? And hold my hand?'

'Of course.'

Joe unbuckled his seatbelt. 'Doing the right thing seems really hard.'

'Tell me about it,' Claire whispered as she stood up and whacked her head on the van's ceiling.

May 14, 1999

10:18 p.m.

Hypnotized by the ceiling fan, Claire leaned against the back wall of the kitchen inside the house on North Harrington Street. Beside her, Stacey's boyfriend, Ethan, tapped a fresh keg, though it was after ten and Claire wished everyone would leave. She was partied out.

She hadn't invited Alex because his parents were in town and because things had been weird since the Captain Ahab career-pep-talk dinner. Claire knew he was trying to inspire and motivate her, but it had had the opposite effect. She felt paralyzed. Pathetic. Tomorrow, she'd pack the rest of her things and move back into her childhood bedroom. She'd barely gotten any response to the résumés she'd sent. Did Alex think less of her because she was jobless? She cringed, remembering how he thought her novel idea was autobiographical. Unemployable *and* unoriginal. Because Neal was so focused on, well, Neal, he'd never really asked about her career plans beyond 'writing'.

'There you are!' Maggie rushed in with a pitcher of punch that was 80 percent rum and 20 percent whatever was left in the fridge and freezer. All appliances needed to be emptied and cleaned by Monday if they wanted the security deposit back.

'Drink up, C.C.' Mags refilled Claire's red Solo cup, shouting above Smash Mouth's 'All Star', which Annabelle played on repeat. 'It's almost our graduation day! We made it, baby!'

In a botched attempt at toasting the occasion, Maggie knocked Claire's cup with such force that sticky pink punch splashed down the front of the white eyelet sundress she'd worn to dinner with her parents and brother.

'Oh shit!' Maggie laughed. 'Sorry!' She spun around to grab paper towels and froze. 'Well look who it is!' she hooted.

Claire lifted her eyes from the punch stain. She hadn't taken any of the mushrooms Annabelle's cousin had offered her, and yet she still thought she might be hallucinating.

'Ladies,' Neal said with a mock hat-tip. 'What's it gonna take to get some real music in this joint?'

Claire's buzz evaporated as every nerve-ending in her body jangled to life.

She hadn't seen her ex-boyfriend since before winter break, when he told her he was graduating early and ending their relationship in a one-two punch that caused Claire to bomb her finals and sob throughout most of the holiday season.

It had only been five months, but he looked better than she'd remembered. A brown leather band circled his forearm. His hair was lighter, longer, wilder.

'You're here,' was all Claire could muster. Maggie's hand on her elbow felt like the only thing holding her upright.

'Observant as ever.' Neal stepped closer and chucked her under the chin. She'd forgotten the roughness of his fingers.

'I mean, I thought you were in LA?' Claire hiccupped, her body betraying her. They were nearly the same height, about five foot seven. She'd forgotten that too. In her mind, she always pictured herself looking up at him. She finally understood why her brother, Kyle, had nicknamed him 'the little drummer boy'.

Like a penetrating pair of light blue lasers, Neal's eyes scanned the inside of her mind, trying to assess how she felt about him. Claire was embarrassed to admit the beer on his breath worked like part-aphrodisiac, part-time-machine, transporting her to their past, to the nights after the bar when he'd undress her with those calloused fingers. She shook herself out of the memory.

'What are you doing here?'

'Back for graduation.' Neal's teeth gleamed whiter against his tanned skin. 'Doin' it for the 'rents.'

Claire frowned, confused.

'My p*arents*,' he said. 'Sheila guilted me into walking in the ceremony tomorrow. Said she and my dad blew all this dough, the least I can do is grant them a photo opp.'

'Right.' Claire nodded, still wondering if maybe this was a dream brought on by whatever Mags had poured into that punch.

Sheila, Neal's mother, was a lawyer. Claire wasn't a fan. The first time she'd stayed at his house, Mrs Callahan asked Claire what she planned to do with her English degree.

Unsure of her career trajectory, Claire had mumbled, 'I'd like to be a journalist or maybe a novelist?'

'Perhaps a ventriloquist?' Neal's mother had swirled her wine. 'You barely moved your lips. Whatever you choose to pursue, do it with conviction or you'll never get anywhere.'

Claire had spent the rest of that weekend hiding from the woman with the loud laugh and diamond earrings the size of baby toes.

'Got in last night,' Neal said, 'thought I'd come by.'

The words 'last night' landed heavy as bowling balls in her gut. She wasn't his first stop. Not even his second or third, probably. She was an afterthought.

'I didn't want things to be weird tomorrow if we're a couple seats away from each other. Callahan, Collins, you know,' he said.

'Yeah, no, right, of course. Why would they be weird?' Claire was desperate to seem cool even though they both knew he'd torched her heart.

She wished Alex were there standing beside her. Let Neal see that she hadn't been sitting around waiting for him. But Alex, his housemates, and their families had gone out for a pre-graduation celebratory dinner. Claire knew because he'd left a message – another of his many calls she hadn't returned.

'Ethan!' Stacey shrieked from the doorway. 'What is taking so long? Where's my . . . Holy shit! Neal?' Claire's housemate dashed over and threw her arms around Neal's neck. 'Wait, are you two back together? Ethan and I haven't signed a lease yet. Maybe the four of us could still . . .'

A spark of rage ignited in Claire's stomach. Yes, her friends were drunk, but where was their loyalty? Mags and Stacey were supposed to be furious with him for the way he'd dumped her. When Ethan reached into a cabinet to grab an actual pint glass so Neal wouldn't have to drink out of a Solo cup, Claire wanted to slap it out of his hand. Neal deserved plastic!

'No!' she said. 'We are definitely not back together.'

She watched Neal's face shift, his lips twisting into a cocky side pucker. He wore that same squint-smirk combo right before he stepped on stage at a Battle of the Bands. It read: Challenge Accepted. Game On.

He took a sip of his beer and raised his eyebrows. 'Let's not be hasty there, Collins, you never know where the night might take us.'

'Seeing you again . . .' Claire smiled '. . . it's made me realize exactly where I'd like the night to take me.' She handed Mags her Solo cup and winked. 'Don't wait up.'

Propelled by punch and giddy excitement, Claire had to stop herself from running the four blocks that separated her from Alex.

Racing up his porch steps, she tripped but grabbed the railing and narrowly avoided falling face-first into the mailbox.

Alex opened the door, his brown eyes brightening at the sight of her.

'Claire. This is a nice surprise. We just got back from din—'

'I'm sorry I've been so weird,' Claire interrupted, breathless. 'This whole graduation thing and getting a job and real life, it's messed with my head and I know you were just trying to help but it made me feel, I don't know, like a loser, I guess, and I haven't returned your calls and I'm so sorry about that. I really like you and I know we don't have much time left and . . .'

Claire was babbling and couldn't seem to stop. *Fewer words, more action.*

'. . . and I'd like to make it up to you.' She waggled her eyebrows. 'Maybe in your bedroom?' She stepped closer and began unbuttoning his pale blue dress shirt.

Alex grinned and bit his bottom lip. He stepped to the side and swept his arm wide like a magician's assistant. 'Claire, I'd like you to meet my parents, Kate and Mike Larson.'

The punch backed up into Claire's mouth as she stared at the couple seated on a beat-up brown leather sofa. Their expressions somewhere between shock and amusement.

Claire took a hard swallow.

'Oh, hello.' She smiled and waved demurely, as if she hadn't just attempted to undress their son in his living room. 'It's lovely to meet you. Goodbye.' Inching her way back onto the porch, Claire mimed 'call me later!' and fled back to North Harrington Street, cheeks as pink as the stain on her dress.

The party had died down. A few stragglers lingered in the kitchen with Ethan, who was determined to kick the keg. Thankfully, Neal was nowhere in sight. Despite the drinks and the impromptu sprint to and from Alex's house, Claire lay in bed wide awake listening to the smoky vocals of Fiona Apple through her headphones.

After midnight, her bedroom door opened a crack and Alex peaked in. 'Hey, Stacey thought you'd still be up. Hope it's cool that I came by.'

'Of course.' Claire turned off the music and scooted over to make room for him on her twin bed. When he was beside her, she sat up and buried her face in his neck. 'Your parents,' she groaned. 'I'm so embarrassed.'

'Don't be.' Alex kissed her and she basked in a moment of temporary amnesia. 'Listen, there's something I wanted to tell you in person.'

Claire's stomach flipped. Good news never began that way. That was how 'I have a serious illness' or 'I've been sleeping with that hippie girl who plays hackie sack in the lower quad' conversations started.

'My new boss wants me to work out of the company's Madrid office.'

His dark eyes shone in the moonlight.

Claire laughed. 'But you don't live in Madrid.' She leaned closer, nibbling his ear, then moving lower, her lips tracing the curve of his neck. His skin tasted salty and sweet.

He drew back to look at her. 'I'm going to give it a shot.'

Claire's heart, which had been galloping like a racehorse's, slowed to a heavy *thunk thunk thunk.*

'Oh,' She scooted toward the wall for stability. The room seemed to be tilting. 'That's . . .' *the end of this* '. . . amazing, Alex.'

'Thanks, I—'

'What a great opportunity.' She choked on the words. 'Really. I'm happy for you.'

She pulled him closer and kissed him. Their relationship was good, fun, but so, so new, not serious enough to even attempt long-distance – certainly not an international courtship.

'Thanks and I'm sorry, I was hoping we'd get a chance to give this – us – a chance but . . .'

'Shhh. Don't.' Claire pressed a finger to his lips and pulled back the top sheet so he could slide in beside her. She couldn't let him say the words, couldn't bear to have two guys tell her goodbye within a six-month period. 'Let's just enjoy the time we have left.'

September 4, 2024

4:56 p.m.

Re-entering the dojo, Joe's deep pockets finally came in handy.

As they stepped onto the welcome mat, an instrumental version of 'You're the Best', *The Karate Kid*'s theme song, began to play.

'What's up?' asked Sensei Ralph, as he stepped away from admiring his moves in the mirror.

'I-I . . .' Joe stammered. 'I took some things that didn't belong to me, and I have to – I want to – give them back.' He pulled assorted gadgets from his cavernous pockets.

Claire could tell by his ragged breathing that he was trying not to cry again. She had a flashback to his earlier sobbing when he thought he was dying from head lice. She hoped he wouldn't blame his stealing spree on vermin eating his scalp, which was absolutely something Max would do. 'I'm sorry. It was wrong to take stuff that doesn't belong to me.'

'First of all, I love how you checked your ego at the door.' Sensei Ralph knelt so he and Joe were eye level. He placed a hand on Joe's shoulder.

Wow, Claire thought, *he's really matured since the days when he delivered my pies upside down and mozzarella cheese dripped like stalactites off the roof of the cardboard pizza box.*

'Second, it's OK, little dude, we all fuck up – excuse me – screw up, from time to time. What's important is you've done the right thing now.'

Joe nodded.

'There will always be temptations, and some will lead you down the wrong path. You just gotta stay strong. As I like to say, our class never ends. We take what we learn here out into the world, and we act with respect – with physical, mental, and spiritual control.'

Joe's head bobbed furiously in agreement.

'Tell you what we're going to do: write a note to put with each of these that says you're very sorry that you took it home by mistake – because that's what this was, Joe, right? A mistake.'

Ralph was laying it on so thick, Claire wondered if she was hallucinating from weariness. But if his speech prevented Joe from continuing with his life of crime, Claire was all for it.

As Joe nodded again, his shoulders retreated from ear level to their regular position.

Sensei Ralph stood and placed his hand on Claire's elbow. *Great*, she thought, *here's where he tells me he's calling the cops. That would be the perfect end to this shitstorm of an afternoon.*

'I've always liked you, Mrs Casey,' Ralph began. 'You're a nice lady and a generous tipper. And your new pink hair is pretty cool too. Aside from this incident, you've raised a good man here.'

Sensei Ralph glanced over each shoulder as if he were about to share a secret.

'I noticed you seem pretty distracted today. I just want to say, for whatever it's worth, I don't believe you bullied that kid at the bus stop.'

'Thank you,' Claire said, wondering if Ralph had heard the story the old-fashioned way – through local gossip – or if he, like her kids and parents, had seen the video.

'But if you had, I wouldn't blame you,' he continued, voice low. 'That little dickwad claims his mom and dad are black belts; he corrects my moves in front of the whole dojo. It's annoying as fuck.'

This seemed not at all like how Mr Miyagi would've handled the situation, but Claire was just relieved Sensei Ralph wasn't going to report her tiny thief to law enforcement.

'Oh, one more thing, Mrs Casey,' the instructor said as she and Joe were almost out the door. 'I think Joe's wearing a Halloween costume. You might want to get him a real gi if he plans to continue.'

September 4, 2024

5:08 p.m.

After collecting Max from the soccer field, Claire pulled into the library parking lot to pick up Henry. She tried to send her middle child a telepathic message to run outside as, once again, she wanted to avoid seeing anyone she knew.

Is this what it's like to be a celebrity or a dirty politician, dodging the public at every turn? Claire wondered. She looked at herself in the rearview mirror. She still hadn't showered and the day had taken a tremendous toll on her. In the fading afternoon light, the lines that crossed her forehead seemed exaggerated. Her facial swelling had lessened to the point that now it merely looked as if she'd taken part in a botched filler experiment. A solitary black hair sprouted from her chin, calling attention to an angry red pimple that blossomed beside it like a flag indicating a hole on a golf course. It seemed outrageously unfair to have the bad skin of a teenager and the whiskers of a housecat simultaneously. She glanced around the playground that sat adjacent to the library, hoping to spot Henry on a swing. He was nowhere in sight.

She would've called him and told him to hustle, but, like Paul, her middle child was a rule-follower. Claire knew he'd have turned off his phone before he'd even reached the book return bin. Plus, he'd never so much as jog indoors unless it was gym class, so asking him to hurry would be futile.

Her ankle ached at the thought of the staircase that led to the basement.

'Max, can you please run into the library and grab Henry? Nana is coming over and she'll be there any minute.'

Despite her mother's prediction that she'd run late, sometimes just the opposite occurred, and she showed up spectacularly early. *No doubt to escape Dad*, Claire often surmised.

'Are you kidding? Look at me, I'm sweating and gross.' Rather than drinking the water he'd brought with him to soccer practice, Max squirted it all over his head. Filthy rivulets streamed down his face. Claire sighed. Just like that, her teen's newfound respect for his 'badass' mother disappeared.

'Fine. I'll get him myself.' She almost added, 'Joe, try not to hot-wire a car while I'm gone,' but she'd read an article that claimed sarcasm and parenting were as toxic a combination as bleach and ammonia, so she simply slammed the door and hobbled toward the entrance.

Inside the library, Claire glanced at the colorful flyers lining the bulletin board. One announced the next meeting of the library's book club. The group would discuss *Madame Bovary*. Claire was embarrassed she'd never finished the classic about the doomed and faithless wife. But she knew how the story concluded. In literature, as in real life, an adulterous woman typically met with an unfortunate end.

She thought about the collapse of her own book club. That term seemed more like a euphemism, as this once-cordial group of women had devolved into a drinking-slash-fight club – one in which a boozy brawl could no longer be ruled out.

For most of the summer, she'd tried not to think about it, but now Claire let her mind wander back to the club's last meeting, which she'd hosted in March. Claire had suggested *Loving Frank*, a fictionalized account of the architect Frank Lloyd Wright's illicit affair with a married mother, Mamah Cheney.

Claire had found their love story compelling and enjoyed the book, but she never anticipated the raucous debate it would spark among the usually mild-mannered group. After the ladies had poured their wine, piled their plates with cheese, crackers and mini-quiches, and shared their summer vacation plans, they got down to discussing the novel.

Claire was shocked to see how Cheney's actions divided the women. Some saw Mamah, who'd left her husband and children to travel the world with the man she believed was her soulmate, as an inspiration. Others viewed her as a wanton woman and a feckless parent who ultimately got what she deserved. Claire's friends and neighbors shouted over each other, fighting to make their points.

'How could she leave her children?'

'No one faults Frank for abandoning *his* kids! Why is it that we're always shaming mothers for pursuing their passions?'

'She followed her heart. Haven't we all done that at some point, or at least wished we had? She was in the presence of genius, and she knew it. He was the world's greatest living architect. Who could resist that?'

'Wait, I thought Frank Lloyd Webber was a Broadway composer. He was an architect?'

'Jesus, did you even read the book or are you just here for free drinks?'

'Mamah wanted to do her own work too. She was a free spirit, a woman ahead of her time!'

'Oh, that's bullshit! She was a mother first and foremost! Her obligation was to her children!'

'Who are you to say that? You travel for work constantly and leave your kids with strangers you find on the internet. You're such a fucking hypocrite!'

Wine spilled. Books, both hardcover and paperback, were slammed against the coffee table for emphasis, until suddenly the group took a dramatic and collective inhale. Claire, tipsy from a day of cleaning and preparing and not much eating, had a vague fear: *Hair-pulling is about to ensue.* As suddenly as the fighting began, it stopped. The group sat frozen. Claire turned around slowly to see Henry standing on the staircase in his pajamas, rubbing his sleepy eyes.

'Did everyone like my fondue?' he asked.

The club promptly dispersed while Claire put Henry back to

bed, assuring him his caramelized shallot and Gruyère recipe had been a hit, and hoping his first words to his teacher the following morning weren't: 'What's a fucking hypocrite?'

After scraping fondue off the carpet and using seltzer and salt to lift wine stains from the couch cushions, Claire pitched her dips into the trash and tiptoed upstairs. She'd expected to hear Paul snoring.

Instead, he'd propped himself up on his elbow as she entered the bedroom and said, 'Are you sure that's a club you want to belong to? It sounded like a *Jerry Springer* meets *Maury* episode down there.'

'I'm sorry.' Claire groaned as she fell into bed. 'Did we keep you up?'

'Nah.' Paul had rolled over on top of her. 'I was actually hoping we could pretend to be the world's greatest living architect and the free-thinking harlot who loves him. I'll be Mamah.'

Claire had laughed, kissed him, and hoped she didn't taste like Swiss cheese and onions. That was the last time they'd made love. It had been nice. Unexpected. They hadn't needed to smoke pot or watch porn the way her MamaRama co-workers insisted was necessary in order to enjoy their partners' company. Why hadn't she and Paul made more time for each other?

As she limped down the steps to the library basement where the debate club met, Claire could still hear the voices of her book club members condemning Mamah, who'd died a century earlier in one of the most horrific ways imaginable. Of course, now Claire sympathized with the woman who was torn between an all-consuming love and maternal responsibility – a woman who tried to recreate domestic bliss only to meet an unfathomable demise.

Peeking into the room, she motioned for Henry to hurry. He and another student were debating whether technology brought people closer together or further isolated them.

She thought of Alex. If it hadn't been for technology, would she have found him and reached out? And had her infatuation led her to ignore Paul?

As Claire tuned back in, it sounded as if Henry were debating himself.

'It's so cool that you can stay in touch with a friend who moved across the country or that you can Tweet at a master chef and get a reply. But while you're doing that, isn't it taking time away from your family? Like the people who are right in your home with you, you know, the people you love who you're ignoring to have this whole conversation with a stranger?'

'Dude! Make up your mind! You have to take a stand,' said the child moderator with an exasperated eye roll.

'I'm sorry.' Henry hung his head and walked toward his mother. 'That's just way too tough a topic.'

Claire mouthed a 'thank you' to the librarian and put her arm around Henry as they walked out to the van.

'How'd it go, nerd?' Max asked through the open window.

'I thought I was going to be great at it. I thought someday I'd be named captain of the debate team.' Henry slumped into his seat and closed the door.

'But now, let me guess, that's *debatable*!' Max turned around and bounced his empty water bottle off Henry's head, a lackluster rim shot.

'The thing is, I'm not a good debater. I can see both sides of, like, every issue; I have trouble picking one and sticking with it. At first, I see it one way, then I can see it the other. What does that make me?'

'Open-minded? Oh, wait, no, maybe you're just wishy-washy. Oh, wait, I don't know. I can't decide,' Max mocked him.

It makes you just like me, thought Claire, who'd spent the past eight hours struggling to figure out what she should do about Alex. *It makes you just like me.*

September 4, 2024

5:12 p.m.

Approaching her driveway, Claire slowed to a crawl and pulled beside the curb. The offending pile of dog's dirt no longer littered her lawn. She smiled, parked, and attempted to process the events of the day.

She'd appeared in a viral video, purchased new underwear, lied to a nun, botched her DIY dye job, possibly conquered head lice, shocked Judy Thompson, middle school PTA president, with a bold 'no', confronted a rude pet owner, attempted to rehabilitate her tiny kleptomaniac, found an unlikely ally in Sensei Ralph, and gotten everyone to and from their activities safely.

Not bad for a day's work, she thought, unlocking the door to her home and breathing a sigh of relief that she'd made it to this point in the afternoon.

Before sinking into the living-room couch, Claire popped two Benadryl, praying it helped her whoopee cushion of a face return to normal. Once seated, she hoisted her swollen ankle onto a throw pillow and pondered her next move. Her cell phone rang inside her purse. MamaRama flashed on the screen. Because it was after five p.m., on principle, Claire didn't want to answer, but she knew her younger colleagues were committed to 'grinding it out 24/7' so she had to play along.

She cleared her throat. 'Hi, this is Claire.'

'Claire, hi, this is Victoria.' Sabrina's boss was like the great Oz, very hard to pin down. Now she was reaching out directly.

For a brief moment, Claire allowed herself to believe that perhaps her single mom daycare drop-off piece had gone viral, and this upper-level editor was calling to lavish her with compliments and gratitude.

'Claire, this is a very difficult conversation to have,' Victoria continued. 'I'm here with our HR rep, Stephanie.'

'Listen,' Claire rubbed her eyes and realized again just how exhausted she was, 'if this is about the exclamation points, fine, I'll use them.'

'Claire, honey, this is so much bigger than that,' said Sabrina, with an uncharacteristic hint of sympathy in her tone.

Wait, how many people were on this call?

'Claire,' Stephanie, the HR rep, took over, 'it's been brought to our attention that you were involved in an incident at a bus stop this morning. It's all over the internet. Attempted kidnapping, bullying? Either way, it's concerning, to say the least. As you know, MamaRama.com is a pro-mom, pro-kid website. We're family champions. Anyway, we've spoken with our legal team, and we feel it's in our best interest to distance ourselves – to cut ties – really, with you.'

Stephanie paused to allow Claire to absorb this information.

'Because of the, um, unusual nature of this termination, we're prepared to offer you three months' salary and the same amount of time in benefits coverage.'

Claire bit her tongue so she wouldn't scream 'Jackpot!' Though she'd held the job for six months, she had never wanted to quit anything so badly in her life, except maybe freshman field hockey.

'I totally understand,' she said, as solemnly as she could while fist-pumping.

'Listen, Claire,' Sabrina was speaking now. 'We think you've got all the talent in the world, but clearly, you're breaking down. If you want another child, you don't have to abduct one! I know you're a lot older than most of us here, but I'm sure a fertility specialist could help. This is exactly where MamaRama.com comes in. Take some time and read our posts: *Geriatric Pregnancy & You*, *Getting Knocked Up After 50*, and our latest, *Rotten Eggs: Why a Donor Is Your New BFF* – those may help. Far too often moms feel like they're alone. You're not. We're here for you. MamaRama.com is here for you. Not as an employer, of course, but as a resource.'

'We think some time off would be good for you,' Victoria said.

'Amen to that,' Claire whispered.

'There's another issue,' Sabrina piped up. 'It's about your superfan.' She cleared her throat. 'We know, Claire.'

'Know what?'

'We know it's you,' Victoria said.

'What?' Claire laughed. She barely had time to brush her teeth; she certainly didn't have the bandwidth to create a fake online persona to pat herself on the back.

'Some of us were suspicious right from the start. Let's face it, HotDogLuvR is the only positive commenter on the entire website,' Sabrina said. 'We had LuLu in IT do a little digging and it turns out your so-called "fan" is connected to the email account . . .'

Claire thought she heard the frantic clicking of a keyboard or maybe her boss was tapping her nails, stretching out this moment for dramatic effect.

'It's tied to Casey5 at gmail dot com. Pretty big coincidence, right?'

'Some of us think it's very creative of you . . .'

'Others think it's kind of psycho . . .'

Claire could no longer tell who was speaking as thoughts tumbled through her mind like wet socks inside a dryer.

'Needless to say, we'll be deleting any positive comments on your work,' Victoria sighed.

That stung. In low moments, Claire had re-read them and felt encouraged, inspired even.

'Anyway,' Stephanie continued, 'when you're up to it – but within forty-eight hours at the latest – please mail your laptop back to HQ.'

'It's *my* laptop,' Claire said. 'I mean, I own it.'

'OK, well, then just keep it, I guess,' Stephanie said.

'I was planning to, duh,' slipped from Claire's lips before she could prevent it.

'We will need those under-eye patch samples back,' Victoria said.

'Gladly.' Claire debated warning them about the brand that caused her face to puff like a soufflé but decided against it.

'And a couple more things, Claire,' Sabrina jumped back in. 'We know this is hard to hear, but there'll be no playroom makeover, and we're going to have to disinvite you to the happy hour at the Slaughtered Lamb tonight. We just can't be seen with—'

Claire pushed the big red hang-up button, disconnecting Sabrina for the second time that day. Then she threw her head back, her spirit soaring like a caged bird finally released.

September 4, 2024

5:36 p.m.

Claire allowed herself a few moments to revel in her newfound freedom. It was a huge relief to know she'd never have to do that job again.

The house was delightfully, almost suspiciously, quiet as Max started his homework and Henry helped Joe craft the vague apology notes he planned to hand out to the kids whose cell phones he'd snatched, or 'borrowed', as he now described his acts of larceny.

Claire was about to head into the shower when she heard yet another ping. Her phone had become an electronic leash, tethering her to so much shit she didn't want to deal with; still she couldn't stop herself from checking it. What if Alex canceled again? What if she'd spent an entire day behaving like an absolute maniac for nothing? She felt lightheaded at the very thought as a new message loaded:

> From: Judy Thompson
> To: Claire Casey
> Sept. 4
> 5:34 p.m.
> Subject: Concerned
>
> Claire, hope you don't mind that I'm reaching out. I have your email from all your past volunteering, which is actually why I'm writing. I'm concerned. You've never been one of the H2O-and-Go moms. (That's my nickname for the women who just sign up for the easiest or cheapest thing, i.e. bottled water, drop it off, and run away from me like my clipboard is a bundle of dynamite.) In fact, people still talk about the lamb kabobs you and Henry made for Greek Day last spring. (Btw, can I get that tzatziki sauce recipe when you have a sec? TIA.) What I'm asking is: Is everything all right? You've never turned down one of my offers to help out before.

Claire stopped reading to laugh. Offers? As if she had nothing better to do than make ninety-six cupcakes for kids who'd invariably leave them icing-side-down on the newly refurbished turf field, prompting a scathing email from the town's parks and rec director.

> You look tired. Are you unwell? (When I'm feeling a little blue, I put on some early Gloria Estefan, and it really seems to help. Try it!) If it's about the gluten-free cupcakes, you can scale back to one dozen. We don't know if anyone actually is gluten-intolerant, we just like to 'be prepared' – you know, like the Boy Scouts say. Speaking of the Scouts, I still can't find that email about the condoms and lice kits. Can you forward it when you have a sec? I want to talk to the den mother about the appropriateness of this request.
>
> Call me if you need anything and let me know if you're good to go if we drop down to seven dozen cupcakes. Maybe you already follow her, but there's this amazing

YouTuber, Alice Masters, and she's got a video where she teaches you how to use frosting to create soccer balls and flaked coconut for the goal's netting. I'll email you the link and drop-off deets. Thanks!

'Judy, Judy, Judy.' Claire shook her head. These women – Judy, Abby, environmental maven Marjorie – they'd become like characters in a sitcom Claire hoped would get canceled, spending their days badgering other people into joining their causes. Did this really make them happy? Or, had they forgotten their own interests and passions along the way too? Claire deleted the email as her phone pinged again. It was Paul.

Big problems with the new platform rollout thnx to one of the brogrammers. I've nearly fixed it. Score one for the IT dept. dinosaur, looks like I live to code another day. Going to miss back-to-school night. Sorry. I know how we used to look forward to these. Don't forget to ask how early we can enroll Joe in Harvard Divinity School's summer camp.

He followed it with a smiley face emoji and then, Sorry, I know how you feel about emojis followed by a skull emoji.

Claire laughed. *We'll be lucky if Joe isn't spending his next summer vacation in a juvenile correctional facility*, she debated typing back.

P.S. I was looking forward to seeing you, Paul added. Had a bottle of your favorite wine chilling in the work fridge. Thought you might need it. What's up with that video, by the way?

She grinned, remembering the fun she and Paul used to have after they'd come home from the boys' back-to-school nights in the early years.

When Max had first started preschool, they'd assumed, wrongly, that most of the parents in their age bracket would be just like them – laid-back and easy-going. But no. Mothers and fathers barked questions like drill instructors while seated at miniature furniture. Paul and Claire returned home, thanked her mom for babysitting, ordered take-out, and sat on throw pillows on the floor around the coffee table, splitting a bottle of wine, and analyzing their evening.

'Did you see the size of the assistant teacher's pupils? I think she may have been 'shrooming. She's gotta be the one with the Phish bumper sticker!' Paul surmised.

'Could you blame her?' Claire refilled their wine glasses. 'Those parents are too much. How about the mom who asked when was a good time to start working on SAT words? For Christ's sake, half these kids are still pooping in their pants!'

'What about those two women who fell racing to sign up for class mom?' Paul teared up laughing, recalling how one had tripped on the leg of an easel, knocking the other into an enormous Paddington Bear. 'And how about when that nanny said she'd been told to ask if the teacher could find alternate ways to instruct shoe-tying so the process didn't negatively impact the children's self-esteem.'

'And that incredibly thin pair who spoke to no one, what's their deal?' Paul continued, frowning. 'What does a couple like that do for fun?'

'I'd bet they call Whole Foods and demand to know where the kale is sourced.'

Their analysis continued until the wine was gone. Then, they'd retreated to bed, drunk, and grateful they had each other.

Claire re-read Paul's message. It was the longest one he'd sent in a while. His spirits were no doubt buoyed by proof that he was still good at his job. And that P.S.— **I was looking forward to seeing you.** His words filled her with a wistful longing, even though he thought it was Joe's elementary school's back-to-school night, when, in fact, it was Max and Henry's. Joe's was slated for the following Thursday.

She was certain she'd already told Paul that. Twice.

September 4, 2024

5:52 p.m.

Claire stared into her closet. She found a white, sleeveless blouse with ruffles lining the V-neck hanging in the back. She couldn't wear her new black bra with it, but the flounces made her size 34B chest appear larger and she liked that. She'd bought it back in late June, but she'd tucked it away after Max took one look at her and said, 'Ahoy, matey!' With jeans and silver sandals, it would be fine. And, really, what were her other options – yoga pants and a tank top?

Putting an outfit together had been a welcome distraction. But Claire could no longer delay deciding where she was going in this recently assembled ensemble. Alex made her feel alive, and his interest in her had boosted her confidence, helping her remember who she once was, what she'd wanted. Somewhere along the way, she'd lost sight of it and stopped believing in herself. Alex had reignited a spark in her. Maybe it was the novel ideas he'd sent or his assurances that there was still time for her to figure it all out and make it happen. Either way, he was like a human wake-up call in really sexy packaging, reminding her of her dreams, her potential, her power.

Before, she'd felt like a cornered animal; now she was rising – not quite like a phoenix, more like a fledgling. Still, she was speaking her mind, living her authentic truth. Granted, she'd lost her job and made several enemies in the last few hours, but she was awake now and listening to her inner voice.

When she thought about Alex, she didn't feel old and depleted. And then there was the chemistry. Passion, she realized, was like really good wine. It was something you didn't realize you were missing until you got a taste of it. And once you did, you thought, 'How can I go back now that I've had *that*?'

To end things with Alex would be like returning to a world without sunshine or podcasts.

But on the other hand, Paul kept her level-headed. Her relationship with her husband had endured, surviving job changes, home purchases, kids – not to mention the tedium of the everyday. She remembered how he'd held her when she sobbed after learning about her mom's diagnosis.

Still, there was no denying the passion they'd felt in the early days was gone, replaced by a shorthand of pecks on the cheek and *love you, byes* they called on their way out the door to drive to yet another activity.

If she pursued a relationship with Alex, if she truly allowed herself to believe it was the real thing, she couldn't help but imagine it might come to the same end, his winking and random spouting of inspirational maxims driving her bananas in mere days. Was there such a thing as being too motivational?

As Claire sat on the edge of the bathtub giving herself an emergency pedicure, she heard her phone ping. *Alex?* On her heels, she hobbled into her bedroom to keep her newly lacquered pink toenails from smudging, and grabbed her phone.

From: Abigail McClaren
To: Claire Casey
Sept. 4
5:37 p.m.
Subject: Worried!!!
Claire,
So sorry to do this, but I'm going to have to ask you to not attend tonight's meeting. I know you were looking forward to it and that's what makes this all the more painful. You probably didn't realize it at the time, but the young woman you viciously attacked in front of your home over something as basic as dog poo is actually Patrick's niece, Harmony. She's been staying with us for a while because she's a little down on her luck. (Fired from her job at the Gap over some missing jean jackets, dog with swollen testicles, boyfriend troubles, etc. etc.)

Anyway, I know I said I had your back after you bullied Parker Westbrook, but in light of this second incident, now I'm rethinking things, and I'm not sure you align with the Something's Brewing image. And where are those edits you promised me? (I heard you have pink hair, btw?! Is this a cry for help!?) Plus, Harmony will be there (awkward!). So . . . No hard feelings, OK?

Also, I don't know if you know this, but Florence and I are Facebook friends (we met at your New Year's Open House and fangirled over Alice Masters), and we're worried your aggression is what's led Paul to spend so much time at his parents' house. Just putting it out there. Maybe get some rest. (I don't think those under-eye patches are working!)
Let's catch up for coffee soon!
XOX
Abs

Harmony? Claire snickered. *What an ironic name for the sullen creature who seemed hell-bent on befouling our neighborhood. The only other names that could've been more ridiculous would've been 'Joy' or 'Hygiene'.*

Kyle often joked that Claire had named her sons after Thomas the Tank Engine trains, but she was glad her boys weren't saddled with strange monikers that offered people misconceptions about their personalities.

Claire debated how to respond. Abby didn't care that her niece was leaving dog shit all over the Caseys' property. She'd pestered Claire for months about her family's business. Now she'd insulted Claire's marriage *and* her appearance. It was too much. She thought of one of Alex's recent posts: *If it doesn't deserve you or serve you, show it the door.*

> From: Claire Casey
> To: Abigail McClaren
> Sept. 4
> 5:57 p.m.
> Subject: Not Worried
> Abby, I'm tightening my friendship circle.

She'd gotten that phrase from a MamaRama piece on ending toxic relationships.

> I'm afraid there's no longer room for you inside my smaller sphere. If I see you in the neighborhood, I'll be cordial, but let's agree to not email or text one another ever again. LOL
> All the best with the coffee shop.

While she had her phone in hand, Claire looked up florists in Connecticut and ordered two dozen Gerbera daisies to send to Maggie.

'And what would you like the note to say?' asked the peppy woman on the other end of the line.

Slightly embarrassed, Claire managed, 'Mags, you will never be anyone's Garfunkel. Let's plan a getaway soon. XO Claire.'

Order placed, Claire put the phone down on the bathroom vanity, turned the shower to full blast, stepped under the pounding spray, and wished she could stay there indefinitely.

September 4, 2024

6:08 p.m.

'Heeeeere's Nana! Where are my little angels!?!' Claire could hear her mother's voice, loud as a train whistle, even over the *whirr* of her hairdryer. A second shampooing had dimmed the pinkish-orange hue, but she still didn't love her new look. But other than wear a tight-fitting baseball cap like some small-time bank robber, she'd just have to own it.

Claire didn't need to wander downstairs to know that her mom would be juggling her purse and assorted grocery bags while her grandsons watched in amazement but didn't offer to carry a thing.

'Nana!' Henry and Joe shouted in unison.

Claire set down the hairdryer, pulled her robe tighter, and went to greet her mother.

'Hi, honey! Don't you look clean! And your hair! It's Pepto Pink . . . how festive! I brought the boys a treat.' Her mother pointed to a half-dozen cupcakes iced with what looked like Crest toothpaste. 'They were on sale. I couldn't resist. Your little fellas are so thin. I know Coupon doesn't like them to have a lot of junk, but what are grandmothers for if not to spoil, spoil, spoil!'

After Claire and Paul had gotten engaged, he'd run a half-marathon and since that time her family had come to mistakenly regard him as a 'health nut'. Her parents deemed exercise the sad pursuit of people who couldn't think of other, more interesting hobbies.

'Thanks for coming.' She kissed her mother on the cheek and watched warily as she unpacked the rest of her grocery bags, which contained enough food to feed several small villages. 'And thanks for bringing all this.'

'Of course, honey. I'm happy to do it,' her mom said, getting right to work with her Shake 'n Bake. 'You know, we never had back-to-school night. We were kept completely in the dark.'

'Lucky you,' Claire wanted to say.

'I would've loved to have heard all about the teachers' backgrounds, about your curriculum, the clubs, and extracurriculars. We had one meeting a year, and unless your child was a total flunky, you could skip it.'

'Since Max is already failing algebra, I guess you still have to go.' Henry smiled, dumping a can of gluey yams into a saucepan.

'It's one grade! Who gives a quiz on the first day?' Max whacked him in the back with a can of biscuits.

'Stop that, Max,' said Claire, making a mental note to find out if extra math help was available. 'Go shower before dinner. I mean it.'

'So, this is a real "Sophie's Choice" for you tonight, isn't it?' Eleanor asked, adding gobs of brown sugar to the pot of baked beans she set on a back burner.

'Huh?' Claire gripped the doorframe. Her mother had always been extremely intuitive. Throughout her teen years, Claire had often surmised that either her mom was psychic, or she had a stellar network of spies set up around town.

One afternoon during the spring of her junior year of high school stood out in her memory. Claire had come home and flopped down on the couch, pulling a throw pillow over her head.

Her mother, who'd been sitting at the dining-room table cubing the potatoes that would ring that evening's pot roast, put down her knife and came to sit on the edge of the hulking coffee table beside her daughter.

'Let me guess,' she'd said, rubbing Claire's back, 'a boy you don't like invited you to the prom. You want to say "no", but you know that's rude and that it takes a lot of courage to ask something like that. But you're also holding out hope the McPherson boy will ask you, so you don't want to say "yes" to anyone else anyway. But if you say "no" and no one else asks you, then what?'

'So, what do I do?' she'd asked, peeking out from beneath the pillow. At almost seventeen, Claire rarely asked her mother's advice anymore and it broke her heart a little to watch her mom visibly brighten from this unexpected consultation.

'The parent in me says "Don't hurt the boy's feelings", but the woman in me says "Follow your heart and wait for the guy you really like to ask you." The older you get, the more you realize how important it is to live without regrets.'

When Claire recalled that moment now, she wished she'd asked her mother what her regrets were. Did they involve her father? Motherhood? At the time, like any self-involved teen, Claire had sat up, and asked, 'How do you always know what I'm thinking?'

Her mom had laughed. 'When you're a mother, you'll be able to do it too.'

Claire had wanted to believe motherhood would give her magical powers, but for the past few weeks – maybe even months – her youngest had stashed a Best Buy aisle's worth of stolen electronics in her car and she hadn't even noticed. Perhaps maternal witchcraft skipped a generation.

'It's a real "Sophie's Choice",' her mother repeated. 'How will you decide whose classes you'll visit? Have you and Coupon flipped a coin for Max's or Henry's? "Sophie's Choice" – get it?'

Eleanor had a knack for latching on to cultural references decades late. Claire overlooked it, while Kyle never missed a chance to mock her for trying – and failing – to be hip.

'Right. It is a tough choice, but, no, I don't know what we're doing yet,' Claire said. *Not a lie.*

'Are you going out for dinner or drinks afterward? Why don't you, honey? Enjoy some time away from work and the kids. You look a little stressed.'

'I really don't know what I'm doing,' Claire said again – more to herself than anyone else.

'Well, you'll figure it out. You always do.' Her mother waved her spoon with a spirited flourish that sent baked beans flying across the kitchen.

Claire winced as they hit the fridge and slowly slid toward the floor.

September 4, 2024

6:16 p.m.

Claire returned to her bedroom to get dressed, put on makeup, and locate the pair of jade earrings Maggie had sent her for her fortieth birthday. She felt as if she were moving underwater. Time was passing too quickly, and she was making so little progress.

Previously, Claire believed she excelled under pressure, but hitting a work deadline or stuffing the boys' birthday piñatas minutes before guests arrived were completely different from deciding her entire future in fewer than a dozen hours.

Throughout the summer, Claire had compartmentalized her relationship with Alex. She'd read (and re-read) the messages he sent each morning, allow herself a few moments to swoon and compose a reply. Then she'd go about her day. Of course, she thought about him, the things he'd written and the way he looked at her at the reunion, as she chauffeured the boys to activities, while she prepared dinner, when she couldn't sleep. But to have only one day to decide the fate of that relationship *and* her marriage wasn't enough. She needed more time to think. Perhaps if she saw him again it would make things clear. She applied the mascara she only wore on special occasions when her phone pinged.

> From: Karen Clarke
> To: Claire Casey
> Sept. 4
> 6:09 p.m.
> Subject: Power walk to BTSN?
> Hey Claire! Susie and I miss you on our daily strolls. Wanted to see if you felt like walking to back-to-school night. (Since it's 1.8 miles, we'll burn at least 140 calories, which means I can have 6 ounces of chardonnay when I get home. If we walk back, double it!) If you're up for it, I'll ring your bell at 6:15. Parking is always such a nightmare. LMK!

> From: Claire Casey
> To: Karen Clarke
> Sept. 4
> 6:18 p.m.
> Re: Power walk to BTSN?
> Thanks for asking. I'm skipping it this year. Enjoy the beautiful weather. And drink the whole 12 ounces either way, you deserve it!

September 4, 2024

6:22 p.m.

Claire floated down the staircase, feeling lighter now that she was clean, dressed, and had decided to skip her sons' school event.

'Kiss me; I'm off,' she called into the family room.

Only her mother appeared to say goodbye.

'Oh, don't you look pretty! I hope you have a nice time, honey.' Her mom smoothed her hair and lowered her voice. 'I packed my nightgown and a change of clothes. They're in the car. If you don't mind, I think I might like to stay over. Your father and I had another disagreement about the recycling, and you know how he gets, sulking around the house like a cat whose fur is too tight. I'd prefer to wait it out here.'

'Of course. We'd love to have you. Thank you for all you do for us, Mom. I probably don't say that enough.' Claire pulled her mother into a long hug and tried not to think about how she'd explain Paul's absence or her own potentially very late return.

More importantly, she hoped there was still time to avoid turning out exactly like her parents.

September 4, 2024

6:29 p.m.

Before backing out of the driveway, Claire grabbed her cell phone and typed the three little words she'd longed to send all day.

On my way.

September 4, 2024

6:30 p.m.

Seated on the bench, Bea used her good wrist to fan herself with a Costco mailer as Claire pulled up to the curb. Lowering the window, Claire called, 'Get in!'

Bea pitched forward. 'Where are we going?'

'To test drive those roads not taken.'

Bea hustled to the van with the vigor of a track star. *Her physical therapist should be commended*, Claire thought as she unlocked the door and patted the passenger seat.

'What's Marty's address?'

'232 Fuller Avenue, Montclair. I know it by heart.' Bea covered her mouth with her hand. 'Am I a cyberstalker?'

'I'll have to check your search history before I can answer that.' Claire laughed. 'Hey, can you text Julie to let her know we're together? I don't want her to worry.'

Bea held up her phone. 'Siri, text Julie. Siri, text Julie. Julie, this is your mother . . .'

Claire pulled onto the highway. They were really doing this – she and Bea on an adventure, just like in her manuscript, *Another Time*.

'That was a good idea.' Bea tucked her phone into her enormous handbag. 'If Julie thinks I'm missing, she'll have a Silver Alert issued before dusk and you've already been accused of kidnapping once today.' She flipped down the visor to retouch her lipstick in the lighted mirror. 'I saw the video while I was Googling Marty. What is wrong with people, filming every move we make? Anyone with an ounce of sense would know that the last thing a mom of three wants is another whining child.'

'Amen!' Claire checked her mirrors then changed to the fast lane.

Bea clutched the door. 'I know you're weighing career options, dear, but are you considering driving for NASCAR? I haven't seen Marty in forty years, I can wait another forty minutes. Not that I don't appreciate the ride. I'm putting twenty dollars for gas in the glovebox. Don't fight me. Uber would've cost me twice that. I'd already checked. And I'll find my own way home.' She winked.

'What was it like to talk to Marty again?'

'It was wonderful.' Bea stretched the last word, her voice hitching upward as she hit all three syllables. 'He said his kids keep telling him to move to Florida but something's been keeping him here. He said he felt like he had unfinished business. It's me, Claire! I'm the business. I feel it in my bones.'

Did her mother have a story like this one? Claire wondered. *Did every woman?*

'Do you want to talk about where you're going, dear? After Fuller Avenue?'

'I thought about what you said.' Claire kept her focus on the road as they zipped toward the exit. 'I don't want to wonder, Bea.'

The older woman nodded. They fell into silence as the map app guided them to Marty's home, a brick stunner, its chimney draped in ivy.

'We're here!' Claire put the car in park. She expected her companion to hop right out but instead she swiveled in her seat and took Claire's hand in hers.

'If I may be so bold, dear, are you hoping to reconnect with an old love or with an old version of yourself?'

Claire pressed her lips together, unsure how to answer Bea's question.

'I ask because the current version is pretty terrific.'

Claire blinked back tears. 'Thank you, Bea.'

'No, Claire, thank you.' She leaned closer and pulled Claire into a gentle hug.

Bea opened the van door, stepped out, and turned around, a worried look clouding her face. 'You don't think he'll expect me to do a cartwheel, do you?'

'Not on the first date.' Claire smiled.

From the curb, she felt as if she were watching a silent film. Bea marched up the slate walkway. Before she rang the bell, the front door opened. A white-haired gentleman dressed in khaki pants and a green polo stepped back then forward, a wide grin brightening his face, bringing him to life. He held out his arms and Bea stepped into them.

Claire's heart fluttered. If she'd done nothing else right that day or even that entire summer, she'd had a hand in this.

Perhaps that was enough.

September 4, 2024

6:47 p.m.

Driving toward Manhattan at rush hour was typically torturous, but tonight when Claire could've used a few extra minutes to prepare herself, it was smooth sailing.

Heading toward the turnpike toll booth, Claire watched planes ascend from Newark Liberty Airport. How amazing would it be to board a flight, see a new landscape, and leave her cares and confusion behind? But who would be there to stop Max from antagonizing his younger brothers, to ensure Henry didn't burn the house down with his crème brûlée torch, to prevent Joe from leading a life of crime?

It felt like years since she'd taken a vacation – a real grown-up vacation; one that didn't involve a theme park, a baseball stadium, or requests for kids' menus and crayons.

She thought back to her trip to London. The day after they'd hooked up, Alex and his pal had left the group and traveled to Edinburgh. When it was time to return to New York, Alex's connection had been delayed. When he hadn't boarded their flight back to JFK, Claire had been an anxious mix of disappointed and annoyed. She'd planned to ask a passenger to switch seats so she and Alex could sit together.

That wasn't the only time his determination to visit as many places as possible had backfired. Over the summer, during one of their lengthy exchanges, he'd confessed that he'd taken a side ski trip in Switzerland while traveling for work and missed the birth of his second son. Claire couldn't imagine the rage that would've ignited in her. Even though Paul primarily dozed in a chair while she'd spent all night writhing with contractions as they'd awaited Henry's arrival, at least physically he was there. He'd taken days off from work to accompany her to their sons' first days of preschool, beaming beside her at their boys. He never would've risked missing anything as significant as their birth.

Claire sped through the toll plaza and headed toward the Holland Tunnel. She looked in the rearview mirror to merge and caught a glimpse of her reflection. After such a rushed makeup and eyebrow tweezing job, she was relieved to see she didn't look like a clown. Recently, she'd discovered that if she spent a few days without wearing makeup, then showered, applied a little eyeliner and the right amount of lipstick, she could go from feeling like a gargoyle to a glamour girl in minutes.

As she wound her way through the busy streets of Hoboken, Claire admired the waning light, the bustle of life as couples pushed strollers, walked dogs, and carted home wine and groceries. But, oh, the parking. On a regular day, Claire tended to circle block after block, willing a spot to appear. But tonight, she was too distracted and didn't trust herself to focus and read the street signs accurately. Considering she'd been fired, she couldn't afford to get her van towed or booted. She decided to park in a garage, regardless of the expense, not knowing how long she'd be gone.

Claire grabbed her ticket from the attendant, whispered 'Thanks', and started hiking up the steep incline that led out of the garage when she heard him calling, 'Ma'am! Ma'am!'

My God, how she hated that – being called 'Ma'am' instead of 'Miss'. She'd never get used to it. She turned around expecting him to ask, 'What time will you be back?' But instead, he held something – a box – out to her.

'Ma'am? You forgot these.'

Claire heard muffled giggles coming from those waiting beside the curb before she realized what he held. Only when she got closer did she recognize the box of condoms, gleaming in all its black and gold glory, beneath the bright fluorescent lights of the parking garage.

What could she do? Yell back, 'They're not mine!' when clearly, he'd found them on the floor of her minivan? Could she say, 'You keep 'em!' and dash out of the garage? Probably not because that would entail darting up what looked like a ninety-degree angle, and though she was filled with adrenaline, the best she could do would be to lunge-walk it at a semi-slow pace.

She had no choice but to grab the box, stuff it in her purse, murmur, 'Thanks,' and avoid all eye contact.

September 4, 2024

6:59 p.m.

The last glimmers of sunlight sparkled across the Hudson River as Claire hurried toward the hotel. Her phone chimed, alerting her to a new voicemail. She'd missed a call from her mother.

'What now?' Claire groaned, pressing the phone to her ear, struggling to hear as she passed bars and restaurants where crowds gathered to savor the warm evening and get a head start on the weekend.

'Honey?' Her mother emitted a soft laugh. 'It's your mom! It's raining in your kitchen. Don't worry, it's more of a drizzle than a downpour, so no need to rush back.'

Claire sighed. Leave it to her mother to put a positive spin on this – as if any amount of water cascading from the ceiling wasn't cause for alarm.

'Your boys are so smart! Just before the sheetrock gave way, Henry said, "That spot is shaped like Venezuela." We were never taught about South American countries in school! Honestly, Claire, you should have them take the test for *Teen Jeopardy!* These kids are geniuses!'

Were they brilliant enough to put pots beneath the drops, or were they standing there slack-jawed, posting videos of their indoor waterfall to social media?

Claire shoved her phone in her back pocket and scowled. She should've been using this time to think about Alex – about what she was going to do, what she was going to say when she saw him. But someone else was on her mind. Paul. 'It's on my to-do list!' Paul!

September 4, 2024

7:02 p.m.

As Claire teetered toward the bar, she forgot about her ankle and focused on her heart, which threatened to beat out of her chest.

She spotted Alex immediately. He looked even better than she remembered in jeans and a crisp blue shirt rolled up at the cuffs, revealing his muscular forearms, sporting the lingering glow of a fading summer tan. Seated in the lounge facing the entrance, he glanced up from his phone and smiled, knocking the breath out of her. Everything she'd thought about, longed for over the past eleven weeks, stood before her – hers for the taking.

Alex rose as she walked toward him. Her legs turned to limp spaghetti, and she prayed her knees wouldn't buckle, leaving her in a heap at his feet. Each step seemed like its own individual mile until she crossed the room, unable to do anything other than marvel at his handsome face and return his smile with equal enthusiasm.

He pulled her toward him, his fingers strong and warm as they curled around her bare arms. 'You're a sight for sore eyes.'

Uncertain if he'd kiss her, Claire bowed her head the way devout old ladies did before receiving communion. His lips, warm but light, brushed the top of her head. Inhaling his scent, vanilla mixed with smoky cedar, desire blossomed like a lotus flower at the bottom of her belly.

'It's great to see you too.' She drew back to look into his deep brown eyes.

'Let's get you a drink,' he said. 'What'll it be? Perhaps rosé to match your hair?'

'I'm thinking of directing our middle school's production of *Pinkalicious*,' Claire fibbed, running her hand over the mess she'd made of her head. 'Just getting in the spirit.'

'Always championing the arts,' Alex smiled, 'that's fantastic!'

Claire wondered if he was truly listening or merely on some kind of super-encouraging leadership autopilot. 'A glass of wine – any color – would be great,' she added, following him to a velvet couch.

Alex summoned the waiter.

'We'll have two Aperol Spritzes.' Alex turned back to her. 'I skimmed your *16 Sexy Summer Cocktails* slideshow last month; I've wanted one ever since.' His eyes drifted to her purse. Maybe he'd been hoping she'd have an overnight bag instead?

She was trying so hard to regulate her breathing and act normal – be normal – that she couldn't attempt to read his mind on top of everything else.

'So, what brings you to town?' Claire asked, as if contemplating adultery in a swanky lounge was part of a routine Thursday night.

The waiter set down their drinks as Alex explained that he was meeting a potential client in Midtown Manhattan to discuss streamlining their operation through his innovative software. Normally, Claire would've paid closer attention, but all she heard was 'words, words, words' as she gulped the colorful cocktail and plotted her next move.

'. . . and the chance to see you is icing on the cake,' he said.

Warmth flooded her chest. It seemed like a lifetime since anyone had spoken to her as if she were special. At home, her titles boiled down to chef, chauffeur, and schedule keeper. There, she was more crumbs than icing.

'And everything worked out with your son today?' Claire stalled for time, hoping the alcohol would settle her nerves and give her some clarity – as if alcohol ever did that.

'Yeah, I'm still not sure exactly what happened.' Alex tapped at his phone before putting it face down on the low table. 'He's supposed to send me the video, but you know kids, they get distracted. His mom wants to take the high road, so I'll follow her lead. She said this parent who yelled at him probably has a lot of pent-up rage, misdirected anger – that sort of thing. Since they're new to town, Jocelyn doesn't want to make trouble.' He sat back and laughed. 'Right there is proof of how different we are. She's so rational. If I were running point on this, I'd rip that parent a new one. I don't care what's going on in your life, you can't go around yelling at other people's children.'

'Totally,' Claire agreed, draining her drink, her cheeks turning as pink as her hair. It was strange how she'd been in a similar situation that morning. She didn't want to argue with Alex, but sometimes kids needed to be reprimanded – like that teen who should've been in school instead of filming her. She blinked, clearing the unpleasant scene from her mind.

'It's great you and your ex get along so well.' She fought the temptation to roll her eyes.

'Absolutely.' Alex turned toward the expansive windows, jutted his chin, and changed the subject. 'Breaks my heart to admit it, but Philly's skyline can't compare. The view's pretty spectacular from my suite.' He arched his eyebrows. 'I don't suppose you'd want to check it out?'

That mischievous twinkle flickered in his eyes as he held her gaze. When was the last time anyone had looked at her that way?

'I'd like that,' she said, operating on instinct, adrenaline.

'Great.' He smiled, snagging the waiter as he passed and handing him a fifty. 'Keep the change.'

Alex rose and Claire followed him into the elevator. They stood side by side, pinkies nearly touching. Watching the floor numbers change, she had a sudden flash of kissing him in the hotel elevator in London. Cold cheeks, warm mouth, so lost in each other they missed his floor. Claire's heart rate skyrocketed at the memory as they climbed higher.

Glancing down, she spotted the box of condoms sticking out of her handbag. No wonder Alex had been staring at it. How had she not learned that everything she stuffed in there eventually popped out at the worst times? She made a mental note to treat herself to the world's smallest clutch for her birthday.

Now that she'd shown up carrying enough prophylactics to supply a Las Vegas brothel, how could she not go ahead with this? Attempting to stuff the box deep inside her bag was futile, so Claire decided to add one more lie to her already-duplicitous day.

'I'm speaking with some at-risk youth tomorrow about the importance of using birth control and stopping the spread of STDs,' she managed. 'I grabbed these at the pharmacy on the corner, you know, save myself a trip in the morning.'

'It's so impressive how you carve out time to volunteer.' Alex placed a hand on the small of her back, sending shockwaves up her spine as the elevator doors opened.

Alex's suite was sleek and modern. She couldn't recall the last time she'd stayed in a hotel that didn't give off the faint scent of mildew. When she and Paul took the boys on vacation, they chose their accommodations based on whichever lodging included a free buffet breakfast.

Amid the fancy bed linens and stunning view, Claire felt out of place for another reason: she hadn't been with another man in eighteen years.

'Come here.' Alex reached for her hand.

Was he going to pull her toward the bed? Claire's mouth went dry.

'I'm just going to use the bathroom.' She stepped away. 'Long car ride.' In her nervousness, Claire rushed into the closet. Wooden hangers clattered to the floor before she shut the door and fumbled her way to the toilet.

Switching on the light, she startled at her reflection. Her eyes were wild; a perspiration mustache beaded above her top lip. Turning on the faucet, she bent forward and guzzled from the tap. What was she going to do? She'd spent weeks thinking about a moment just like this one. How could she come this far and still not know what was in her heart?

She shut off the water, closed the toilet lid and sat. As she took a deep breath, her phone pinged. Was her kitchen flooded? Had the ceiling finally collapsed? What bad news was her mother relaying now? She braced for the worst.

It was a text from Marcy, her agent.

Read your pitch and pages, Claire. All I have to say is 'More please!' Can you send the next few chapters and a synopsis by mid-October? Then we'll set up a call. Nice work!

Claire's already-racing heart kicked into overdrive. Marcy had never used an exclamation point before – not even when *A Panda for Amanda* was translated into French. Claire believed in this project, made space for it, and now she'd (finally!) piqued her agent's interest.

Through the door, voices filtered in. Alex must've gotten a call. Claire unlocked her phone to re-read Marcy's message and a new one loaded.

Siri, text Claire. Claire, it's Bea, Watch this.

She'd pasted a link to Alice Masters's latest newsletter. A video appeared mid-page. Claire pressed the play arrow.

'Hi Everyone!' Alice stood inside a warehouse. She removed

her hard hat and shook out her loose blond curls. 'Today I want to share a very special project I've been working on.'

The envy that often consumed Claire when she watched Alice show off her work was gone. Marcy loved her pages. Claire had a project too.

'This summer a neighbor asked for my help.' The camera pulled back to reveal Alice looking tall and strong at the top of a wooden ramp. Leave it to Alice to make denim overalls look sexy. 'He said a family member is facing a health challenge that makes it difficult to climb her steep porch steps, yet she's reluctant to leave her lovingly restored Victorian. Who can blame her, right?' Alice lowered her voice. She had a knack for making it seem as if she were talking only to you. 'My neighbor asked me if I'd design a ramp that attached to the back of the house so his mother-in-law could comfortably and safely stay in her home.'

Despite her chunky tan work boots, Alice strutted down the ramp like a runway model.

'Before I show you how we built this baby, I'd like to give you a bit of backstory. This neighbor? He and his wife hit a rough patch. Who doesn't, right?'

A tingle began at the base of Claire's neck. Alice was talking about *her*.

'Claire,' the camera zoomed in on Alice's flawless face, 'your husband loves you. This is his grand gesture and, no, it's not a field of daffodils or a serenade beneath your window – and honestly, he barely helped because he doesn't know a crowbar from a claw hammer – but my point is this guy cares deeply about you, your family, the life you've built.' She revved her pink power drill. 'Like love itself, this ramp will endure. It's thoughtful, it's practical, and I'd say that makes it . . .'

'Pretty darn perfect,' Claire whispered. Paul had done this for her mom. *For her*. He'd been listening; he'd heard her. This was his secret project.

'Claire?' Alex knocked on the bathroom door. 'You OK in there?'

His voice snapped her out of her trance. She looked up from her phone, disoriented. What was she doing in her former boyfriend's hotel bathroom?

'Uh, yeah, give me a sec.' As Claire stood, a sweeping sense of vertigo sent her lurching forward. She clutched the towel bar to steady herself.

'Claire, can you come out? I'd really like to show you something.'

Something like his genitals?! Had he taken his pants off? Could she feign diarrhea and ask him to leave the suite so she could disappear down the stairwell and race back to the parking garage? No. She'd faced every other part of this crazy day head-on; she'd do it again.

Claire ran cold water over her wrists, dried her hands, smoothed her pink hair, and stared at her face, paler than a roll of toilet paper.

A woman's muffled voice traveled through the door. Had Alex ordered room service? Turned on the TV?

Stepping out of the bathroom, she found him sitting on the edge of the king-sized bed.

The woman's voice came again, louder, more shrill, more . . . familiar. 'Geez, what a baby! Hey! Why don't you put that phone down and do something useful!'

Alex turned the phone toward her, his voice half-laugh, half-accusation. 'Is this *you* yelling at my son?'

Claire's mind spun to that famous scene in *Casablanca*. Of all the neighborhoods in New Jersey, Alex's ex and kids had to move into hers? What were the odds? Why hadn't she paid more attention when he mentioned Jocelyn? How had she not put it together sooner?

'"Yelling" is a strong word.' Claire felt as if she'd slipped into an alternate universe. How had it started? *I offered a boy a ride because the school bus never showed, and . . . and . . . and . . .*

'I know you're under a lot of pressure right now; I get it. But *this* . . .' Alex stood and held the phone to her face. With the video paused, frozen on her half-open mouth, she really did look like a T-Rex. 'This isn't the Claire I know.' Alex stepped closer. His signature scent – a hint of vanilla mixed with cedar – so lovely in the hotel lobby, now seemed sickeningly sweet, making her a little queasy. It was so different from Paul's. Her husband smelled like Tide muddled with fresh air, leaves, and grass from playing outdoors with their sons. This new, foreign fragrance suddenly smelled much less appealing.

'You've been under a lot of pressure lately,' Alex continued. 'You're a newly single mom stuck in an unfulfilling career. Let's chalk this,' he waved his phone, 'up to a moment of stress-induced madness, OK? You've been going through a lot, Claire. I think Jocelyn nailed it with the "pent-up rage and misdirected anger" stuff. We all become a little unhinged every now and then.'

Was she unhinged or was she thinking clearly, speaking up for herself, aware of what she wanted, not afraid to go after it?

Alex tossed the phone onto the bed and traced circles up and down her bare arms. With his thick fingers, he tilted her chin upward. 'I *really* want this to work out,' he inhaled deeply, 'so I'm willing to overlook this . . . I wouldn't call it a *red* flag . . . more pinkish, like your hair.'

As he reached toward her rosy locks, Claire reared back and squared her shoulders. 'Your son should've been in school, not filming his neighbors, and certainly not sharing videos that get misconstrued and repackaged as kidnapping attempts and bullying!' She paused, dizzy from the cocktail and the anger coursing through her bloodstream. 'I lost my job because of that video!'

'Claire.' Alex shifted his weight from foot to foot as if he were losing patience. 'You complained about that job non-stop. It sounds like Noah did you a favor. Plus, he wasn't intending to film you. He was documenting traffic patterns for his Geo-studies class.' He paused, smiled, and made the slight screeching sound of a car veering off-course. 'Proud dad detour: Noah's hoping to major in urban planning and development. A lofty goal, but he's an exceptional student; he'll breeze right through.'

Claire dug her nails into her palms.

'Look' – Alex reached for his phone – 'I think you might feel better if you apologized to Noah – and maybe even Jocelyn. They've had a rough day. Give and get some closure, some clarity.'

Claire's eyes narrowed.

'Or shoot them a text?' Alex held the phone out to her.

'"Never apologize for how you feel. It's like saying sorry for being your authentic self." Isn't that one of your mantras?'

'I-I don't remember saying that.' Alex frowned.

'On LinkedIn – you just posted it last week. It was one of your morning meditations!'

'Oh, Claire, I barely even read those,' Alex confessed, his expression shifting to pity before turning upbeat again. 'But I'm glad someone does. My assistant finds them. It's good for my brand. She gets them from this thought leadership calendar a client sent last Christmas. Sounds like it might make a nice gift for someone else I know.' He winked.

Claire looked at him. *Who was this man?*

He stepped toward her, slid the phone into his pocket, and placed his hands on her shoulders.

'Maybe this is a teachable moment for Noah. He'll understand that sometimes grown-ups don't know what we're doing either. You overreacted; maybe I overreacted.' His fingers caressed her cheek. 'We have so little time together. Let's not waste another second of it.' He leaned in, lips parting.

And just like that, Claire's entire life crashed into focus. She saw herself as a child sitting in her closet, wishing her parents would work on their marriage. She pictured her father walking her down the aisle, Paul waiting at the end, smiling, blue eyes gleaming, then Max as a toddler in a swing under the oak tree in their backyard. Henry flipping pancakes for the whole family on a summer Saturday morning, oven mitts up to his elbows. Joe reading to her hours earlier. Alice Masters speaking directly to her: 'Claire, your husband loves you.'

'Alex, I . . .' She stepped back. Over email, she'd never been at a loss for words, but now, in person, she stumbled. Her mouth hung open. She shut it quickly to avoid resembling a dinosaur again. She needed to deliver her own version of those painful pre-proposal *Bachelor* speeches that began with flattery and quickly changed course: '*I think you're amazing, but I have a stronger connection with someone else.*'

'Alex,' she started again. 'You have no idea what you – what this – has meant to me these past few months. You came into my life at a time when I was asleep, and I didn't even know it. You woke me up. I'd forgotten who I was, and you helped me remember, and I'm so, so grateful for that.'

Before she could continue, the light in Alex's eyes faded, his shoulders sagged, a wave of recognition crossed his face. He'd been in sales long enough to know when a deal couldn't be closed.

'I'm so sorry I've misled you.' She took his hand. 'But I can't do this. I think – no, I know – I can't keep emailing you either. I came here because I wanted to see you again,' she paused, 'but I think I also wanted to see me. The me I used to be. I'm still trying to find her, actually. Seems I've got a bit more work to do.'

Alex shook his head. 'Don't do this, Claire. What we have is special. Rare. This is our second chance. Don't you want to see where it goes this time?'

'I thought I did, but I think I was confused. You made me remember the girl I was when we were together all those years ago. I wanted to be that girl again.'

Alex rubbed his face and blew out a long exhale. 'I get it,' he said. 'I'd be lying if I didn't say I'm disappointed, but I get it.' He sank to the bed. 'Completely. When I saw you back in June, I realized I'd been kind of hiding out since my divorce. I'd forgotten how to be myself beyond work and parenting, if that makes any sense.'

Claire nodded. 'It does.'

'I had no idea what I was missing. I missed *you*, Claire. And you pushed me. You'd die if you knew how long it took me to compose some of those emails.'

'I struggled too.' Claire laughed and sat beside him. 'And I'm a writer.'

'Yeah, but those emails – you – all of it – made me feel things again,' Alex continued. 'Good things. I always knew you – *this* – was a long shot. But you know the thing about long shots? When they come in, the payoff is pretty phenomenal.'

Claire caught herself slipping under his spell again. She shook it off and squeezed his hand before releasing it.

'Thank you,' Claire said.

'For what?'

'Being kind and . . .' she stumbled again, lost in this lexicon.

'And gracious in defeat? For you, Claire, anything.' He offered her a slow smile.

'I should probably . . .' Claire gestured toward the door.

'Who knows, maybe we'll see each other again in another twenty-five years?' Alex winked. 'They say the third time's the charm.'

'That's what I hear.' She thought of Bea and Marty, joy rippling inside her.

'What will you do now? I mean for work. I have plenty of connections. I'd love to help you.'

'You have helped. More than you know. I'm finally writing that novel. You inspired me.'

Alex smiled more broadly this time and Claire thought she spotted a faint blush, though it may have been the soft twilight giving him a rosy radiance.

'The one about the Girl Scout who stashes listening devices inside the cookie boxes and spies on her neighbors only to realize the people next door are terrorists and it's up to her troop to stop them before they blow up the bridge that's the only way off their island?'

Claire shook her head. 'No, but if my current idea doesn't pan out, that's a close second.'

'The Uber driver-slash-serial killer who finds redemption through Christian rock radio?'

'Nope, sorry,' Claire shook her head.

'OK, I give up.'

'This. Our story.'

Surprised, Alex took a beat before nodding. 'Ah, yes, the old "Girl walks into a bar, breaks guy's heart" story. Know it well.'

'There's a bit more to it than that,' Claire corrected. 'It's more "woman travels back in time with a new friend to see if they can rewrite the past." A little out there, but inspired by true events . . .' Claire touched Alex's arm softly. 'And we both know that guy's heart will be just fine.'

Alex pulled her into a quick hug before letting her go. 'We'll see. Just do me one favor?'

'Name it,' Claire said.

'When you write it, change this ending.'

September 4, 2024

7:32 p.m.

It would be quicker to leave the van in the parking garage and take mass transit. As Claire hurried toward the PATH train station, she detected the first hint of fall in the undercurrent of the gentle breeze. Yes, summer, and all it brought with it, was coming to an end.

A small knot of sorrow the size of a peach pit rested at the bottom of her stomach. To have spent months stoking an internal fire, to have cultivated an elaborate fantasy, only to snuff it out in mere minutes felt like almost too much to bear.

There would be no more witty emails, no promise of cigarettes and cocktails. She could no longer allow her thoughts to linger on the June evening when she and Alex had held hands as they crossed the street on their way to the next bar and she'd believed their palms were secretly communicating.

Still, saying goodbye to Alex was for the best. Whatever was wrong or had gone missing between her and Paul in recent years, how they'd flipped into some robotic way of going through the motions rather than connecting and appreciating each other as they once had, she knew there was still love beneath it. The foundation, though weathered, remained intact. And after all, wasn't marriage just one long endurance test? Like the ultimate staring contest, wasn't each partner out-waiting the other to see who would flinch first? As long as you didn't blink at the same time, you could carry on, good days giving way to bad and vice versa.

She dropped the box of condoms in a garbage can, and rushed through the turnstile to board the Thirty-Third Street train. As it lurched toward Manhattan, Claire checked her watch. She thought about Paul, and hoped he'd be happily surprised to see her.

When the boys were little, she'd take them to visit him at his office. She'd dress them alike so they'd look as cute as possible in case they behaved like tiny demons. Plus, that way she'd have an easier time keeping track of them, counting off 'one, two, three' on escalators and elevators. But once they'd started school, they'd stopped that tradition. Occasionally, she'd suggest that Paul stay in the city, and she'd meet him for dinner, a concert, or maybe a play, but he usually said he was tired and preferred to come home.

If she arrived in time to catch Paul before he left – if this wasn't a complete fool's errand – what would she say? Where would she begin? The rocking of the train car helped her think.

I came this close to having an affair. But I'm choosing you, so please make it worth it.

Our son has head lice. He's also a kleptomaniac. But don't worry, I've taken care of it all.

I lost my job. And I'm thrilled about it.

I caught the person who won't clean up after her dog and I scared the shit out of her. You're welcome.

You don't have to worry about hosting a New Year's Day open house this year. In fact, we may have to move; I've alienated a lot of people today.

I still love you, but I don't want to feel invisible any longer. We need to fix this.

Bingo. That was the one.

As she hurried across town, she tried to recall the last time she'd been in Manhattan. It was a shame because, here they were, so close to what many considered the center of the universe, and she had the nerve to complain about a forty-five-minute express train ride. Not appreciating what she had was becoming a recurring theme. She needed to change that too.

As Claire approached Paul's building, fear notched up her spine. Had his office moved? If she was completely honest, Paul wasn't the only one guilty of being distracted and unfocused much of the time. Had he mentioned it one night as they watched the boys' swim meet? It seemed plausible. Still, that would be a big thing to forget. She scanned the building's directory. Relief swept through her as she spotted the company's name on the roster.

She took the elevator to the twelfth floor and experienced a momentary panic. What if Paul was making love to a flexible young woman atop an office copier? She couldn't rule it out based on the turns Stacey and Maggie's marriages had taken. She was glad to see the door propped open by a high-top, no doubt placed there to allow a delivery person to drop off dinner without needing to get buzzed in.

She stepped lightly through the lobby in case Paul was engaged in the sort of behavior you'd expect at a *Mad Men* Christmas party. Peering into his office, she found him facing multiple monitors, pointing to something on the screen while his colleagues stood behind him, spellbound. He looked different – confident – in his element. Paul and the brogrammers turned to look at her one by one like a pack of curious prairie dogs.

'Yo, yo! It's the "Geez, what a baby!" lady!' one said, pointing.

'Claire?' Paul looked confused.

'Dude, you know her?' Another worker frowned.

'Are the boys OK?' Paul asked.

'It *is* the "Geez, what a baby!" lady!' a third guy exclaimed, looking from his phone to Claire and back again. 'Come on. Get in!' he roared like a T-Rex the way Henry had in the van that afternoon.

'The boys are fine,' Claire assured Paul, realizing her out-of-the-blue appearance must've been concerning.

'Seriously, are you really the woman in the video?' asked the first guy, who looked not much older than Max. 'Your hair is, like, way pink IRL. Am I right?'

'Claire, this is my team. Team, this is my . . . this is Claire,' Paul said. 'In addition to being the star of a viral video, she's also an expert cupcake baker and a damn fine bowler.'

A small man in the back of the room bowed.

'Hi,' Claire said, surprised and slightly embarrassed by the attention.

'Can you say it, you know, "Come on. Get in!" while I film it?' another asked. 'Or, wait, how about a selfie?'

'OK, fellas, that's enough. I think we can pick this up tomorrow. Thanks for your hard work today.' Paul gestured toward the door.

'It was all you, man,' another guy fist-bumped him.

As the team dispersed, Claire studied Paul's desk. A silver frame held a black-and-white photo of them on their wedding day, a candid shot of Paul whispering in her ear. What had he said? How could she not remember? Maybe she didn't need to – her broad smile said it all.

Beside that frame was a picture of the boys on their first day of school, taken a few years ago. In it, Joe, a full-fledged kindergartner, looked the happiest, while Henry and Max made faces for the camera and gave each other bunny ears. Still, they appeared impossibly young and sweet. How had time passed so quickly?

'So, to what do I owe this pleasure?' Paul swept a mess of documents into a sloppy stack. 'Aren't you supposed to be at back-to-school night finding out what Max should be doing now to secure his spot at a top veterinary program?'

'I'm playing hooky this year.' Claire swayed, the cocktail she'd consumed on an empty stomach loosening the knot between her shoulders.

'Is your new punk hairdo bringing out a more rebellious side?' Paul smirked. 'Or is it part of a disguise now that you're famous?'

'I was trying to save some money and time,' Claire ran her fingers through her tresses, 'with mixed results.'

'I'm all about saving money.' Paul smiled. 'Your family doesn't call me "Coupon" for nothing.' He waited for that to land and continued, 'Oh, I know a bit more than you think I do.'

All the blood in Claire's body seemed to rush to her face. She had no idea he knew about her family's nickname for him. Did he also know about Alex? Afraid she'd blurt a full confession, Claire kept her mouth shut and her eyes on her husband, who stepped out from behind his desk to stand just inches from her.

'It's OK,' he said. 'I kind of like it. Your hair, I mean – not being called "Coupon".'

'I'll talk to them about that.' Claire laughed, relief making her knees buckle – or maybe that was the cocktail mixing with the Benadryl. 'I'm starving. You?'

'Follow me,' Paul said.

Together, they walked to the office kitchen, where pizza boxes formed a tower on a center island. Paul lifted lids and moved empties toward the recycling area before finally locating a full pie at the bottom of the pile.

'It's pepperoni, but don't worry, I'll pick it off for you,' he said, acknowledging Claire's aversion to the slimy little discs of meat.

There it was. The shorthand they shared. All the things they never had to say. All the things no one else knew.

Paul opened the fridge and grabbed a bottle of white wine covered in Post-its that read: 'Do Not Touch!' 'I MEAN IT!' He peeled them off, revealing the label – the same as the one she found on their porch in August with the smudged note: *Wish I could be there to toast your success.*

'*You* sent me that?' She pointed at the bottle.

Paul frowned.

'I mean, you sent me *that*.' She changed her inflection. 'I-I don't think I thanked you.'

He opened a drawer, dug out a corkscrew.

'Thank you,' she said as Paul placed two coffee mugs atop the pizza. 'Here, let me carry something.'

Claire expected them to sit at one of the kitchen's tiny plastic tables.

'Come with me.' He handed her the chilled bottle and nodded toward the door. As they wound their way past dozens of cubicles, Claire remembered that she'd lost her job. She had so many things to tell her husband, she had no idea where or how to start.

Paul led her to a door at the end of a corridor. Inside the stairwell, they climbed two flights before he opened a door that led to the roof.

As Claire stepped out, a warm breeze lifted the ruffles of her blouse, and she watched as the city lit up around them – offices and apartments winking like fireflies, the setting sun sinking low, the pink sky giving way to a sleepy silver. Using a brick, Paul wedged the door open, while Claire poured the wine into the mugs.

Several folding chairs, anchored to pipes, awaited them. They faced west toward home. She pictured the boys feasting while her mother doled out second and third helpings of pork chops and baked beans. She imagined her dad, brooding over recyclables and tuning in to *Jeopardy!* alone, Bea and Marty remembering the summer they met. Somewhere Stacey, Maggie, and Kristie were off reinventing themselves, and Alex, on the other side of the Hudson, was probably admiring this same view only in reverse. No matter where you stood, the world kept turning. You lost something, but you picked up what you had left, and you tried to reshape it and make it every bit as good as what had been.

Together, Claire and Paul sat facing the skyscrapers, so enormous they looked like a model city the boys built with Legos on a snow day. She passed Paul a mug while he handed her a slice of pizza on a cardboard plate he'd fashioned from the lid of the box.

'I've been feeling pretty invisible for a while now.' Claire hoped it came off more matter-of-fact than needy or desperate. If they were going to make this work, she needed to share her feelings and ask for what she needed.

'I see you, Claire.' He turned to face her. 'But I also see the boys. The bills. I see the layoffs all around me. I see my dad forgetting the kids' names and my mom covering for him. I see time speed up a little bit more every day – except in our dining room, where it is always two fifteen.'

Claire smiled. He *had* noticed.

'Don't worry, I've got batteries on my list. And a new toilet paper holder too. I've picked up some tips from Alice Masters.' He grinned and then drew a long breath. 'I want to talk to you about this project we – Alice and I – have been working on . . .'

'Paul, I know about it.'

He frowned. 'Joe squealed?'

'No, I saw Alice's video. Thank you. I had no idea.'

'Say the word and we'll – she'll – install it.'

Claire felt a catch in her throat as her eyes welled up. 'Thank you. I—'

'I know things are about to get a lot harder, Claire, and I know you're on the frontlines, but I'm with you. I guess this whole time

I'd been thinking that someday we'd get back to being how we were. The boys would grow up and life would slow down. It never occurred to me that I'd dropped out of the present. Or, that you wouldn't be right there with me when we finally got to the easy part.' He took a sip of wine and licked his top lip.

'After everything that happened here today, I'm asking for a promotion. If it doesn't come through, I'll find another job. I've updated my résumé, and I've been sending it out.'

'I didn't know you were doing that.' Claire took a long sip. The wine, fruity and delicious, tasted even better now than it had in August.

'When you only have basic cable, you find yourself with a lot of free time.' Paul smiled. 'I've been sitting on the sidelines long enough. Plus, it kills me knowing that you're forced to write about *14 Ways to Incorporate Pumpkin Spice into Your Lovemaking*.'

Claire almost spit out her mouthful of wine. 'How—'

'My mom sent me the link.'

She slumped lower in the folding chair and half laughed, half moaned before clearing her throat. 'I got fired today.'

'Because of the bus stop video?'

Claire nodded. 'Want me to tell you what happened?'

'Not unless you want to. You know I'm always going to take your side.' He looked out at the setting sun in its pink and orange splendor. 'It's for the best, Claire. You have too much talent to waste at that place.'

A jolt shot through her as puzzle pieces clicked inside her head. 'It's you!' She clapped her hands. 'You're HotDogLuvR!'

Paul nodded and held up his palms. 'Guilty as charged.'

'Why? How?' Claire shook her head.

'I've always believed in you, in your writing. But you stopped believing me.'

'That's not—'

'No, I mean, it's like when your mom says you're smart or handsome or a great athlete. It's nice, but it's not the same as hearing it from a stranger, right? That job was killing you and I wanted you to know how good you are.'

Claire didn't know what to say so she went with the easiest question. 'Why "HotDogLuvR"?'

'I'd been helping Henry whip up his signature chorizo dogs with that smokey red relish when the idea came to me.'

'Well, thank you. Thinking of you reading all those slideshows and stories means a lot. And those comments were really nice.' The light breeze gave Claire goosebumps. 'I'm working on a new project, actually. Marcy likes the pitch and some early pages.'

'That's amazing.' Paul squeezed her hand.

'It may go nowhere, but I have to try.'

'I think of us kind of like a story, too,' Paul said. 'We're in the middle, the conflict, the toughest part. It'll get better – at least I like to think it will. Who knows? Maybe it'll actually get worse for a while. Have you met our kids? We'll have three teenagers in the blink of an eye and already they can be . . . a lot.'

Claire laughed. She knew this was Paul's way of letting her know he did really see it all.

'I don't know what else to say other than we're in it – this story – together.'

She wanted to savor this moment, but she needed to know one more thing.

'Why did you just walk out? Why didn't you fight to win me back?'

'You asked for space. I wanted to let you decide what *you* wanted. You've got enough people badgering you all day. I also thought I needed to work on myself a bit. I never thought it was the end of us. Just a chapter break.'

Claire experienced a pang of guilt thinking about Alex and how differently the night might've ended. But really, it was because of Alex's reminder of all that she'd been, all that she'd once wanted, that she'd felt more like herself than she'd had in years. And how could that be considered a bad thing?

'Did you tell Joe that I wasn't fun?' The wine erased any order she might have intended for this conversation, but she couldn't hold her thoughts in any longer.

'Claire, he'd asked me if we could set up a zip-line that led from his bedroom window straight to the trampoline. I said, "Probably not." I had to tell him that sometimes, when you're a parent, safety comes before fun. I told him that even if I said OK, you'd definitely veto it.'

'Well, I would,' Claire admitted. 'But I want to be fun again. I want to feel lighter. Loved.'

Paul set his mug and his slice, loaded with Claire's pepperoni, on the asphalt and took her hands in his. 'Claire, you're the most fun person I've ever met.'

She frowned. 'Show don't tell,' she wanted to say, but she didn't have to because he knew what she was thinking.

'Remember when we went to visit my parents and it was their block party and you agreed to sit in the dunk tank because that kid asked you to?'

'He was cute.' Claire recalled the chubby-cheeked, freckle-faced tween who'd pleaded with her to dangle above the murky water.

'He was totally trying to see through your T-shirt,' Paul said. 'But, anyway, you did it, and you were the hit of the party.'

'I did it because your mom kept refilling my cup with her famous sangria. For me, it was more like a drunk tank.'

'Well, all night everyone kept asking me, "Where'd you find this girl? She's amazing." And you know what I told them?'

Claire smiled. She knew this one. 'Bed Bath & Beyond.'

'That's right. I told them I had a coupon.'

Claire rested her head on his shoulder.

'Speaking of the drunk tank, had you been drinking before you got here? You seemed a little wobbly.'

How much did the truth help in this case? Claire wondered.

'Yes, I had a drink with an old college friend on my way here,' she said.

'Got any good stories for me?'

'Not really. I cut the visit short to see you,' she said. *Not a lie.*

'I'm glad you did. You definitely upped my street cred with the brogrammers.' He laughed.

They sat for a bit, eating the cold pizza, finishing the wine. Late summer stars began to glimmer against the darkening sky.

Paul laced his fingers through Claire's. 'We should make more time for this – us. Maybe put a standing date on the calendar.'

'That's a nice idea.' Claire nodded, knowing that perhaps it would happen once, maybe even twice, before things – life – got in the way again.

But maybe that was OK, because while it wasn't perfect, it was the life they'd made. Their story.

Book Club Discussion Questions

Could you relate to Claire's day-to-day life and her longing for something different? If so, in what way?

Does Claire cross a line by keeping up a correspondence with Alex?

Who is the bigger influence on Claire: Alex or Bea?

At one point Claire states: 'But what was marriage if not recognizing someone's shortcomings and loving them anyway?' Do you agree?

Do you think that Claire was chasing Alex or a former version of herself?

Can someone from the past change your future?

Referring to Bea, Claire asks, 'Why was it sometimes easier to love people who weren't family?' What are your thoughts on that?

Claire talks about running away from home. Have you ever felt this way?

Does society expect far too much from women and mothers? For example, the school nurse calls Claire about her son Joe's head lice rather than Paul. Has this been your experience? Discuss the emotional labor of caring for children and aging parents.

Claire considers writing an essay on this topic: *Why do we go to so much trouble to build up friendships for our children without tending our own?* Did that resonate with you?

Claire and Alex come up with ideas for novels that Claire could write. Was there one you think Claire should pursue?

Claire decides to end her relationship with Abby. Do you agree with her choice? Have you ever severed a friendship that no longer served you?

At one point Claire wonders if she is 'a good mother, daughter, friend, tipper'. How do you think she measures up?

How were you hoping the book would end?

Do you have a passion project? If so, or if not, how does that impact your wellbeing?

Acknowledgments

Thank you to the women who helped me shape Claire and bring her to life: Rose Casanova, who suggested our writing group attempt NaNoWriMo (National Novel Writing Month) in 2017, (it took me closer to a decade than a month to write this novel, but who's counting?); Bonnie Taggart and Deb McCoy, who read early drafts and encouraged me to keep going; Lucy Dauman, Amy Tipton, and Jodi Warshaw, who offered invaluable edits; Vic Britton, who offered Claire a home; and Laurie Johnson and Mary Karayel, who saw a brighter future for Claire than I initially imagined.

I'm so grateful to Camille Pagán, Ann Garvin, and Catherine McKenzie for taking time away from their own writing to read this novel and lend their support and incredibly kind words.

Thank you to my husband and sons, who've been hearing about Claire for far longer than any of us would like to admit.

To all the reviewers, librarians, and booksellers who've recommended my work to readers, I appreciate you more than you could ever know. Thank you to the book clubs who've welcomed me into your homes, both in person and via Zoom. It is an honor and a gift to have the opportunity to meet you.

Thank you to everyone who read *Claire Casey's Had Enough*. If you enjoyed the story, please consider leaving a rating or review. Your feedback helps other readers discover the book.

For more information or to simply say 'hi" please visit LizAlterman.com where you'll find information about events, workshops, and my monthly newsletter.

Thank you again!